Brizio DeLuca

Savage Bloodline Series

Mafia Romance

By:

Keta Kendric

Brizio DeLuca

Copyright © 2023 by <u>Keta Kendric</u>

This is a work of fiction. Names, characters, places, and incidents are a product of the author's imagination. Locales and public names are sometimes used for atmospheric purposes. Any resemblance to actual people, living or dead, or to businesses, companies, events, institutions, or locales is completely coincidental.

Cover: <u>Cosmic Letterz</u>

Editing: <u>A. L Barron</u>, One Last Glance Editing and <u>Tammy Jernigan</u>, publisherchick1@gmail.com.

ISBN: 978-1-956650-06-8

Table of Contents

Dedication

To the fierce Savage readers. You are my best motivation.

Synopsis:

Maya: I couldn't leave well enough alone. My obsession with finding out what happened to my brother led me into the hands of Brizio DeLuca. His offer to help me came with a set of rules and instructions that set me on a path lined with torture, death, and destruction.

Brizio: I was minding my business and working on becoming a better man. *And here she comes.* Maya waltzed into my club and brought with her a mountain of trouble, the kind of trouble that whispered sweet nothings to my dark side.

Warning: This book is a multicultural romance that contains explicit language, graphic violence, and strong sexual content. It is intended for adults.

.

CHAPTER ONE

Brizio

Who the hell is that and why is she questioning my customers?

My eyes squinted into slits, while reading her lips. The large monitors I stood behind in my club's office aided me in making out enough to know that she was asking questions about the person in the picture she would occasionally flash.

First, Primo, my cousin and Capo of St. Louis, with his new girlfriend showing up out of the blue tonight. Now *her*. She was in my club a few weeks ago, and although she exhibited strange behavior like she was casing the place, I hadn't confronted her.

Now, she solicited men, feigning interest to gain their attention so she could question them. From what I could tell, they weren't taking her interrogation sessions well, some threatening to hurt her.

There was something about her even at a distance and scaled down to a stilled image on one of my monitors that didn't give off a cop vibe. She was too reckless. The person she was asking about had to have been a missing or dead loved one. A sister, brother, or close friend.

Shit!

An exhausting sigh did nothing to alleviate my building tension. There was more important shit going on in my family than for me to be dealing with this shit. I would have to go and break this up before she ended up in a physical altercation. Surely the woman had enough sense to know that being sexy wasn't enough to keep a man from laying hands on her.

Threading through the crowd I picked up bits of conversation here and there, but nothing stood out. The accidental bumps, seductive smiles, and admiring eyes from females and the occasional male was the norm. I pretended to be flattered by the attention and handed out a few cheek and back of the hand kisses because it was good for business.

Truth was, it took a lot for a woman to keep my interest, more than a lot of these women were willing to give, I was sure. Therefore, I didn't stick around long enough to lavish them with too much attention.

Dammit!

I sped up, bumping into people in an attempt to get to the woman before the man she augered with decked her. He had already gripped her by the shoulders and shook her, but the aggressive action had no effect on the determined woman. Now, his fists were balled up at his sides and his eyes narrowed into slits.

"Is everything all right here?" I questioned, stepping between the two and invading their personal spaces. The man stood to my left, the woman to my right. My gaze landed on the woman.

Damn!

Up close, she was gorgeous. Her perfectly symmetrical face showed off lush pouty lips, a cute nose, and big expressive eyes, all aligned just right. Five-seven. My quick eye captured her height in a second flat. Body fit, but with enough curves to give those jeans and the top she wore enough definition to drag in major attention.

The light bounced off her sugary-brown skin tone, so unblemished it begged for a few bruises, or perhaps a little rope burn. Images of me yanking those shoulder length reddish-brown untamed curls, while slapping her round, drool worthy ass was already on replay in my head.

A light touch of dark, smokey makeup encircled big brown eyes while the blush red lipstick on her lush lips was sending me a personal request to be smeared.

How could this woman be so damn right and ready for me and not even know my name?

She'd made me forget why I was here in the first place, a sign that I needed to turn my ass around and leave her alone. I rarely get distracted, and she'd done it without even trying.

"This is none of your concern," she stated, leveling me with a side-eye dangerous enough to cause physical damage.

In my peripheral vision, the man bristled. He had enough sense to keep his mouth shut, an indication that he at least had a clue as to who I was in name or in ownership of this club. Didn't matter to me either way.

Since it would be a waste of time talking to the mouthy woman , I turned my gaze on the man.

4 · KETA KENDRIC

"Walk away now, while you still have the legs to do so."

He scoffed and threw up his hands.

"She's not worth the trouble," he muttered before turning abruptly in the opposite direction. He was a damned liar. Little Ms. Mouthy was worth some trouble, I just hadn't determined how much yet.

"I'm out of here," the man muttered over his shoulder before stepping off and mingling with a crowd of dancers flashing white teeth and welcoming him with open arms.

Hands on sexy ass hips. Big brown eyes leveled on me, squinting. I ignored the stare and took my time letting my gaze travel from the top of her head to her feet and back up. Sexy as hell-lit sin, any idiot who walked away from her had a weak ass ego.

"I should charge you for looking at me that way," she said. "Why are you all up in my…"

"Brizio," I said, cutting into a statement I knew would be full of venom based on the danger in her one-eyed squint and the wrinkle above her nose like I gave off an odor.

She wanted a fight, of that I was sure. Someone hadn't just pissed in her cereal this morning, they had dropped their pants and taken a shit in it .

"You're inside my establishment, so your business is my business," I stated, taking a deliberate step closer, although I was sure intimidation wasn't a tactic that worked on this woman. She was as wild as a stallion that needed to be broken, and I had just the thing to tame her sexy ass.

"Look B3co, or whatever your name is."

She knew damn well what I'd told her my name was, but she could have that one jab.

"Just because this is your little club," she said, dragging out the word club like it tasted nasty on her tongue. "It doesn't mean you can tell me who I can and can't talk to. You can move it right along and pretend to be the boss of someone else."

She actually sized me up, running a scathing gaze up and down my body like I bothered her trouble-making ass. And she wasn't done.

"I don't care if this club belongs to the Pope. I'll ask whoever I want, whatever I want."

I wasn't used to anyone speaking to me this way. Normally, I wouldn't tolerate this kind of lip from anyone, but something about this particular mouthy ass woman made me like the opposition she posed.

She was a challenge if I ever saw one and although her vibe and expressions breathed a serious attitude, there was a vulnerability hidden within the depths of her eyes that revealed itself to me.

I took another half step, so close now, her warm breath breezed along my face. My voice dropped an octave lower, my unflinching gaze at war with hers.

"I'll pick you up and carry you out of here myself if you're here to start trouble."

"I wish like hell you would put your hands on me."
She edged closer, throwing her chin up in defiance, her
eyes projecting a dare so serious, I hiked up a brow.

"Try it, and this club will be mine by next week,"
she spat, dripping sass like her body was oversaturated
with it.

Her words sliced through me like a flaming knife
through butter, and although her attitude irked my damn
nerves, I liked the kind of whiplash her tongue was capable of dishing out.

If only she knew how badly I wanted to toss her
across my shoulder and spank her ass until it was raw.
Even better, marching her down to my sandbox so we
can play adults games that would have her begging me to
untie her or pull the rope tighter.

"Is everything okay?" a female voice broke into
our stare off. When I managed to lure my gaze away
from the piercing gaze of the unruly woman in front of
me, it landed on a familiar face.

I was tempted to crack a smile at the woman who
may as well have been my new cousin-in-law the way
Primo had been holding her a little while ago in our
meeting. His body language clearly conveyed that she
was his and if anybody was bold enough to say differently, balls were getting cut off.

She stood beside the mess-starter I was currently in
battle with, her posture fierce and territorial. Were they
sisters?

"Everything is fine. I'm just playing the part of
Peacekeeper, so your friend here will stop stirring up
trouble in my club. She's agitating my customers," I

said, my eyes back on the one I was still tempted to toss across my shoulder.

"I'm sorry to hear that," Primo's woman stated before snatching the messy one by the arm and dragging her away. I turned and stared after them, catching the eyes of my opponent when she glanced back and tossed a teasing smirk across her shoulder. My gaze chased them until the crowd hid them from view.

My interest was piqued now. Who was she and why had she been acting like a rookie detective with my customers?

***

Once I was back in my office, I rewound the surveillance footage to capture a clear image of the object of my intrigue. With a message attached to a clear photo of her, I sent it to my detective contact, head of homicide for the SLPD, Johne Crawford. For ten grand a month, he was my loyal eyes and ears in the precinct.

Although a quarter of law enforcement in this city was on the DeLuca payroll in some capacity or other, Johne was known for being straight-laced and by the book. In the four years that I've been dealing with him he was so meticulously careful that he'd never been caught doing anything outside the law. Had even earned several bonuses for finding two double agents who worked for us as well as reported information on us back to the Soldanos family against us.

Lifting my phone to my ear, I focused on the frozen image of Ms. Messy on the screen.

The line finally clicked on but Johne didn't say a word. He never did. He cleared his throat two consecutive times, letting me know his line was secure and that he was listening.

"I just sent you a picture. Find out who she is and why she would be in my club asking questions like she's the police."

He cleared his throat once more and hung up.

My lips bent into a sneaky smile while continuing to stare at the monitor.

"Soon, I'm going to know who you are. May even get a chance to make you…"

My attention was drawn to another monitor. Primo had eyes on him and it wasn't from one of the many admiring women he had a habit of ignoring.

We would be engaged in a bloody, possibly deadly game, if the two men currently spying on him were angling for trouble.

CHAPTER TWO

Maya

The sight of Nevah's retreating back while leaving me standing at the bathroom door tore at my heart. She'd had to drag me away from B3co so she could give me one of her motherly talks.

Nevah and Tracy weren't blood, but they were my best friends, my sisters. I hadn't shared with them that I was back on the hunt to find my brother's killer. They would want to help, and I didn't want to risk them getting into trouble or hurt because of me.

My desire to find answers concerning my brother's death was a twisted obsession I couldn't shake. He had been beaten to death, so violently I hardly recognized his face when I identified him.

The sight was permanently etched in my brain, each memory of the image a rip in my heart. My brother had suffered. Based on the police reports I had begged and bribed to get my hands on, he had fought hard for his life.

All I received was a bunch of 'I don't knows' and 'we're investigating it' without a single clue as to who had savagely murdered him. Eric was too good a person to die so viciously only to have the detectives gloss over his case. They didn't have any witnesses or informants who could help solve their case for them. Not even a flimsy lead had surfaced.

I sucked in a deep, chest lifting breath and prepared to return to the club area. At this point, my motivation was shot and all I wanted was a few drinks and to call it a night.

The vibrating beat of the music welcomed me back with open arms. I appreciated the distraction more than I expected. The noise helped drown out all the nagging voices in my head, urging me to question anyone suspicious. Nevah was right in the little speech she'd just given me, I needed to chill.

I headed to the bar, not caring about the not so subtle bumps from men attempting to get my attention. I ignored them all. My new objective was to get wasted.

"Crown and coke," I told the bartender, who ignored the man attempting to get his attention to fix his smiling eyes on me. He nodded at my request, before turning away to go and fix my drink. He hadn't responded to the man beside me who amped up his huffing and puffing to gain the bartender's attention. A lazy smile crept onto my lips.

The joys of being a woman could be fun at times. At other times, womanhood was an ugly bitch, especially when men treated you like you were mindless, weak, and helpless. God forbid, you attempt to try and get one to listen to your ideas where it concerned subjects deemed unfit for a woman. A perfect example were the assholes down at the police precinct who wouldn't hear reason to investigate the few hunches I had...

"Stop it. Chill the fuck out," I muttered under my breath to stop myself from getting upset all over again.

"Crown and coke," the bartender said, his pearly white smile on display.

Cute.

"On the house," he announced before winking and walking away with a smooth stride that had me checking him out. Nice body, nice smile, and good looking in a rugged sort of way.

If he kept smiling like he wanted to suck up my pussy juices with a straw, I just may have to fuck him. Lord knows I needed a good sex session to put my mind back on track.

Five minutes later, I stood and mouthed, "Next time," to the cute bartender and laughed when he mouthed back "Okay," understanding my drift.

I walked off in the direction I last saw Tracy and spotted her immediately. She was the only one of our little group who actually enjoyed herself when we went out. I headed in her direction and something, intuition I suppose, made me glance up at the recessed blacked out area adjacent to the second level VIP area.

I got the sense I was being watched and knew who those eyes belonged to. I kept my eyes pinned on the area before I lifted my hand and licked up my middle finger. I sat the finger in front of my face, ensuring the watcher saw my gesture.

The act was childish, but there was something about the man, B3co. Tall, lean, sexy, and toned like the gym was his playground. His low scruffy beard and all that dark curly hair made my damn fingers tingle. He had all the qualities that reeled in women from miles around. As much as his sexy ass turned me on, he also irritated the hell out of me.

Cocky son-of-a-bitch.

"You ready," Tracy asked, breaking me out of my stupid act of rebellion against a man that could care less about my childish antics.

"Yeah. Did you have fun?"

She nodded, and dropped her gaze quickly, but I didn't miss that bashful glint that peeked through her gaze.

"I just ran into a priest when I was coming out of the bathroom. Surprised the shit out of me...because, what the hell is a priest doing in a place like this?"

I shrugged.

"Exactly," she said, taking my shrug for the run-on sentence it represented.

"I took it as a sign that it was time to go home," she stated, aiming a finger in the general direction of the front door.

With that, she waved at the company she was keeping with a cute Hispanic guy, and we headed for the door. She expressed a pleasant smile, but I knew when her smile was genuine. She wasn't ready to go back home, priest sighting or not. Her reality at home came with a lot of stress that I didn't envy.

I gripped her hand and swung it back and forth like we were kids. All I cared about was the genuine smile that appeared at my action.

Tracy would go home to three kids that came with a man who was more in love with the streets than he was a wife that did everything in her power to make them a family. Every once in a while Nevah and I would take the kids for a weekend so Tracy could get a break. The hours the three of us just spent in this club Tracy would consider vacation time.

I didn't have the kind of dedication she possessed. I would have left Kahlil's ass staring at my back the moment he informed me of his ex-wife walking out on him and leaving him with three bad ass kids to raise alone.

The urge to glance back again lured me from my thoughts, but I maintained my pace to the front door. At 1:45 in the morning this crowd was just getting energized. Unable to stop myself, I took one last lingering glance at the shiny pitch-black glass before we pushed our way through the exit.

CHAPTER THREE

Brizio

Two weeks later.

"Dammit woman, give me a fucking break," I muttered when *she* popped up on the monitor.

Maya Daniels.

With her rough upbringing, no wonder she wasn't afraid to get in a man's face. According to what was reported back to me about the neighborhood she grew up in, half the kids didn't make it into adulthood.

My fingers brushed the report sitting atop my desk, but my eyes remained on the monitor. The death of her brother was what was making her a thorn in my side. There was no connection I'd found between her brother and my club.

Why are you targeting Hard Rain?

Although I didn't see it in the reports, this may well have been one of the last places he visited before he was killed. How would she know that information though?

I placed my hand to my forehead and massaged my temples while her beautiful image danced across the monitors. She was at it again, harassing my customers which meant I'd have to go and put a stop to the shit.

A stupid smile filled my face. I couldn't put my finger on the reason for it other than wanting to see her again up close and hear what that sassy mouth of hers would say tonight.

Admitting a truth I had been ignoring, I'd wanted her to return despite the trouble she could get into by testing this world. The trouble she *would* get into if she didn't stop the quest she appeared determined to carry out.

She was playing detective because the one assigned to her brother's case was a fucking joke who couldn't solve the mystery of his own ass crack let alone a murder case. And it was reported that she marched down to that precinct and stayed on his ass enough for him to hide from her when she showed up.

A few quick strides put me outside my office door. I drew it closed behind me and waited until the beeps alerted that the room was secure.

Minutes later and after having been stopped several times, I finally located my little trouble maker in a dark corner flashing a picture in front of Jed's face.

My right brow lifted high on my forehead when she became the center of my focus. The way those ripped jeans hugged her ass had my gaze zeroing in on the delicious area.

Damn. Why did she have to be sexy? Was she a test sent to put my willpower in jeopardy after I'd vowed to stay away from trouble?

For the past week, I'd been doing well in my new vow, not angling to find someone to hurt, torture, or *kill*. I'd even let Victor from the Soldanos family slide for drilling one of my informants for information about my family.

A pair of shiny tan heels cupping pretty feet with red painted toenails caught my attention. Her sunbaked skin peeked from tiny cut outs in a trendy black top. Her tone was so syrupy and creamy it made me want to lick her to see if I could guess her flavor. Her skin was as tempting as the rest of her, beckoning for a touch, when I already knew one caress would destroy my vow of becoming a better Brizio.

I reminded myself of the subject at hand. Stop her from pestering customers, no more.

Jed was a regular, rich and older. Told me he was searching until he found a wife half his age that was likable and compatible with him.

"Good luck with that shit," I'd told him several times. Here he was a year later, continuing the search and no closer to finding his magical wife. He was fifty and had a lot of good years remaining that would allow him to fuck and forget he even wanted a wife. Despite the odds stacked against him, I rooted for him to find what he was determined to find.

However, it wasn't going to be that sexy-sassy one hounding him for answers he didn't have. Her mouth was working overtime, but those scanning eyes of hers landed on me.

She squinted and I couldn't tell what the little twitch in her facial expression meant until it became the lead up to a dramatic eye roll and a visible sigh. Her action caused Jed to glance in my direction.

"Brizio," he greeted with a nod and wide smile.

"Jed," I returned. "Is this woman bothering you?" I motioned in her direction with a dismissive hand gesture.

Jed's eyes flicked back to Maya which caused his smile to grow about as wide as the Grand Canyon. She could have been bothering the hell out of him, but her looks had him willing to deal with whatever she dished out.

"Not at all," he replied. His eyes practically undressed her although she was dressed somewhat tame compared to the bits and pieces of outfits being modeled tonight.

At a closer observation , I noticed a hint of cleavage, her chest impressive enough to call out loudly to my attention. Her eyes had never left me, scanning and sizing me up.

"B...3...C...O," she finally greeted, her tone dripping so much contempt, I swore I heard some splash on the floor. She mocked my name, converting it to numbers and letters, but it *did* sound like she was saying it correctly, something I wasn't admitting to her smart-mouthed ass.

"I see you choose the kindergarten's way of saying my name. If you need pronunciation lessons, I'll be happy to give you a few."

She managed to squint and side-eye me at the same time, cursing me with a look like I'd stole something from her. I didn't notice I'd stepped into her personal space until Jed was forced to take a step back. She didn't.

"Jed," I called to him without unpinning my gaze from her razor sharp one.

"Yeah," he replied, his head rocking back and forth between the two of us. She and I remained locked in a standoff that we didn't initiate or intend, but neither of us would relent.

"This one's not for you. She's my little *pet.*" I spit out the world pet like it stung my lips. "You're going to have to find a future wife somewhere else."

"Pet! Who the fuck are you calling a pet?" Maya questioned, waving her hand like a blunt object in my face. Back and forth that hand danced to add serious emphasis to each of her biting words.

Jed lifted his hands, "Sure Brizio, I didn't know she was one of yours."

"His?"

I read her lips as her head jerked back in dismay at Jed's statement.

Jed backed off. His abrupt departure drew her attention before she leveled her fire-blazing gaze back on me. The raw energy she gave off and the crease of tension that was a resting staple between her eyes said she could rip a man apart with just a look.

She jammed a stiff angry finger in my face, aiming it inches from my left eye. Hostility swirled in her fiery gaze and sparked a magnetic charge that rolled off of her and struck me like an invisible slap.

I fucking liked it. I like that I could get her this upset. Calling her my pet had done the trick.

"You must have lost the one rusty screw keeping your brains pinned to the inside of your head, calling me your pet, you limp dick loser."

Her wicked words were a backhand to my cheek, and I along with anyone within earshot paused.

"Calm down, you sour pussy skeezer." I slung an insult right back at her in a relaxed tone, leveling my hands down to indicate she needed to take her tone and attitude down a notch.

She jerked her head back, her lips parting at the insult. I know she didn't think she could toss out insults and not be given one in return.

"Pet is a term of endearment, not a derogatory saying. All you need is a good belly rub and scratch in the right places and you will be back on the path of righteousness."

She huffed and puffed, her words an explosion in her brain based on her widened eyes and sharp head snap. My justification for calling her my pet did nothing but heighten her already amped up attitude.

"Just because these weak ass women you're used to dealing with let you talk to them in any kind of way, doesn't mean that I will. You can go to the kennel and rescue a dog if you want a pet. I'm no man's fucking *pet*."

She spit out the word pet like a bitter pill melting on her tongue. I pinched my forehead between my fingers, squeezing and rubbing the throbbing in my temples that pulsed harder each time she spoke.

"You've obviously lost your diseased ridden mind, but I'm just the one to help you find it," she muttered. Her wicked tongue sliced through her aggressive words like a blade through hot fat meat.

Tuning her out wasn't easy because she had the unique ability to lure me into her chaos. I pictured her naked, tits bouncing while she bobbed up and down my dick instead of listening to all that shit she was talking.

The only reason we hadn't been approached during this little standoff was that most of the regulars knew I was the owner and a DeLuca. A small percentage also knew what went down in the basement of my club.

Before I noticed what I was doing, my fingers tightened around her right arm, and I dragged her in the direction of my office. She labeled me several types of sons-of-bitches and motherfuckers for this stunt.

I leaned in, placing my lips against her ear.

"We need to have a fucking talk," I muttered through gritted teeth.

"Yes, we fucking do," she spat right back.

Although her facial expression revealed the depth of her anger, she didn't jerk away from me. I eased up on the hold I had on her arm. We had drawn enough attention. The last thing I needed was for her to go off and get herself killed after hundreds of eye witnesses had seen us in a heated debate and me dragging her off like a jealous lover.

"Brizio fucking DeLuca!" a strong male voice shouted from the crowd behind us.

Not fucking now!

I didn't have time to deal with him and his bullshit right now. My abrupt stop at the irritating voice caused Maya to bump into my side.

She was more worried about who called me out than plowing into me. She turned to see who she was in competition with for my attention.

"Detective Limp Dick," I called out to Detective Lincoln Marx. "How the fuck did you get into my club?" I asked him, finally turning fully to see the irritating as fuck smug grin I knew would be on his face.

"I have my ways. But, that's beside the point," he said, casting a lingering glance at Maya. A hint of knowing flashed in his eyes before he fixed his stringent gaze back on me.

"I have a few questions to ask you about a homicide that took place in a burned down warehouse…"

I jumped in his face, slamming my chest against his, shoving him back and cutting him off. His loud ass was drawing the wrong kind of attention. He was doing the shit on purpose. Marx was known for harassing DeLucas on every trumped up nugget of information he believed he knew.

"You better contact my lawyer and get the fuck out of my club before I have you tossed out on your ass," I spit the words in his face.

He drew closer, his eyes dead locked on mine, face drawn back in a snarl. At this point, all eyes were on us.

"I'd like to see you try. You touch a hair on my head, and I'll have you behind bars within minutes. Now, I asked you a question: De...Lu...ca." He sounded out every syllable of my last name, the hate in his tone undeniable.

"And I said get the fuck out before you piss me off," I growled, my nostrils flaring as rage ripped through me like rolling thunder. All that kept me from exploding was the crowd and a part of my brain reminding me that Maya stood next to me.

He snickered but was smart enough to back off.

"You are going to fuck up and I'm going to be right there, waiting to slap handcuffs on your want-to-be-mob-boss ass."

"Your little fantasy has about a raindrop's chance in hell of coming true. You've been trying for what, years now? You couldn't take down a stale donut much less a DeLuca. Be gone pig before you stink up my establishment."

I waved him away with the flick of my hand, loving that tick of frustration under his right eye. He wanted me and anyone in my family in jail so badly, it was only a matter of time before his by-the-book ass did something illegal to make it happen.

He turned with a sharp snap and stomped off. After he faded into the crowd my rage settled to a low hum of energy versus the serge of blazing fire it had become seconds ago.

"You have interesting friends," Maya said, drawing my attention.

"You have no idea," I replied before turning to continue our journey. I took a hold of her arm, not because I was afraid she would turn around but because of my roaring need to touch her. I dragged her stubborn ass along, making her heels *click clack* loud enough to be heard despite the crowd and music.

Once we cleared the first level hall, the flight of stairs, and were out of eyesight of the public, she swung on me. Ripped her arm out of my hand and nearly took my head off. If I didn't have any training, she would have decked me with a wicked right hook. Hard.

"Look, you camel-toe-faced asshole, the next time you grab me like I'm one of these skanks you're used to manhandling, you're going to end up being dubbed the one-handed mute, because I'm going to chop your hand off and use it to snatch your tongue out of your mouth." *Dayem!*

I blinked. And blinked a few more times for good measure. I couldn't let her have the last word.

"Look you slimy faced slut, the day you put those crusty claws of yours on me is the day you're going to draw back a stump."

She threw her hand on her hip, jerked her neck back, and stared me down, daring me to touch her again. I was rarely stunned by anything, but this spitfire of a woman was pissing me the hell off and at the same time about to make me come on myself.

I was still processing that she'd swung on me and insulted my face. A lesser man would have been crying by now.

"And I didn't forget the slick shit you said, calling me your damn pet."

My face bunched into a tight knot and a flood of emotions or *something* chose this moment to silence me. She was hot and sexy and fuck, so much more than met the eyes. I sensed it but I didn't know how to interpret the shit.

She was also serious, and I couldn't figure out if I was angry or turned on. Tempers flaring be damned, we needed to talk.

"First, calm the hell down. Second, you're going to get yourself hurt asking questions about a subject that raises red flags. Third, get your ass moving so we can talk in private." I barked, deciding after all that it was anger that pulsed through me.

"Be glad I didn't toss you out of here with the limp dick detective. You got some damn nerve and if you keep running that mouth, I'm going to put a ball gag in it."

She got in my face, that evil finger of hers nearly taking out my eye.

"You fucking…"

It was all she got out before I snatched her ass, spinning her around and shoving her towards my office door. I pinned her between my body and the door at her back. I slapped my palm against the glossy surface next to my door and allowed it to scan my palm before keying in the six digit pin that popped the door open.

She breathed out her anger, hard and fast, eyeballing me with murder in her gaze the entire time. We were so close, her warm breaths winded against my chin, her body heat mingling with mine.

Once the door was open, I spun her ass around again, placed a firm palm in the center of her back, and shoved her into my dark office.

"Get your hard headed ass in there!" I ordered, giving her more of that manhandling she claimed she didn't like but was getting today.

Whatever she was about to say died on her tongue. My office, once I flipped on the lights, became way more interesting than the shit she was about to say. She glanced around, taking in all of the equipment. Her eyes stopped on the large display of monitors.

"Maya Daniels," I said, my voice low, firm, and edgy from her getting my nerves charged up.

Me calling her name pulled her gaze away from the monitors. Her sharp-eyed gaze strolled over me, her observation deliberate, like she was seeing me for the first time. Although I knew it killed her to stay quiet, she did and I was grateful she knew when to shut up after all.

"I know about your brother. Know the authorities aren't doing anything to solve his case. Know that you're attempting to do it yourself. But, you're going about it all wrong."

She lifted a curious brow and folded her arms across her chest.

"If you're the paradigm of knowledge and infinite wisdom, then by all means, tell me how I'm supposed to be handling it," she spit at me.

"With a lot more finesse. You want anything done in this city, in this type of environment, you have to do it from a dark place. A place where no one knows you're even looking. A place where you may have to and are willing to get your hands dirty, maybe even bloody to get the answers you're searching for."

I stepped closer, so near, her warmth and invigorating scent flowed over me like a sheet warm from the dryer.

Why was this my first time getting a good whiff of her? Did she have me so upset that I had ignored that scent. *Fuck!* Spicy amber, lavender flowers, and…*stop.* I was allowing her to distract me again.

"So, you used all of your finessing and dark skills to find out who I was? And about what I was doing?"

She still hadn't lost that hard edge I liked.

"Yes," I said, proud of myself, although her pursed lips and stiff eyes suggested she wasn't the least bit impressed.

"So what?" she shrugged. "You know who I'm and why I'm doing what I'm doing. What does that have to do with why you brought me in this…"

She turned and took in my office that contained a surveillance area just as big as the one in my basement.

"…Office," she decided.

I released a long sigh.

"I may regret this, but I want to help you."

"Why?" She squinted and placed a hand on her sexy ass hip and dared me not to lie with her rigid glare.

"If I don't help you, you're going to end up getting yourself killed. I know where you grew up, know you're a lot tougher than you look. But, some of my customers are not your average everyday criminals. There are people out there who would snuff you out with a snap of their finger and no one will ever know you existed."

Her face softened for the first time and the crease between her forehead disappeared.

"Why do you care what happens to me? I'm none of your concern."

"I don't care."

Liar! The voice in my head called my ass out.

I didn't know this woman on a personal level and until I dragged her into my office, I hadn't planned on offering her help.

"I don't want detectives sniffing around my place looking for your dead body because the last place anyone saw you was in my club asking the wrong kind of questions. I don't need that kind of heat. You already met Detective Limp Dick sniffing around here like a let loose bloodhound."

She placed a manicured finger against her lips, *very sexy ass lips*, and her eyes narrowed into a hard squint before she lifted them to meet mine. I could see her thinking.

"So let me get this straight, you want to avoid the heat the cops will bring, but you're willing to get involved with the kind of trouble I'm stirring?"

The gleam in her eyes brightened or maybe it was the way her eyes widened when an idea popped into her head. Her sexy lips curled into a smile.

"What am I saying? You're the mob. Of course you don't want to draw any attention. Cops are either trouble for you or the solution. I get that part, but I can't figure out why you would help me? It doesn't benefit you. And what does this help of yours entail, anyway?"

She was right. Me helping her didn't benefit me or my family, but I felt the strange need to do it anyway. I also knew that my club wasn't the only one she'd been visiting on her journey to the grave.

"I can use my connections to find out what happened to your brother."

She shook her head. "And that's it. What do you want in return? I know damn well you're not volunteering your services out of the goodness of your heart."

I considered what she was saying. When I dragged her into this office it was pure impulse and male ego driving my behavior. The last thing I wanted to do was offer her help. I blinked, my face drawn in tight contemplation.

Why did I volunteer to help her? What did I want from her? This was some strange behavior, even for me.

"I can tell by the constipated look on your face you probably want something that I'm probably going to tell you to go fuck yourself for asking me."

She took a deliberate step closer, not the least bit afraid of me. She didn't have much in the way of brains, by how recklessly she was managing her life, but she had balls, big ones.

"You think you know all about me, but I know your last name. Mr. DeLuca," she spit out the syllables of DeLuca like she was hawking up a big wad of spit.

"I'm in just as much, if not more danger, from your family taking me out than the people I'm questioning. I'm better off on my own."

She wiggled a finger around in my face while talking. The act would have been comical if we weren't discussing something as serious as her life. Did she want to die? Was she on a suicide mission?

She turned and stepped towards the door. I followed, getting in her face and shoving my hand against the door to keep it closed.

"I'm trying to save your life. Are you suicidal or something?"

"If finding out who killed my brother makes me suicidal, then the answer is yes. Besides, I'm sure getting tangled up with you in any situation is more detrimental to my health than anything else out there."

I lifted an eyebrow. The DeLucas did love to flirt with death and disaster, but that wasn't the point. There were things just as dangerous, if not more so than us out there and she needed to get it through that thick skull of hers.

She continued to pull effortlessly at the door. The hot headed ass woman was going to end up getting herself killed, and for some irritating as fuck reason, I didn't want to see that happen.

I shoved my face closer to hers, so close her breath blew against my lips. But, she didn't back down and the challenge in her eyes made me want to do all sorts of mean and nasty shit.

"Go ahead, you will probably end up dead long before you find any answers. See if I give a damn. Just don't bring your ass back to this club with that shit."

She released a long-winded sigh. Released it all into my face before she rolled her eyes and snatched the door open. She shoved her shoulder into my arm, knocking me out of her path before she stomped off, leaving the door open.

"Fucking straight trouble," I muttered through gritted teeth. Why on this earth was I forcing myself to believe that she needed me? Needed my help. Needed me to save her from herself before she ended up like her brother.

I placed my phone to my ear after I'd listened to it ring for the third time.

"Brizio," Jay called into the phone. "Everything is set up. When are you coming down?"

Jay and I conducted shows of a kinky nature down in the Devil's Sandbox, the dungeon in the basement level of Hard Rain. The secrecy of its existence and exclusive admission process was known to less than one percent of the people who frequented my club. Occasionally, we took in a select few invites.

"You're going to have to run the show tonight," I told Jay. "There's a bit of an emergency I need to handle."

There was an emergency all right, a hard-headed ass woman who wouldn't listen to a damn thing I had to say. It irritated the fuck out of me that she hadn't taken me up on my offer to help her.

"Okay. I'll make you proud," Jay stated.

"Thank you." I clicked off, but my phone was right back at my ear. I was talking as soon as Vance, my club manager, said hello.

"I need to leave the property and I'm not sure when I'll return."

"Okay. Call me if you need me," he replied.

"Thank you." I hung up. Vance wasn't a DeLuca, but he was my right hand at the club and had put in work as a cleaner for my family for nearly a decade. He called the job his retirement plan. I still didn't know which job was the side job, being my club manager or our family cleaner.

I snatched my keys and headed out the door. Although muffled a bit, the pulse of the music beat against my skin as soon as I stepped into the hallway. Once I cleared the stairs and cracked the back door open, I was gripped by a different intensity. Silence. It pricked at my skin, but was tinged with random sounds that traveled among the warm currents of the night.

From the shadows, I started my car remotely, checking out my surroundings. A carefree life would never be something I'd ever experience. Even as a young child I was taught to check my surroundings, keep my head on a swivel, and always invest in information and knowledge.

When I was sure the coast was clear, I stepped out of the clingy shadows and hopped into my car. Once inside, I called up the app attached to the tracker I had stuck inside the wheel well of Maya's silver BMW when I saw her on the monitors pulling up and parking over an hour ago. I didn't expect to have to turn on the tracker, but it appeared this woman was determined to make me chase her.

CHAPER FOUR

Maya

My thoughts were as lit as struck matches while I sped along the interstate on autopilot.

Brizio DeLuca wanted to help me. Yeah right. And what would I have to give up? My soul? Rat on somebody? Kill someone for his family? Hell no, I wasn't getting in more shit than I needed to.

Despite what he and my friends assumed they knew, I wasn't suicidal. I was passionate and dedicated to my brother who had been cheated out of his life before he even had a chance to live any of it.

"Who the hell…"

I squinted while attempting to make sense of what popped up in my rearview mirror. Why was this crazy asshole riding my ass so close? I switched lanes so he or she could go the hell around me if they needed to be somewhere so damn bad.

"Go around," I yelled although the ass-riding asshole couldn't hear me. I'm sure they saw my gesture in the mirror."

"Hoot! Hoot!"

The loud horn sounded while their lights flashed like giant strobes behind me.

"Scared the shit out of me," I muttered. "Why the fuck don't you just go around you fucking idiot?"

I leaned across the center console to reach for my glove compartment and....

"Oh shiiiit!"

The hard impact took my breath. I fought the steering wheel for control when my car skidded into a neck-snatching swerve across the road. When I straightened and lifted my foot to stomp on the brake, another harsh clap of metal sounded as the impact took my breath and damn near snatched me through the front seat.

The road raging asshole behind me wanted to play bumper cars.

"Son of a bitch!" I cursed, steering into the harsh turn in an attempt to keep from going into a spin out. Thankfully, this stretch of I-270 wasn't that busy. Unfortunately, it meant that this asshole could run me off the road and get away with it.

He came at me again. I saw his move in time to cut a hard right to the far lane and out of his reach. I floored my car and the idiot followed, wanting a road war.

"Okay, motherfucker. You don't know me. My ass is as crazy as you are." I slammed on breaks so he was on my driver's side with his bumper at my back door. I banked hard to the left, cursing while sending what I now saw was a dark gray Honda into a deadly swerve of screaming tires and burnt rubber.

"You wanna play rough?" I quoted Tony Montana from one of my favorite movies. I floored my now damaged BMW due to that asshole. He remained hot on my trail, determined to destroy me and my car.

Maybe B3co was right. I had gone too far and had finally gone and pissed off the wrong person.

My instincts told me, whoever it was, was out for blood. This wasn't a road rage situation. I hadn't cut anyone off, hadn't even flashed or zoomed past anyone.

The Honda was coming after me full force again, but I dodged it in a nick of time, swerving hard and giving my tires a good workout.

"Bam!"

The impact sent my car sideways and me ripped away from my seat, but the seatbelt snatched me back in place. The Honda had knocked the shit out of my car, making the sharp edges of my dented door poked me in the arm as I fought to keep my car on the road.

As soon as I was able to shake off the first impact, the dented front fender of the Honda was coming straight at my door. All I could do to save myself was turn into the car and pray the impact hit my driver's side fender and not me.

We collided hard, the medal on medal impact thundering like an explosion. The sharp ache that exploded in the left side of my head had me believing my left eardrum had been blown out. The car went airborne, lifting me off the seat for a second. The force of the impact sent our cars in opposite directions.

The Honda swerved across two lanes towards the barrier dividing the southbound traffic from our northbound side and stopped with a thundering crash. My headlights revealed a double stack of thick orange jersey barriers I was closing in on. The reflective signs cautioned drivers about the hill of gravel sitting right behind them.

"Lord, if you hear me. I'm sorry!" I screamed, gripping the steering wheel while my life played out on a fast-moving reel in my head. I had no idea how fast I traveled and couldn't look down because my gaze was locked on the orange barriers and the giant hill of gravel behind them that I was about to plow into head on.

"Lord, help me!" I cried and my yell kept going while death closed in on me. I slammed my feet down on the breaks so hard my legs shook to maintain the pressure. Nothing stopped my car's relentless pursuit as it kept hurdling forward despite the smoke from the rubber scratching to get a grip on the highway.

With my eyes shut tight, I instinctively lifted my arms to protect my face. It was all out of my hands now. *Damn.* I was about to die without knowing who killed me or my brother. My hard-headed stubborn ass should have been more careful. Will those thick plastic barriers be enough to soften the blow?

A loud *bang* sounded off before everything went pitch black.

***

Brizio

Fuck!

I saw the accident before it happened. The moment she turned into the car that was attempting to ram her. Each vehicle came apart and shot off in opposite directions, like two lit rockets. The Honda hit the concrete divider on the driver's side. The passenger side door of it sprang open but I didn't see the driver.

Maya's car ran head on into some barriers before plowing into a mound of gravel. The impact caused the back of the car to lift. She'd mowed down the orange barriers, so her car was angled up on a slight incline like it was getting into position to ram its way through the hill.

The impact had pushed her hood back to the engine. She would live, but may have suffered some serious injuries.

I was closing in on her location with my heart pumping as fast as my engine's pistons. Was I having a damn panic attack? I couldn't inhale a deep breath no matter how hard I sucked in air.

Out of the darkness, a man stumbled across the road. It was the one she'd rammed into the center divider. He didn't appear to notice my approach, his gaze focused on Maya. I drew my gun when he took up a defensive posture the closer he got to her car.

The bold motherfucker walked up to her window and peeked in, so focused on Maya he hadn't noticed me rolling up and closing the distance to the back of her car now.

I came to a screeching halt, about fifty feet behind her car, purposely keeping my car in the darkest patch on the roadside. I hopped out of the car leaving my door open and sprinted in the direction of her car. My nerves were as charged as the atmosphere around me.

Even at a distance I made out her face planted in the airbag and visible signs of blood in the dim light shining down from the high telephone poles.

There was another car approaching from a distance in my rear, and I prayed it was people who weren't interested in lending a helping hand. I didn't need any witnesses to what was about to go down.

Thankfully, the car rolled by, slowing to see what was happening, but not stopping. It was two o'clock in the morning, so the road was relatively deserted and provided a deterrent for Good Samaritans. If they called the authorities, I will have taken Maya and gone long before they arrived.

The gleam of the weapon caught my attention when the man sent it crashing into Maya's driver's side glass. The loud shattering was followed by the metallic click of his weapon.

"You move one muscle and a thunderstorm will be the only force strong enough to clean this highway of your brains."

At the sound of my voice, he glanced in my direction and...

Pop!

Pop!

The man clamped a useless hand around his neck, blood squirting between his fingers. His Adam's apple bobbed frantically. I hadn't squeezed my trigger which meant Maya had to have been the shooter.

The man staggered away from the car and headed towards the mound of gravel in front of Maya's crashed car on wobbling legs.

"Don't shoot," I called out, making my careful approach to the driver's side window to see how badly she was injured.

Bam!

If I had stepped any closer, and hadn't dropped beside the car, the crazy ass woman would have shot me. My heart hammered at just how close she'd gotten me to meeting the devil.

"Hold your goddamned fire! It's me, Brizio!" I yelled at the top of my lungs. The asshole she shot was cast in the dull light of the moon, his body slumped against the rocky hillside. His ass was dead or dying.

I lifted to chance a peek at her and all I saw was the shiny top of her pistol before it nudged my chest.

"B3co," she muttered, weak and barely holding up the shaky gun.

"Crazy ass woman, I came here to help you."

"What are you, my stalker now?" Her eyes widened one second and slammed shut the next, fighting to keep me in focus. Her head jerked from her attempting to keep it up right.

My gaze fell to the gun sitting at the center of my chest before I lifted it to meet hers.

"Will you take that gun out of my chest so I can help your hard headed ass?"

The gun dropped. She was so weak, I had to catch it before it fell to the ground.

"I'm going to pass out now," she said before she slumped in the seat, her head lulling to the side.

CHAPTER FIVE

Maya

A jolt of awareness hit me like a ghostly slap. My eyes snapped open right before the rest of me jerked awake. Wrong move. My eyes slammed back shut and my muscles tensed against the explosion of aches that followed my movement.

I squinted, but it had nothing to do with finding focus and everything to do with combating the fierce ache relentlessly tormenting me. I wanted to cry, shout my frustrations, and fall back into the abyss of sleep.

My head. My neck. My chest. Had parts of me been set aflame? Time was the only thing that would wedge me from under this weight of crushing discomfort.

Where the hell was I? My eyes darted around a pristine bedroom, colorless enough to be a hotel room, but personal enough with its long white drapes and knick-knacks throughout it to be a room in someone's house.

Where is this?

How did I get here?

Why was I here?

Think Maya. Think.

I forced myself to grasp what was dangling right at the tip of my consciousness. The club. Searching for my brother's killer. Getting confronted by B3co. Leaving. Getting followed. Getting run off the road. Shooting someone.

There was too much information coming at me too fast now.

I shot someone?

I glanced around the room again. Why wasn't I in jail? I didn't recall any police coming to the scene. Had I dreamed all the shit I believed happened tonight? Had I finally pushed myself to my mental breaking point? Was this a mental hospital?

I scratched absently at the side of my head, thinking, grasping a hold of memories that didn't make any sense and some that could have been a product of my imagination.

I shot someone.

Someone who would have killed me. The crazy ass man raised a gun and aimed it at my head. His eyes burned with the kind of empty darkness that said he would have done it, if I hadn't shot him first.

B3co was there also, wasn't he?

"Welcome back, Trouble."

I jumped when he stepped from the darkest corner of the room. Had he been there the entire time, watching me drag my mind for answers?

I hefted myself up a few inches, my body screaming for me to stop my foolish attempt at sitting up. Brizio
placed a firm hand on my shoulder, nudging me back
down.

"You may want to stay down," he suggested, leaning closer to get a better look at me.

He looked different. His hair. It was straighter,
longer than it had been at the club, like he had blown it
dry. It now fell over his shoulders, like it was reaching
out to me, the dark tresses beckoning me to reach up and
touch. I broke out of my feeble-minded moment of
weakness.

"What happened? Did I shoot..." I didn't want to
say it out loud.

"Yes. You did and he deserved it. He would have
killed you."

That much I knew based on the man's determined
expression alone.

"Is he dead?"

Brizio nodded but didn't elaborate.

His lips were rosy against his olive complexion,
sexy, kissable, the bottom slightly bigger than the top.
My tongue skimmed across my bottom lip and I caught
myself, clamping my lips shut. I must have been half
dead to be thinking about lips. Hadn't he just confirmed
that I had killed a man?

"You followed me. How did you even know where
to find me?" I questioned, still piecing together all that
had happened in my head.

I reached up and touched where my head ached most and found what I believed were stitches. *Thank fuck.* The wires in my brain were still crossed. That explained why I was checking this man out instead of worrying about what was more important.

"You said earlier that my family name makes me dangerous. Well, it also makes me well informed," B3co said smugly.

I was smart enough to grasp what he was getting at without knowing all of the details.

"You...helped...me?" I glanced down at herself. "Is this your place?"

He nodded again.

"The man I shot?"

"He's taken care of," he said, cutting me off before I could say more. I don't believe he wanted me repeating out loud anything that happened tonight. I swallowed hard when his statement about the man being taken care of finally soaked into my brain.

"The police. My car. Shouldn't I be in jail?" I whispered and despite all the shit swirling around in my brain, I couldn't help checking him out again. His eyes, a brown that reminded me of hot embers waiting to be stoked back into a flame.

The way his toned frame pushed at that designer T-shirt he wore. The way his lower half gave those jeans purpose, letting me know he had a good relationship with the gym and didn't miss leg day.

I swallowed hard. Yep, my ass was definitely injured. I didn't fawn over men, not like this and especially not at times when I had more important shit to worry about.

Brizio leaned in closer, his eyes scanning like he could detect the mix of crazy shit rattling off in my head.

"All taken care of," he reiterated, his eyes narrowing, still observing me.

His statement brought me back to the seriousness of my current reality. I wanted to ask how everything was taken care of, but I learned a long time ago, not to ask a criminal for details unless you wanted to take ownership of something that could end up biting you in the ass.

"I appreciate you helping me."

"Was that a thank you?" he questioned, that arrogant smirk making its first appearance.

"Yes. That was a thank you. That was also me revealing that my ego is not too big for me to be humbled. I should have listened to my friends, and even you, when you all kept warning me about stoking a fire that could burn me. Now, I have blood on my hands and I'm no closer to the truth than I was when I started this months ago."

It took a lot of effort, but I forced myself up onto my elbows. I swayed to the left, my body telling me it wanted more rest. However, I needed to get home. I needed the familiarity of my surroundings to ease the heavy tension weighing me down.

I had to get my head straight. I also had to stop checking this man out before he thought I was interested.

"You may want to rest for a few hours," B3co said, placing a delicate hand on my shoulder again.

"I need to get home. I need a change of clothes," I said, glancing down at the long-black T-shirt I wore for a hospital gown before tossing my legs over the side of the bed. The task was easy but it was the standing part that nearly put me on my ass if B3co hadn't caught me.

"Why are you so damned hard headed?" he questioned, while helping me back into the bed.

"Think Maya. You can't go home. Whoever came after you tonight could have someone there waiting for you."

Fuck, he was right. This was something I should have already known, but I still wasn't in my right frame of mind. And why did his bicep flex and tease the inside of my palm when he caught me and I caught his arm for support to keep from falling on my ass?

"Besides, I've been to your place already. I grabbed you some clothes."

This got my attention.

"You have? You did?"

I was about to ask him how he'd gotten in but there was no point. Even without my keys, he'd have found a way to enter.

"Why don't you try listening to someone for once in your hard-of-hearing ass life," he chastised me. His fussing made me smile because it sounded like he cared.

"You don't have a concussion, but you hit that cement pillar you call a head. Had to get five stitches right at your hairline and three more on your left forearm. You are also going to be sore from the impact."

My lips twitched at his insult about my head, but I managed a serious face.

"So, what are you, a doctor? Doctor Hot-Ass-Mess," I mumbled the smart remark, not because I was mad at him but because I enjoyed pissing him off.

He hit me with a wicked side eye, his unblinking gaze disciplining me like a teacher's ruler.

"No, but I had one check you out," he replied and a glint of concern flashed that put an end to the next smart remark I had prepared.

He drew the covers up to my chest. At this point, my effort to be hard headed had been zapped away and I fought to preserve the little strength I possessed. I was hurt worse than my brain would allow me to think. My eyes were just as weighted down as the rest of me now.

"Why are you helping me?"

My heavy gaze dropped before I snapped my eyes back open.

"Because I don't want you to die," is what I think he said.

I faded out, snuffed out by the grips of exhaustion spiked with a shot of straight, take-your-ass-to-sleep. Silence. Blackness. Nothing. This was the crowd that greeted me at the doorway to sleep.

***

Brizio

Maya was growing on me. I liked her. I liked that she was willing to fight for herself. I adored that sassy mouth. Even if I hadn't shown up, she'd have saved herself from that asshole intending to kill her.

Even now, when I should have been back at work or at least gone out with the cleaner to see if I could figure out who the guy was, I was at her bedside.

Why?

I couldn't figure out why I liked her even though she got on my damned nerves. My phone buzzed, dragging me out of my state of uncertainty and more than likely my misguided intentions towards Maya.

"Yes."

"Alfonzo Dominquez, a member of DG6," my cousin Romigi revealed.

Romigi wasn't always available, but when he had free time on his hands, crime scene cleanups were one of his favorite pastimes. For him, it was like putting together a piece of life's puzzle. He communed with the dead. Since he was a priest, he prayed over them, talked to them, and I believed saw something in them in death that others couldn't see. He also found clues, got names and leads faster than anyone else who cleaned for the family.

"DG6. Didn't they disband? Wasn't there too much infighting after the entire upper echelon of their crew got whacked?"

"I believed the same," he agreed. "But, the question we need to find an answer to is what is a member of a disbanded or rebranding cartel doing in St. Louis, thinking he's going to kill your lady?"

I laughed. Romigi might have been a priest, but he possessed a slick DeLuca tongue. I wasn't going to dignify his fishing attempt about me and Maya with a reply.

"I don't know what he's doing here, but I'm sure there's probably more to him than meets the eye. Think he could be working with another crime organization?"

"It's possible. I'll see what I can find out. But, it looks like you have a lot of work to do if you are going to help her. She may not have known her brother as well as she assumed she did."

I stared at a sleeping Maya. She was no stranger to the streets based on where she'd grown up. Was that what got her brother killed?

"Thanks for the information," I told Romigi before clicking off.

I already had enough on my plate dealing with a traitor in our family who may have been the same one hell bent on sending assassins to take out my cousin Primo. Did I have room in my life to take on more *Trouble*? Because like it or not, Maya was all sorts of trouble; good, bad, and ugly.

CHAPTER SIX

Maya

Three days later.

My fingers worked the keyboard of my work laptop. Thankfully, Brizio with his forward thinking had not only grabbed me a few changes of clothing, but he'd also been wise enough to grab my work laptop, work phone and spare keys.

It surprised me that I still knew how to put in for leave since I hadn't done so in nearly a year. Until I got my damned head straight, I didn't need to be at work. Despite my hard head and smart mouth, I actually cared about my job and helping people, especially when they depended on me for their medical safety and security.

The last thing I needed on my conscience was a bad diagnosis, issuing the wrong treatment, or God forbid, prescribing the wrong medication. People were already at their wits end by the time they got to me, so I wanted them to be aware that I didn't play around when it came to my work.

Would two weeks off be long enough for me to resolve this mess I'd gotten myself into? My supervisor had been on my ass about taking leave and since I was on use-or-lose status, taking off wasn't a problem.

I heaved a deep breath, fighting to get B3co out of my head. He hated me calling him that, and I loved that he hated it. The idea of pissing him off had me smiling.

It boggled my mind that he went out of his way to help me when I was clearly a pain in his ass. I didn't get it. He'd saved me from prison. I was grateful, thankful that he'd decided to help me after I'd walked out on him.

Why was he helping me?

The question kept springing up in my head like weeds.

I promised I wouldn't question it anymore, however, him helping me was one among a list of questions torturing my mind. Not to mention a member of DG6 at my car window about to take my life. Although I'd heard of the gang in the past, Brizio had to give me a quick history lesson on the once infamous organization.

Who did I piss off? Who did I question and what did I ask them that set them off enough to come for me? Maybe it wasn't someone I'd questioned. Did the person who'd killed my brother know I was looking for them and had sent someone to take me out?

Another long sigh. *Fuck my life.* I was making a mess of it, but I couldn't shake the notion of finding out what happened to my brother. He'd suffered too much. Died in the worst possible way. Someone had to pay and as much of a mess I was making in my attempts to find his killer, I knew I wouldn't stop looking, couldn't stop.

Now, I had to stuff all my feelings deep inside because I had another important duty to perform. Tonight, I had to be there for Nevah, who I hadn't seen in damn near two weeks. Me and Tracy were set to link up, carpool, and to meet her in Mt. Vernon, Illinois of all places.

***

The temporary break away from my current reality was one I wasn't aware I needed. Outside of work, I hadn't been doing a good job of managing my life.

Hiding my activities from the two ladies who meant the world to me wasn't an easy task as they usually found ways to make me spill my guts. Not this time. I couldn't tell Nevah or Tracy that I killed a man and a member of the mob helped me cover it up.

Jesus.

The idea of it alone was enough to make me shiver.

"You alright?" Tracy asked, flashing that questioning squint like she did when she suspected one of us of hiding something from her.

"I'm fine." I lied. "I was thinking I needed this break to let my hair down, enjoy some drinks and laugh with my girls."

She bumped my shoulder before leaning in and placing her head against mine.

"Awe," Nevah said, her tone dripping raw emotion, her gaze projecting care despite all the drinks we'd consumed. I had a tendency to get loud when I drank, but we were the kinds of drunks that loved on people, wanting to hug each other as well as drag strangers into our emotional reunions.

"I'm dating someone," Nevah blurted.

The soft music playing, people's muffled conversations, and other background noises faded out. I couldn't believe Nevah's ass was sitting there sipping on her margarita and pretending like me and Tracy weren't staring holes in her flesh.

Tracy slapped the shit out of her forearm, making her jump and spill some of her drink.

"Are you going to tell us who the fuck you're dating, or are we going to have to tie your secret-keeping ass down and torture it out of you?" I questioned, my eyes fixed on her lips anticipating her words, any words.

"He's probably not someone you'll approve of me dating. Kind of dangerous, but he treats me really well," Nevah blessedly continued.

"How long have you been dating this guy?" Tracy asked, flashing her famous squint that said Nevah better not lie.

"I met him at the club a few weeks ago when we were there."

"That's why your fast ass wanted to leave so soon after we arrived. You could have told us you were sneaking off with a man. Who the hell is this miracle worker that had you ditching your friends these past few weeks?" Tracy questioned. She was spot on with her line of questioning, asking what was on my mind before I could spit out a word.

"His name is Primo DeLuca."

At that revelation, I choked so hard on the sip of drink I'd taken that Tracy grew concerned enough to slap my back like she did one of her kids when something went down the wrong way. Primo DeLuca was a big shot in the same mob as the cousin who had taken it upon himself to help me.

Not that I wasn't grateful for the help, but when dealing with the mob, you never knew if you were better off dealing with whatever came at you on your own because the mob came with a certain level of danger that even the law was afraid to touch. I had to keep reminding myself of this because Brizio had a way of making me forget that he was a part of a crime family.

"It happened by accident. I was searching for Maya and the guy she walked away with and sort of just ran into him when I peeked into one of the back offices. We talked and hit it off."

"What?"

The most simple of my questions remained stuck inside my head, buried under a sea of all the questions I couldn't organize to voice out loud. Tracy sat staring, unmoved. She was apparently as stunned as me.

"You're serious?" Tracy finally asked Nevah, her voice a harsh whisper.

Nevah nodded, but her face didn't give the appearance that she was in trouble. She looked relaxed, happy even.

"We are not together at the moment because he's taking care of a family problem," Nevah added.

I was usually the one with all the opinions and questions, but my voice was lost in the dark cloud of trouble hanging over my head. The idea of Nevah dating someone from the mob was the last thing I expected to hear.

"Um," Tracy dragged out, gathering herself, "Once you're in one of those kinds of families, you can't get out of it, right?"

I shook my head at Tracy when ideas finally formed into words that marched down to my tongue, itching to be set free.

"That's not true. The men date, dump, and marry whoever they want. However, they are selective about the women they choose. It's usually women who are in similar families."

I flashed a fake smile, expressing the emotion to hide the fear I felt for my friend.

"Is this a relationship you want?" I questioned Nevah. My forehead creased with the stress I fought to contain. The idea of Nevah being pressured into a relationship she didn't want to be in had me ready to go and curse someone out. She took too long to reply, causing the frayed edges of my nerves to sharpen.

"Some of those men *take* whatever they want, and it's my fault if you are stuck. If you hadn't been looking for me, you wouldn't be in this situation, hiding out and waiting until he *fixes* what I'm guessing is a dangerous situation since he obviously doesn't want you anywhere near it."

Nevah placed a hand atop mine, her eyes projecting a relaxed vibe, her smile calming.

"I'm not being forced into this situation," she reassured, glancing at me and Tracy.

"At first, I was against us having a relationship, but after spending time around him, I honestly believe we can make it work."

This time we must have taken too long to respond because Nevah continued.

"I'd certainly understand if you guys would want to keep your distance. I don't want…"

Tracy lifted a hand, cutting her off before I did.

"I know what you're about to say, and you can chill with that shit. We are your girls, and I don't care who you're dating. It's not going to stop me from being your friend. Do I want you with someone a little more…safe? Shit, yes. But we are all placed in certain situations for reasons we may never understand. If you and that fine ass Primo DeLuca are meant to be, his job and who his family is don't matter."

"What she said," I agreed, pointing at Tracy who proudly displayed a big grin.

"Here we are trying to force you down random men's throats, and you're dating one of the finest men in the damn city." I added to let her know that I was okay with whoever she wanted to date even if the idea stressed me out.

"Thank you. I appreciate you ladies wanting to keep me, but my life may become a lot more complicated than me hanging out in a hotel," she said, eyeing each of us.

"I know you can't disclose family secrets or anything, but if he said he needs to work something out, that means he's probably planning on killing people, right?" I questioned, gauging if Primo was in fact one of the big shots in his family.

Nevah's eyes rested on mine until mine dropped. I was asking too much which meant there was a lot she couldn't say, which translated to yes, he was way more than a working member of his family.

The mood around the table was getting too serious and I knew a way to bring their smiles back.

"How's the dick? That man, although I've only seen his elusive ass once, looks like he could put it down," I questioned and commented.

The way Nevah's ass was smiling and staring off into space, said more than she needed to say out loud.

"That damn good, huh? He got any more cousins? My poor pussy is starving, and if there is one thing I know, the more dangerous a man is, the more he knows how to lay the smack down in the bedroom. It's like the danger enhances their instincts, especially their sexual instincts."

Nevah shook her head at me while I was high-fiving Tracy. Little did they know, I was already acquainted with a cousin. I wasn't sure I wanted to spill the beans about the mess I had gotten myself into yet.

"Facts!" Tracy added.

We drank and laughed about the good ole days at college while Nevah continued to dodge most of our questions about Primo. I wasn't as relentless as I knew I could be because I was sitting there holding on to a big secret too.

Speaking of secrets, my phone buzzed and a quick peek revealed that it was Brizio calling.

Dammit! I needed to take this call.

"I need to go to the little girl's room," I announced, before taking a big gulp of my fourth or fifth drink. Seeing their smiles was an assurance that everything would be all right whether I believed it or not.

Standing, I walked away, heading towards the bathroom. Once inside, I checked to make sure it was empty and locked myself inside. I dialed Brizio back.

"B3co," I greeted when the line clicked on.

"I'm trying to figure out if I like that name or not," he returned.

"You like it," I assured him, smiling way too big for no apparent reason.

Brizio had done his best to try to convince me to stay at his house, but three days of laying around and allowing him and his house-visiting doctor to take care of me would give him the impression that he had some kind of power over me. I checked into a hotel, one he insisted on picking out and had paid for before I even got there.

"I have a lead," he said, regaining my attention. "I know you're with your friends right now, so I'll see you tomorrow at the club, six pm sharp. Don't be late. Oh, and I'm shortening your hotel stay, it's not safe for you there anymore. You'll be coming back home with me after we finish up at the club tomorrow."

Click.

I glanced down at the phone in my hand, lips parted and tongue still itching to spit out the choice words I had for him. Who the hell did Brizio 'B3co' DeLuca think he was? My husband?

Coming back home.

He would get enough of trying to boss me around. And why was there a silly smile spreading across my face at his antics?

I still hadn't found an answer to the question that had been burning a hole in my brain since we'd met.

Why was Brizio DeLuca helping me?

Tracy's abrupt silence at my approach let me know that they had been talking about me. They were worried about me continuing to pursue my brother's case and how promiscuous they assumed I was with men lately. I was willing to leap head-first into danger to find justice for my brother, but I'd be damned if I put them at risk.

It's why I wasn't going to tell them I was involved with Brizio. Which likely meant he would need to keep his trap shut to his cousin Primo about helping me.

I dropped back into my seat and continued where I left off, picking up my drink and sipping. An odd silence filled the space, but when we all glanced up at each other, we couldn't help cracking silly smiles.

"It's getting late," Nevah said. "I don't want to stay out too late considering the new dynamics of my life."

Tracy's face crinkled. "Don't you mean reintroduction? We grew up in The Grind. If you had never seen a hood in your life, I think you would have packed up and run by now."

I nodded reminiscing on the good old days.

"We might have all found a way out of the hood, but the lessons remain inside each of us. We don't run from a fight because we weren't raised to. We don't take shit from anyone because we weren't taught to," I preached.

In a way, I was proud that we had grown up tough. It made us stronger women.

We'd all had our run-ins with the law and God only knew how our records had remained untouched. Everything from grand-theft-auto, to being caught in police chases, to being caught in the middle of an active shoot out, bullet wounds, witnessing crimes, stab wounds, and now a covered up homicide. Although, I could argue it was self-defense. We had been through more than the average group of women that's for sure.

"Don't ever think that we would walk out on our friendship because your guy is not one of those squares that I like to take advantage of," I blurted, reminding Nevah that I would always be there for her.

Tracy nodded in agreement and Nevah swiped at her eyes, fighting to hold back tears.

"If that big, fine ass man of yours is ever in trouble, my advice to you is to help him. If you ever need a little help from me, I'm game," I stated, genuinely willing to help with whatever she needed.

"You ladies being here for me is all I need. Besides, I've seen Primo in action, and I don't think he's going to need my lightweight help."

I bet he didn't. Based on the way Brizio could steal me away from the scene of an accident and a death involved shooting and make it look like the scene had never happened, I could imagine what Nevah's new man was capable of doing.

An hour later, we hugged for what felt like an hour so Nevah could return to her hotel. Tracy and I were too damn drunk to attempt to drive back to St. Louis.

We opted for a hotel across the street from the restaurant and staggered our drunk asses across the road to hug and harass the people at the front desk.

I hadn't had a good night's sleep in weeks, so getting tipsy and going to bed wasn't a bad idea. Besides, I needed to be ready to meet Mr. Want-to-be-my-boss tomorrow and there was no telling what he had in store for me.

CHAPTER SEVEN

Maya

This crazy ass man wanted me to meet him in the basement of his club. I didn't even know the place had a basement. It sounded like trouble and based on his family name alone it was probably where they took people they planned to kill.

For all I knew, Brizio's basement was a damn prison. But, here my crazy ass was, parking this rental that he'd paid for to go down there and meet with him. A man who'd told me just last night that I was *coming back home* like he'd staked some type of claim on me.

Was I *this* desperate to find out what happened to my brother? Hadn't I already survived and gotten away with enough? Was I about to tempt fate further by meeting up with Brizio to pursue this lead he claimed to have found?

I nodded like someone else had asked me the questions. I owed it to my brother to find out what happened so he could rest in peace. It was the least I could do for him in death, since I failed to take care of him in life.

Nevah and Tracy insisted that I was punishing myself. Maybe I was, but there was something inside me, something gnawing at my spirit that wouldn't let up, wouldn't allow me to stop this path it insisted I keep traveling. I had to see this through.

Darkness lurked, like a heavy cloak of iron thrown across my shoulders, but I dragged myself closer to the door and the big brutish man standing guard outside Hard Rain. The usual line that wrapped around the block to get in, wasn't out here tonight. Those same people had probably attended church this morning and confessed the sins that manifested within them inside the club the previous night.

There was however a small crowd of women waiting out front that the guard was turning away. Did Brizio let his guards know that I was coming? I marched up to the line of women. Didn't they know the club wasn't open?

My question about the guard expecting me was answered quickly when the big brute of a man gestured me forward with the wave of his hand. The woman, about ten, standing before him continued trying to get inside the club. Were they holding job interviews?

When I stepped past the women, eyes followed, necks jerked, and frowns and gasps of protest ensued. The guard turned away from the group to open the door for me.

"How does she get in and I can't?" One of the women shouted at the guard. He ignored the outburst and stepped inside with me.

"Is she a Mistress?" another shouted before the door closed behind us.

Mistress?

"Mr. DeLuca wants you to meet him in the basement. Have a good night Ms. Daniels," he said, waving his hand to the interior door that led into the club. He turned and stepped back outside before I could reply.

Out of nowhere, another big man appeared, this one with a gun visibly holstered over a crisp white button up. He must have gotten rid of his suit jacket at some point.

"This way Ms. Daniels," he said, stretching his hand past the doorway he stood in. I stepped inside and followed the man to the area that would lead to the office locations.

I hadn't missed that these men knew my name. I didn't know how I felt about it. But, I had to consider that I was dealing with a professional criminal who could cover up a car accident and death without so much as a question being asked. How the heck had he pulled it off? Would he tell me if I asked?

The man stopped at what appeared to be a broom closet. When he lifted a panel I didn't notice at first sight and keyed in an eight digit number, my brows lifted. A spike of intrigue at the action made my brain cells tingle.

The door opened with a little *pop*. The guard pushed it open further and gestured towards the opening for me to enter.

"Have a good evening Ms. Daniels," he said before tipping his head at my low, "Thank you."

He stepped away, and I stood in place, contemplating stepping down. My hand remained pressed against the door behind me, keeping it open.

Taking these steps could mean me reaching a point of no return in this situation. My eyes fell closed on a long inhale and when I released it I also released the doubt that kept clawing at the back of my mind.

I took my first few steps down the dimly lit stairway and whirled around at the sound of the door closing behind me. The stairs turned at a sharp ninety degree angle and led me into an empty entryway facing a giant hardwood black door wrapped in barbed wire of all things.

The door resembled something designed for the devil himself, and the title above it, dripped paint resembling blood and spelled out the words, Devil's Sandbox.

Standing in place, I stared at the knob made of the same barbed wire as the door, reluctant to grip, turn, and push the door open. I tapped the knob to see if it was as deadly as it appeared. The view of it was deceptive. It wasn't as spiky as the metal sight of it suggested. However, turning the knob left a prickly ache in my palm. The door must have been a test, like a prerequisite you needed to pass to enter this place.

Darkness swallowed me when I walked past the doorway.

"Ahh!"

The sound of a woman screaming stopped me in my tracks. My head jerked around in every direction as I attempted to stretch my focus through the dark space.

What the fuck?

She was in trouble so my instinct to help her got me moving again. Light danced lazily from wall sconces that narrowly illuminated the space. A more luminescent glow of light drew me closer despite my nerves going haywire.

I placed a hand inside my purse in case this was a set up to kill my ass. This *was* the mob I was dealing with after all. Brizio stuck his neck out to help me, but he could be one of those people who enjoyed playing cat and mouse games with his victims.

"Ahh!" The scream grew more intense, sharp. "Pl...pl...please," the woman shuddered while a long black weapon sailed through the air and struck her body.

The shadows grew clearer, the dark fog lifting the closer I came to a stage lit by a series of small candles. The set-up wasn't romantic but more along the lines of dark and dirty romance.

Spiced lavender permeated the air, the calming effect seeping into my raging anxiety level. A low melody that could only be described as toxic-tragedy played low in the background.

When the scene came into full focus, Brizio stood before a woman who was tied to a big black cross. Her pale skin pierced the darkness better than the flickering light surrounding them. I picked up my pace, making my already erratic breaths kick up a notch.

"Stop that shit!" I yelled out, my voice stopping Brizio's next strike with his arm aimed away from the woman. He held up a funny looking belt.

"Are you out of your fucking mind? That's a fucking woman your about to hit. If she crossed you, you could mess up her credit, total her car, or find another way to get back at her. Don't do this sick shit."

He smiled. The crazy ass man flashed a big bright smile at me. The poor woman lifted her head that appeared to be too heavy for her limp and trembling body.

"Sir," the woman called breathlessly, her shaky tone matched the visible tremble in her body.

Before I could get another word out, he hit her again. The fringe of the belt connected across her stomach and the next across her hips.

Did he think I would be interested in watching this shit? *Hell no!* I marched my ass around to the three wide steps that took me up and onto the stage.

"Nice. This should be fun," he said, looking at me while striking the woman again, making her howl like a wounded animal.

He threw his arm back to hit her again, but I caught a hold of the fringed edges of the belt and yanked.

"Are you fucking crazy?" I pulled against his hold on the strap.

"Please Sir. Don't stop. Please. Please. Please," the woman begged.

What the...

His head tilted before he glanced at the strap, at where my firm grip had a hold on it.

"You heard the lady. You are messing up her session. She doesn't need to be saved. She needs to be set free."

I glanced at the woman, whose wide expectant eyes were aimed at the strap stretched taut between me and Brizio's grips.

"Sir Please," she cried.

Who?

What?

The crazy and obviously brain washed woman was crying hard, tears slipping down her cheeks like raindrops. I released the belt and lifted my hands.

"You two can have this sick ass shit," I said, my eyes bouncing back and forth between the two. No less than a second later, he struck her again and again, until...

What the double fuck?

The woman was in the throes of a full-blown orgasm. I'd heard about this freaky shit, but if you had told me I'd see something like this with my own two eyes, I wouldn't have believed it.

"Thank you, Sir," the woman kept repeating in a low shuttering voice while her body continued to shiver, limp with satisfaction.

I shook my head, reluctant to believe what I was seeing. When I assumed I had seen it all, this was added to my collection of crazy.

When I managed to draw my gaze away from the woman it landed on Brizio. He stood there tapping that strap against his legs with his eyes glued on me. I didn't need a lot of light to see the lust in his heavy gaze.

"You want a turn? Trust me, it will be a favor. My waiting list is about a year long. You probably walked past a few fighting to get in tonight."

"No, absolutely not. Getting my ass beat doesn't turn me on in any way. You can keep your freak shit between you and crazy ass broads like that one. "

I can't believe there was a line of women, damn near fighting that big ass, armed guard to get this sick shit done to them. That sneaky smile of Brizio's widened like he knew what I was thinking.

"Don't knock it until you've tried it," he had the nerve to say.

My lips pursed. "Look, I didn't come here to watch you beat the shit out of someone who gets off on it. I'm here on time because this is where you told me to be right now. Can we get on with our business? Are you done with this or do you have to flip her so you can catch the back side of her body?"

"Already done that, but yes, we're done," he replied with equal sarcasm.

When he stepped off and walked in my direction, I jerked my head back.

"Aren't you going to take her off that thing?"

"It's a St. Andrew's Cross, and no. She needs to stew in the punishment I owe her."

For how long?

I didn't ask the question out loud because I wasn't sure I wanted to know the answer. I had better things to worry about than the sexual habits of crazy people.

However, if this crazy man could help me figure out the mystery surrounding my brother's death, I'll certainly take the help.

He opened the barbed wire wrapped door for me and aimed his hand into the hall entryway. He secured the Devil's Sandbox before leading the way up the stairs, light taps against the hard wood the only sound between us.

Once we traveled along a hallway that I was sure I'd not seen before, we ended up at his office that housed the monitors. One screen provided an outside view of the club. The guard had managed to get rid of the line of women. Another monitor showed the woman he'd beaten, her head hanging low like she was asleep.

"What do you know about my family?"

His question drew my attention away from the monitors.

"I know that you are the infamous DeLuca family. Most things I hear about you are all centered around violence or death."

He shook his head.

"We are more than the rumors you hear. People are only going to talk about the negative aspects of us. We do community services, charity events, own non-profits and on and on, things you would never hear about. However..."

His eyes leveled before he pinned his gaze to mine. "We are dangerous people when we have to be. There are no other options when you carry this last name. You are associated with us now, which means I had to do a more thorough background check on you."

I wanted to be surprised, but it was something I assumed would happen sooner or later.

"I know you took on the responsibility of taking care of your brother after your parents were killed. And in doing so, I know you had to make certain choices."

He had my full attention now.

"I know that you sold crack cocaine for two years to put food on your table and to take care of your brother. You used your apartment as a stash house for one of the most notorious dealers in the state until he was gunned down."

My face creased into such a tight knot, it ached. He knew shit the police didn't even know.

"I said all of that to say that, if you attempt to or even think about ratting, trading, and selling any information on me or my family to anybody, you will go down, and I can guarantee you that we won't. You understand?"

I nodded, but he had to know that I wasn't easily intimidated.

"While you were doing all of this digging into my past, I'm sure you found out where I grew up. You probably also know how many laws I've broken in my attempts to track down my brother's killer."

I walked up close, getting into his face. "Snitching hasn't been, nor will it ever be an option I choose. I have enough street class to know better."

One more step had me close enough for his fresh breath to breeze along my face. He didn't even flinch. "Loyalty has been and always will be embedded in my soul. The last thing you have to worry about is me running my mouth and that is a guarantee no matter what goes down."

After a long stare off, the corner of his lips twitched before he nodded approvingly and stepped away. He rounded his desk and sat behind it before ushering his hand to the chair he dragged next to his for me to have a seat.

Once I was seated, he opened several documents on his laptop. I had to admit, I was kind of impressed at how well he knew his way around that computer.

"What I'm going to reveal to you may be a bit unsettling, but you're going to need the guts I know you have to see beyond what's on the surface."

"O...kay," I replied, unsure of what he was about to show me.

"Being the infamous DeLucas as you called us, we have to be connected to a lot of legal and illegal shit. I have a contact, a detective that provides me with information. This recording was compiled from multiple surveillance cameras in the area during the night of January 25th."

My neck jerked around at the mention of that date, the day the cops were saying my brother was killed. Before I could respond, Brizio pressed play on the first recording.

The sight of my brother climbing out of an Uber made me swallow a knot of regret so thick, I massaged my throat to help it down. My hand shot up to my parted lips that I couldn't seem to make shut. The slight tremble in my hand and the tears stinging the backs of my eyes were ignored.

Eric walked into the Calabresi Hotel and into the lobby where he fell out of the camera frame. Brizio pulled up the next video, showing him being scanned to get into club Bella Vita inside the hotel.

My brother did love the club scene, mainly because he was studying every aspect of the industry because he wanted to own his own club someday. He was three classes away from earning his bachelor's degree in business and very enthusiastic about starting his career.

A big burly Hispanic security guard patted him down. When Eric turned his back to the man and lifted his arms, the man whispered something in his ear. The smile my brother flashed at whatever the man said, indicated that he, that they, were flirting.

"He's gay?" I muttered to myself. My face creased and my eyes squinted hard enough for my vision to blur for a second.

Common sense told me that gay wasn't a look or even an act, but in my eyes, I never saw my brother as gay or even bi-sexual. He'd always dated women as far as I knew.

In my quest to find my brother's killer, I was learning some interesting discoveries about the life he was building. I was discovering a lot more than he ever shared with me.

Did he think I would judge him if he was gay? Had I said some homophobic shit in front of him? Why wouldn't he tell me about this part of his life? Was I reading too much into what I was seeing on the monitor?

A deep breath calmed me, as I forced myself not to get lost in the emotions raging through me. I shook off the attack. Feelings, especially mine, didn't matter. My thirst for justice and maybe even vengeance was my main driving force.

Once Eric was cleared to enter, he glanced back and winked at the security guard before stepping inside the club. The darkness inside the space swallowed him, making him disappear from the camera again.

Brizio loaded another video, his fingers gliding with a rapid, familiar rhythm that let me know he did this type of work more often than I would have assumed. I also reminded myself of what he'd said about glancing deeper than the surface.

"11:55," I mumbled to myself, noting the time on the recording stamped in the corner of the video and re-alizing my brother had a few hours according to the time of death that was officially recorded.

The video brought up several people dancing until I found Eric in the crowd, laughing and dancing. He shared a festive vibe with the crowd without a care in the world.

Brizio fast-forwarded through fifteen minutes of him dancing and stopped at him ordering a drink at the bar. The bartender pointed out someone outside the cam-era angle. Eric lifted the glass towards the person in appreciation of them buying his drink.

He didn't approach the person, but turned back to the dance floor, sipping the drink and observing the crowd with a big grin on his face. I believe it was appreciation for seeing people happy. I often listened to him for hours tell me his plans for his future club and how he would accommodate his customers.

My eyes narrowed, studying him. Why hadn't he at least gone to the person who bought him the drink?

"Will you return to where he received the drink?"

Without question, Brizio backed the recording up to where the bartender handed Eric his drink and leaned towards him to point out who had bought the drink.

"Stop," I called out, unaware that Brizio could react so quickly to my demands although I was off in my own head. The video froze this time with Eric smiling and lifting the drink in thanks to a person out of view.

"It looks like he may know the person who bought the drink or at least may be familiar with them. He didn't go over to thank them, which is not like him. Instead, he placed his attention back on the crowd and never looked back in the direction of the person like he was avoiding them."

I finally shut down my runaway ideas to acknowledge Brizio. "Is there any way to see who bought him the drink?"

Brizio shook his head.

"I've tried everything. The individual knew how to stay off camera which tells me he was familiar with the place or had studied it."

My unblinking gaze sat on Brizio. While I was in Mt. Vernon getting sloppy drunk with my friends, he was back here working on behalf of me and my brother. No one went through this type of trouble for no reason. What did he want from me?

"Thank you for getting and checking out this footage."

I stared at him with a newfound respect that stalled my words and left my lips parted for a few seconds.

"You think the person who bought my brother the drink could be the owner of the club or at least an employee?"

Brizio gave a small nod. "We are thinking along the same line. I happen to know the owner of this club. He's all about the money and rarely mingles inside his establishments. Are you up for paying a club a visit tonight?"

I glanced at Brizio, my forehead tight with questions while concern tapped at my shoulders.

"Why are you helping me B3co? Seriously. What do you get out of helping me relieve my thirst for justice, or vengeance or both? I don't get it. I don't understand. Why would you use your contacts and basically put yourself at risk when all I've been is a pain in your ass?"

He released a deep sigh, a smile teasing the corners of his lips. He glanced up at me and the seriousness etched in the depths of his gaze jarred me, kept me pinned in an unshakable hold.

"I'd rather not say right now."

I studied him, my gaze roaming over him slowly. He sat comfortably under my assessing gaze, enjoying the attention. After what had to be a solid minute of me staring and him staring back with an indiscernible glint flashing in his gaze, I returned my attention to the monitor. He proceeded to click the next video without a word.

The next video was of Eric leaving the dance floor and heading towards what I assumed were the restrooms. It was 12:45 am. When he disappeared from view, I expected another video, but Brizio's eyes rested on me with the most sincere gleam of sorrow I'd ever seen in them.

"That's it?" I asked, interpreting his look. He nodded. That couldn't have been it. Someone had to be hiding more footage.

"He was found in the penthouse suite of a hotel on the outskirts of the city at least a thirty minutes' drive away from that club, if the traffic isn't bad." I was speaking more to myself than Brizio, attempting to piece things together in my head.

"There were no recordings of him leaving the area," Brizio stated what I already assumed. "None showed him leaving that hotel."

"Someone is covering up something in that club and hotel. How did he get from that bathroom to another hotel? As far as the detectives that are so-called working his case are concerned, he died at the hotel he was found in. But, these videos suggest that he could have died at this club."

Brizio stared straight ahead, his brain processing the information he'd acquired.

"My brother and I aren't poor, but we don't have the kind of money for the suite he was found in. It was in his name and cost over seven grand a night. It gave the detectives something to think about, but they didn't want to hear shit I had to say."

That bit of information got Brizio's attention.

"My cousin Aurelio is in town. I asked yesterday if he could use his special skills to see if he could find out anything connected to your brother's disappearance from one hotel and his miraculous reemergence at another. If your brother didn't pay for that suite, who did? If we can find that out, I believe we will find your brother's killer," Brizio said, thinking while he talked.

I nodded absently.

"The person who killed him could have booked that room across town as a cover. If they did, it means they are rich enough to purchase an expensive cover up. It will also make them that much harder to find," I stated.

Brizio remained silent, his eyes fixed in a tight squint, his lips a thin line. He nodded at my attempts to ease my troubled mind with multiple scenarios.

"This seems too easy," I blurted. "How was your contact able to get this information when the detectives working Eric's case started their search at the expensive hotel he was found in? They, as far as I know, don't know anything about him being at that club hours before he was killed? I'm starting to think the place he was found in could very well be a set-up location?"

"I'm not sure. I'm not even sure your brother's gay," Brizio blurted.

"What?" My head whipped around in a flash. My forehead creased.

"What do you mean?"

"I've watched those videos several times. And my gut is telling me all types of shit about this situation is off. Could your brother have been looking into something or investigating something, anything that could have warranted what is starting to look more and more like a cover up for a murder that may have happened at that club?"

I gulped down a hard swallow.

"No. He was interested in becoming a club owner. His interest is what got me interested in frequenting clubs more often to get ideas and information for him. When he wasn't working or in class he was studying, researching, speaking with prospective investors and partners. He was insanely invested in pursuing his dream of owning his own club."

Brizio replayed the videos, pointing out things I had missed. One thing in particular was how often it appeared my brother was asking questions, some causing people to frown and even a few to walk away from him.

"Doesn't it look like your brother was doing exactly what you have been doing in my club, asking unwanted questions that may have sent the wrong message or pissed the wrong person off? It doesn't look like he was researching nightclub ethics 101."

I sat, blinking and staring at the screen. Brizio was right. On several occasions, it appeared my brother was almost demanding an answer to his questions. Was he on a quest to find answers to a mystery? Had Eric gotten into something that got him killed?

"We are going to pay club Bella Vita a visit to-night?" Brizio announced, tapping his finger against the monitor.

I nodded absently. The notion that this was the closest I'd come to finding out what happened to my brother and why he was killed gave me an edgy vibe, like there was a secret implanted in my head that I needed to tell myself.

"Will you run those videos one more time?"

Brizio nodded. This time, I concentrated so hard my vision blurred. At round number four of running the videos back, Brizio gripped the top of the Laptop and closed it, putting an end to my obsessive need to analyze every detail.

CHAPTER EIGHT

Brizio

I had a problem, a major fucking one I didn't want but had no choice but to acknowledge. The shit made no sense. And this problem, this wasn't one I could fix with a cleaner, make fall into submission at my commands, or make disappear when it got out of hand.

Fucking Maya Daniels.

I wanted her. I wanted to fuck her. I wanted to mark her, tame her, but at the same time I loved her wild, reckless, and disobedient nature. I didn't want to change her, I just wanted to disrupt her flow, throw her sassy ass off guard.

Her reaction to my disciplining one of my many pets earlier today revealed all I needed to know. She knew very little about BDSM and what a good old fashioned spanking could do for her libido.

She could fuck a hundred men and it wouldn't measure up to the satisfaction she could experience if she would just let me...

"That's what you're wearing?"

Her dry as toast tone lured me away from the idea of hard leather smacking against her exposed ass. It took great effort to keep my eyes from bugging out of my fucking head at the sight of her. When she said she had a change of clothing in her car, I assumed it was something casual like her usual jeans and heels.

Instead, the fucking woman was a walking cloud of seduction. My shit was hard at first sight, like she was wired into my dick. Black leather against her brown skin, the little black dress was made specifically to tease the senses.

Her knees peeked from behind the material when she walked, the length and design added class. The rest of it didn't hug or even kiss her skin, it gripped waist, squeezed tits just right, and tugged at her flesh with every step she took.

The damn dress was doing what my hands ached to do to her. Those I-know-you-want-to-fuck-me black stilettos had a peep toe that would taunt anyone with a foot fetish.

Although she wasn't a part of the D/s life, she naturally carried herself with a dominating quality that radiated off her like sunbeams. Maya was dressed like a female Dom, one with class, and didn't even know it. She had no idea what she gave off sexually was likely the only reason she'd gotten away with the dangerous stunts she'd been pulling for months.

Now, I would be forced to control my dick and eyes while conducting serious business.

"That's what you're wearing?" she asked me again, her eyes strolling leisurely up my body.

"What's wrong with what I'm wearing?" I asked, smoothing down one side of my charcoal suit jacket.

"Clubs, unless they advertise otherwise, are casual dress areas. You're in a full suit, like you're about to conduct a funeral. Do you and your family own several suit manufacturing companies or something?"

I was sexy and she damn well knew it based on the way her eyes kept raking over me. A twitch of my lips was all I offered in response before I let my gaze dance up her body one more time.

"Are you ready?" my gaze collided with hers. "Looks like I'm going to have to start calling you, *Mouth*. You make me want to muzzle you, or better yet, put something in that mouth of yours so you'd know when to shut the hell up."

I glanced down at my dick to make sure she got my drift. I just couldn't help myself. I had to find a way to put her in her place for making me want her so damn bad.

The dangerous glint in her eyes from my comment was sharp enough to cut straight through bone. I loved that shit. Loved that she was either too crazy to be afraid of me or insane enough to go toe-to-toe with me. Either way, I loved the shit out of it all.

She pursed her lips and wrinkled her nose like something stunk. My comment about putting something in her mouth left me absorbing the blows her dangerous side eye delivered.

"Hell will be flooded with water. The earth will spin backwards. And the devil will ask to borrow my lipstick if I ever let you close enough to put your Vienna sausage anywhere near my face."

My lips twitched so hard, I had no choice but to re-lease a loud outburst of laughter. She turned away to face the door, but I didn't miss her attempts to keep from laughing at her own clapback.

She liked this crazy fake hate we had going for each other too. Her stubborn ass knew she liked me and would probably never admit to the shit.

Ten minutes into the drive and I couldn't allow the stilted silence that climbed into the car with us to continue. The need to pluck Maya's nerves just for the hell of it, had risen, and I had to satisfy it.

"How does someone like *you* become a nurse practitioner? I'm just saying, you're barely functional enough to run your own life, and you're advising others about their medical health, diagnosing people, and prescribing medication?"

The number of insults I dished out in that one statement should do the trick. I'd seen her background, her impressive college transcripts, and career path, but the insult would touch that one nerve of hers I liked plucking.

And...three...two...one.

"What the hell do you mean someone like me?"

She didn't even give herself time to take a breath.

"First of all, you shady ass preacher man with that suit you just ripped off the dead body your back-alley church buried, you don't know a damn thing about me other than what you saw on paper. Second, all that crazy you're carrying around is snacking on the last few functioning brain cells swimming around in that empty sponge you call a brain."

She leaned in and glanced at the side of my head. I purposely ignored her, hoping it would irritate her further.

"Can you understand the words coming out of my mouth?" she pronounced every word loudly like I was also deaf.

"I understand the words all right. I understand that there is a lot of hot garbage coming out of that trashcan you call a mouth," I replied, hoping she couldn't hear the laughter I fought to keep out of my voice.

"Trashcan," she huffed. "With that toxic waste dump cut across your face, you got some nerves."

"We're almost here," I said, cutting into the companionable tension I'd purposely created. "I need you to act like you have command of your senses for a little while," I sneaked in the last jab before I whipped the car onto the tight alley leading to the parking garage near the location we were visiting.

Maya tossed me a devastating eye roll before she straightened in her seat. Whatever anger my words caused immediately evaporated. She was serious Maya now, ready to rip the throat from whoever killed her brother.

That she was willing to die to avenge him was strangely admirable. And why did the idea of her being harmed or dying stir up so much unease within me?

"I'm going to need you to let me do all the talking," I said. Her head snapped around so fast, I expected it to fly off and hit the steering wheel. She didn't know it, but she could get away with saying whatever she wanted and no one better not even look at her funny or they would have to deal with me.

However, I did enjoy the sight of her facial expressions when I said anything she didn't like. The unblinking death stare, the flaring nostrils, and clenched jaw. She was ready to rip me a new one right now.

"On second thought, I'll let you at least say hi and bye," I said, making that deadly gleam in her eyes go even more evil.

"You..." was all she spit out before I whipped the car again, turning sharply around the curve and into the parking garage across the street from the club we would undoubtedly fill with drama if Maya had anything to do with it.

CHAPTER NINE

Maya

"I'm going to need you to behave once we step inside," Brizio warned, again. I huffed but didn't reply. I didn't miss the twisted smile he fought to hide before he gripped the handle of the tall, wide hardwood door. The door creaked open, the sound thick and heavy like a warning of what awaited us on the other side.

Once we stepped inside, Brizio's hand immediately touched the small of my back. I didn't recall us discussing playing a couple, but it felt that way.

I doubt we had taken five full strides before, "Brizio!" was shouted over the sound of the pounding music and voices pouring over us from the mingling crowd.

"Brizio, how have you been?" The sleaze in the man's tone was acknowledged before I saw his face.

Middle-aged and balding with a pot belly, the man was dressed in expensive clothing that did nothing to enhance his features. I'd seen men with a build far worse than his pull off swagger, but this man lacked that particular type of confidence.

His up close view looked about as sleazy as his voice had indicated. His face was etched in a permanent frown even when he smiled, and his beady eyes scanned me for only a second, but it felt like an irritating minute.

He was the kind of guy that could only be described as being a dirtbag, a grimy motherfucker. He looked like he would fuck over his own mother to stay out of trouble, or if the price was right.

Brizio didn't offer him anything but a quick dismissive glance before he let his attention linger on the crowd. It was an action that poured truth into my assessment of the man.

"It's been a long time," the man continued, his smile widening like Brizio hadn't just brushed his ass off.

"Aren't you going to introduce me to your lady?" He asked Brizio who continued to ignore him. Brizio's face or body didn't show a thing, but I could sense the storm churning below all that calm. Did this man not know he was in physical danger?

"I'm not his lady," I said, just to cut through the tension swirling in the air. "Not in this lifetime or the next," I informed the man, fighting to keep from frowning at him. His whole vibe rubbed me the wrong way, making me better understand Brizio's rudeness.

"I'm Nicole," I introduced myself and pretended I didn't see the man reaching out his hand. I was following Brizio's direction on this one and not touching the man.

"She's delusional," Brizio said, finally glancing in the man's direction. "She was my woman before she even knew my name," he added, his eyes dropping to the hand the man still had extended to me.

The man who I still didn't know the name of was smart enough to drop that hand at the devilish glint aimed at him. For once, I was glad for Brizio's arrogance or protection, or whatever it was he was offering me.

"Damn women these days don't even know when they've stumbled upon a treasure," Brizio stated with confidence, like he spoke nothing but the truth.

My sarcastic cackle sounded before my dramatic eye roll was delivered. The man's eyes bounced back and forth between me and Brizio, his lips parted like he was trying to determine if we were serious or playing. The crease between his brow indicated his confusion.

"The club looks good," Brizio complimented.

Pride flashed in the man's eyes. "Thank you."

"Where's your brother?" Brizio asked, cutting into the man's only moment of satisfaction in his presence.

The man, whose name I *still* didn't know, glanced up at the VIP area.

"He's in his..."

Brizio stepped off before the man could finish his sentence.

"...Office," I heard him finish after I turned to follow Brizio. I cast a quick wave over my shoulder at the man who hadn't gotten an ounce of respect from Brizio. Why?

"Do you hate them both or just the sleazy one we just left?"

"Just the sleazy one."

"Why?" I asked. I was all up in mob business and being nosey. These brothers had to be connected to the mob, and I would venture to say that they'd had a run-in with the DeLucas at some point.

"Motherfucker tried to get my cousin killed over a fucking card game. His brother cut a deal with us to spare his life. Every time I see him, I remind myself of what we gained to spare his miserable life."

There was no use in me asking what cousin the man had set up. I was learning that the DeLuca bloodline ran deep. And it appeared the DeLuca wives and women birthed only sons. I hadn't met or heard the mention of a DeLuca borne female yet.

"Hey. Hey. Hey," a guy called out to me. His baby face along with the Greek letters embroidered on his button up indicated he was fresh from a college frat party. He turned and trailed me despite me walking besides Brizio.

"You are so fucking pretty," the man said, his hot breath reaching my ear. "I like me some brown sugar," he continued digging the hole in which he was about to be buried.

Brizio whirled around on the man so fast, I jumped back.

"You can either walk away while you can or be prepared to crawl away on your belly," he promised the younger man. His tone was so low and thick with the truth of his intention, the man threw up his hands and cautiously backed away.

I was well versed on how to handle a pest, but I didn't have shit to say about Brizio's method. If he wanted to be my asshole-be-gone-spray, I was all for it. I hated the way men treated and talked to me like my brain didn't work. Some saw me as nothing more than something for them to fuck, so I enjoyed seeing them get their egos ripped in half.

We climbed a set of stairs, our steps in sync. This time Brizio was closer, his body leaning slightly in my direction. I couldn't help myself, I itched to say something smart.

"You know, just because I'm on an important mission doesn't mean I'm dead. How do you know I wasn't interested in that guy you just chased away?"

"He's not your type. Besides, there wasn't shit a douche bag like that could do for a woman like you."

My face squinted. What did that mean? It sounded like a compliment.

Brizio knocked twice, turned the door knob, and pushed it open before I could formulate a reply to his comments.

I stepped into the office and Brizio faced me before reaching around to close the door. The front of his body connected lightly with the front of mine. Forever was the space of time passing before he reached the door knob, to our gazes connecting, to my nostrils flaring, from the up close view of his eyes, to the warmth radiating between us.

Why was he staring at me like he was enjoying a view he rarely got to see? Why weren't we moving? The flow of our connection put me in a dreamlike state that I couldn't move or shake myself awake from. What were we doing?

Before another question invaded my brain, he turned away as quickly as he had faced me. The same shit happened the first night we met. He got all up in my face and although we were fussing, something else was going on between us.

An uneasy silence fell between us during the short walk into the office. A man stood in front of a wall of monitors, displaying multiple angles inside the club. He turned his head across his shoulder at our approach, his smile nothing like his brothers.

When he turned and faced us, I would have been impressed if he wasn't a suspect in my eyes. Tall, with thick wavy hair cut low to his skull, the man was good looking, but there was nothing spectacularly unique about him. When he stepped closer and reached out a hand, Brizio took it, indicating a level of respect they had for each other.

He reached out for my hand when Brizio's rude ass didn't introduce me. I took his hand, which was cal-loused, like the hands of a working man versus a rich pampered one.

"I'm Federico Romano," he stated, his eyes heavy with interest. I sensed Brizio's gaze burning a hole in us, but unlike his brother, Federico ignored Brizio.

"I'm Maya."

He leaned down and placed a delicate kiss on my hand. The fumes coming off of Brizio threatened to suffocate everyone in the building. Federico let go of my hand before we ended up going up in flames.

"Maya, Brizio informed me of your situation. And I can assure you that I want to find out what happened as badly as you do. If something happened here that had no business happening, you can be rest assured, I'll find out. And it will be dealt with."

He reached out a hand, pointing us to two chairs before he walked around his big gray oak desk and sat. I was glad Brizio trusted him enough to tell him about my situation because I was just now realizing that I'd been so busy staring, I'd given the man my real name.

"I checked into what we discussed," he met Brizio's gaze. "I can assure you, nothing shady happened at my club or hotel," Federico stated. Although I wasn't an expert, it appeared he was sincere, believable.

"I reviewed the surveillance myself from that night. The individual you mentioned wasn't here."

Brizio and I glanced at each other, our faces squinted in confusion.

"What do you mean he wasn't here? You checked surveillance for January 25th right?"

"Yes. I didn't see the individual entering or departing that day. However, I did see the individual here, alive, on the day prior," he paused glancing at me and Brizio. "I tracked him coming into the club and leaving. I can even give you a partial description of the vehicle he climbed into later that night."

"What?" I questioned, sliding to the edge of my seat. My face was squinted into a tight knot, wondering if this man was a master liar.

"Are you sure you're tracking the right person? I sent you more than enough to properly identify him," Brizio stated.

Federico nodded. "I'm sure. You're welcome to review the data. I'll show you everything you'd like to see. I have nothing to hide. But, I must mention the original footage from that day got wiped out by some type of power outage. But, in our world you can't be too careful, so I always have a backup plan."

Power outage my ass. That shit sounded suspect as hell. Federico picked up the remote and hit play. Immediately, I noted the date, January 24th. Brizio must have also noticed.

We glanced at each other but didn't say anything. It was the same video of my brother arriving at the club, being checked by security, entering and dancing.

We sat through the footage, fast forwarding through the parts my brother wasn't captured in. There was a very distinct difference in this set of videos. This time, the video continued on to show Eric exiting the bathroom area and leaving the club.

Federico clicked off the video and began a new one. "This is the next night. January 25th. It doesn't show him arriving, entering, or leaving the premises."

I wanted to say something so fucking bad my teeth ached, but Brizio was quiet, thinking. He wasn't talking for a reason, and I sensed that this wasn't the time to shoot my mouth off.

"Is this the authentic digital footage from those two nights," Brizio asked.

"Yes," Federico answered, clicking off the footage. "I can send it to you right now."

"Do that," was all Brizio stated, before he stood. My head kept bouncing back and forth between the men, not missing the tension riding the air.

"Are we good?" Federico asked Brizio before casting a quick glance in my direction.

"We're good. For now. I'll get back with you in a few days."

Brizio turned and marched to the door. I took that as my cue to leave as well. As soon as the door closed behind us, the urge to spill my guts took over.

"Did you see that shit? Different dates, more footage added. Do you think he doctored up the footage to clear himself?"

Brizio was quiet for a long time, the silence fighting the sound of the music as it traveled up the stairs and found us.

"Before I jump to any conclusions, I need to see what my cousin Aurelio found out as well as check the authenticity of the different sets of videos. Someone is lying and covering up shit, and I will find out who the hell it is one way or the other."

"Are you saying that everything we just saw could have been true?"

He nodded absently.

"At this point, it could have been," he replied and the distant glint in his gaze kept me in as much suspense as the two different versions of video footage. Brizio was a lot smarter than he let on, therefore I believe he was already sure about something he didn't want to admit to me yet.

"So..."

The music pounded louder in my ears like a hard gust of wind, stopping my question since we were back on the main floor. Brizio's strong hand was at my back again. He leaned down, aiming for my ear.

Damn he smells good.

The damn irritating compliment snuck out before I could stop it from manifesting.

"Let's hang out, have a few drinks," he suggested.

At least we were thinking on the same wavelength again. I wanted to stick around, feel out this place, sense the people, see if I could spot anything or anyone suspicious.

***

I believe the mystery surrounding my brother's death intrigued Brizio. Someone was going through great lengths to cover it up. It meant that his death was tied to something else the person or even a group didn't want discovered. But what? Why had someone who'd never been in trouble, end up dead in such a brutal way?

And what was up with the recordings? Could Brizio's cop friend be trusted to deliver authentic evidence?

I'm sure harsh punishments were delivered to those who dared to double cross the mob, law enforcement or not. Therefore, it was hard to believe that the cop would supply false evidence, unless he too was being fooled.

"Crown and coke. Two," Brizio called to the bartender. This damn man knew too damn much about what I liked, already.

We waited for our drinks with our backs turned to the bar, taking in the scene. Mingling couples and friends having drinks and observing others. There were a few loners, people watching from quiet corners. The music provided a pulse that energized you no matter your mood. Overly aggressive men, shooting their shots, some getting lucky, some, not so much.

Although my brother's dream was to own one, I hated clubs. Always did. Tracy would go to a stuffed animal fight if it gave her time away from those bratty ass kids she was raising and her husband. Nevah was that good-hearted friend who had gone along with my sudden desire in the last few years to go clubbing all the time. They didn't know my interest at first lay in helping my brother pursue his dream, but now lied solely in finding his killer.

I hadn't noticed when Brizio had turned to retrieve our drinks, and I had no idea how long he'd been handing me mine.

"Thank you."

I took it and gulped some while processing all that I'd learned since I began this new journey with Brizio.

"Let's have a seat," Brizio suggested, aiming his head in the direction of a fancy couch a group of four had vacated. I gladly followed, wanting to take the pressure off my feet in these heels. I'd have much preferred flats but wore heels more often now than I had in the past.

Brizio stood in front of the couch and waited until I was seated before he took his seat. His ass had barely touched down on the seat before a slut appeared out of nowhere and was in his face, flirting and smiling.

"Hi, mind if I join you?" She asked him, not even casting a glance in my direction. Her level of utter disrespect made me feel a type of way I couldn't tag with an accurate description. Brizio wasn't my man so I had no right to curse that bitch out.

"Not right now," he told her, glancing at me with a teasing smile.

Not right now? What was he planning, to save her for later, like when he was ready to tie her up and beat her ass?

"Okay," she said, the stupid smile on her face revealing her desperation. "My friend is also interested," she told him, glancing back at whoever she was referencing.

My head shook in disgust. This bitch was offering up her and her friend's pussy like they were buffet choices.

I'll admit that I flirted my ass off, propositioned men like there was no tomorrow, but when they found out what I wanted they got the hell away from me with a quickness.

I released a sigh and took another long swig of my drink. Another woman had sprouted up like a weed, her bleached smile revealing damn near every tooth in her mouth.

Had Brizio sprayed on some type of secret love potion? Big milky white tits sat one breath from popping out of her toddler's shirt. Her lips moved, but I no longer cared what the bitch was saying.

Was this how it would be sitting here with him? I admitted to myself the first time I met him that Brizio was one sexy ass man, but his family, along with his depraved sexual habits ripped apart the desire. I had sense enough to be wary before I found myself tied to a damn cross.

Finally, a smiling Asian man stepped his fine self in my direction with a drink in his hand.

"I'm Ryn. Care to dance?"

I was up before he finished the question. He sat his drink on the table at my reaction.

"Nicole, let's go." I stepped off in the direction the man had danced in from, which was behind Brizio. I sensed his eyes on me when I started to dance about ten feet away from where we had sat.

Ryn had rhythm. Missy blasting through the speakers brought a big smile to my face. The arrogant asshole back there flirting was already forgotten.

Ryn eased closer dancing to the beat, his smile wide and bright. I lifted my arms and swayed my hips to the music, letting go of my stress and going with the flow.

Ryn took it as an opportunity to place his hands on my hips. His caress was smooth, relaxing for a stranger.

Leaning in close, Ryn's words brushed warm against my ear. "I can't believe I'm dancing with the sexiest woman in the building."

His line was corny and unoriginal, but he could at least form complete sentences and didn't look at me like I was a brainless fuck-doll.

"Thank you," I told him. His gaze lifted, and the smile melted clean off his face at what he spotted behind me. I sensed him before a shadow slithered up beside me.

"If you want to know what it's like to choke on your own blood, keep touching her."

The words were a low hum, but a deadly edge rode them, the sound making me shiver. Ryn jerked his hands from my waist and lifted them in the air like he was be-ing held at gunpoint.

"Hey man, I didn't know she...I didn't know," he said, backing off so fast it made me wonder if it was a man or monster standing behind me.

Was I the only one not afraid of this big DeLuca bully? I spun on him, my finger aimed, my mouth ready to shoot off.

"Was that necessary? How the hell..."

A big gust of air flew from my mouth and it remained open from the impact of me slamming into Brizio's chest.

"Shut the hell up and dance with me," he said, his eyes locked on mine briefly before he lifted them.

Grind With Me by Pretty Ricky was playing, giving the crowd a reason to get one grind away from fucking on the dance floor.

"You..."

"While you're over here shaking your ass," he blurted, cutting me off like he often did. "Shit is going down between Federico and his weird ass brother Franko," he finished.

Franko was the dirt bag's name. Brizio's quick hand against my cheek stopped me from turning my head to see what drew his attention. He shoved me back before his hands zipped up my arms to grip my shoulders. He spun me, making my back collide with his chest hard enough to make my insides shake.

The shit happened so fast, I didn't even have a second to get upset. My eyes found the two brothers on the edge of the dance floor crowd, exchanging heated words. The dirt bag aimed a stiff finger in Federico's face, that he stared and frowned at like it was a piece of shit.

It was too bad I couldn't read lips because this was interesting and had me wondering if one of those two had something to do with Eric's death. The dirt bag stormed off, while the other spun and greeted clubgoers like he hadn't just been in a heated battle with his brother. Whatever charming comments he said put a wide smile on the surrounding crowd of men and women's faces.

I was whipped through the air again, spun so fast, my feet wobbled on my heels. I glanced up at Brizio, nostrils flaring, eyes no doubt deadly.

"You have one more time to manhandle me." I warned, pretending like I didn't like it.

"Or what?" he questioned, drawing me clean into his chest and leaving my arms pinned on either side of my body.

I didn't even bother replying to his question. This man enjoyed baiting me into fights and like his little fool, I always fell for it. A part of me enjoyed it. Too fucking much.

"You plan on letting me go?" I questioned. The music was another upbeat tune, so we stood out by continuing on with our version of an odd-moving tango.

"Let's go home," he said, tightening his grip on me. My strong side eye met his smiling gaze.

"What? It's going to be your home sooner or later, anyway."

The loud outburst of laughter I released didn't even phase him. He simply gripped my hand and dragged my stubborn ass behind him. I glanced across my shoulder for one last glimpse at either of the Romano brothers, but neither was in sight.

However, I sensed eyes on us as we marched towards the exit. There was no use in me fighting this crazy man who assumed I was supposed to fall all over myself for him.

A sick smile bent my lips. It was probably the reason he was being so possessive. I didn't fawn over him like these club sluts.

He opened the car door for me after the valet drove up, a gesture that proved he could be a gentleman. He was also such a dick at times, it was like hanging out with Doctor Jekyll and Mr. Hyde.

After he climbed into his pitch black Challenger SRT Demon, we didn't drive off right away.

"Is there a reason you're staring at me like that, B3co?"

"Just admiring your beauty," he replied.

I couldn't stifle the loud peels of continuous laughter.

"That sounded like a load of sarcasm tucked in a shit wrapped sandwich to me," I blurted, despite the underlying surge of unease his compliment caused.

"You have a mouth on you. But, I think I like it," he said nonchalantly before finally slamming his foot on the gas, and darting from the parking lot.

Whatever I was about to say was thrown to the back of my throat from the force of his take off and now reckless driving. I was often worried about him being a member of the mob but after riding with him a few times I realized it was his driving that would end up killing me faster than any member of the mob.

CHAPTER TEN

Maya

The silence inside the cab of the car grew so thick, it settled into my nerves. I was used to Brizio shooting off his mouth, thinking he was bossing me around, not allowing this depressing silence to dominate us. My right leg jumped, and I couldn't shake a chill riding me so hard I kept lifting and dropping my shoulders.

"Brizio…"

"I know," he said. I sensed his eyes on me.

"We've had a tail since we left the club."

"What?" I said, fighting to keep from turning to witness what I must have been sensing.

Brizio picked up his ringing phone and slid his finger across the screen.

"Cousin," the man on the other end of the line called and made the one word sound like a term of endearment.

"Aurelio," Brizio replied, the sound of his voice a loud echo pouring into the cabin of the car.

"I have a lead and you are not going to like it," his cousin stated.

Brizio remained expressionless while I choked down a storm of anticipation before sucking in a breath I couldn't release.

Silence.

Dead motherfucking silence stretched on for an eternity. Was Brizio not going to say anything else?

"I need to talk to you in person," Aurelio blessedly said, allowing me to finally release the breath I held. Excitement and dread crept through me.

"I've picked up a tail or two," Brizio stated, his eyes on the rearview mirror. "Let me take care of this, and I'll see you in about an hour, maybe two."

If he wanted to see Brizio in person, it meant he was in possession of something good. On the other hand, waiting to hear what he had to say would kill me. A glimpse in the mirror didn't reveal anything out of the ordinary.

"How can you spot a tail? I don't see shit but headlights. A lot of them."

"Silver Expedition about eight cars back. A gray Altima far left lane six cars back."

It took me a while, but I used the mirror, my eyes straining to spot the vehicles and track them making every turn we made.

"So, what now?" I asked. "Do we attempt to lose the tail, so we can go and find out about this lead your cousin discovered?"

"Stay calm. It's time for patience. It will help you make excellent decisions in the midst of...trouble."

"Yeah. Whatever. I don't have as much experience with trouble as you do," I told him with my wide eyes glued to the rear view.

"We're going back to my club," Brizio stated.

He was too calm about all the trouble stirring around us while my damn nerves went haywire.

"Are you hungry? Let's stop for food. I can't cook and I can't have my woman starving now can I?"

My neck snatched around, his words drawing my attention away from the rearview mirror.

"What the hell are you talking about? First, in what lifetime did I agree to be your woman? Second, you just said we were swinging back by your club, where I know there are more DeLucas. Third, why does your twisted up brain think it's a good time to stop for food?"

He didn't reply to my questions right away. His head was tilted slightly keeping an eyes on the tail, but I sensed him watching me also. A smile twisted his lips.

"I want to see something. And if you don't want to pick up take out, we can have something delivered."

He was talking casually, like we didn't have an unknown threat on our asses.

"You truly are crazy huh? I mean, straight up loco, aren't you?"

He grinned.

"Many have described me as such, but I can assure you I'm of sound mind and body."

My brow lifted at the statement. I begged to differ.

"Yet, you're asking me about food and want to make a stop while we're being tailed by someone who's gunning for me or you, or us?"

"The ones tailing us isn't the point. The point is, we still have to eat. And I don't know about you, but I'm hungry."

I continued to peek in the rearview, but a question came to mind, *Had Brizio been dropped on his head as a baby?*

This line of conversation had to have been his way of distracting me, to lure me away from the nervous tension I'd allowed to consume me. Okay, so maybe he wasn't dropped, but something had fallen on his head, right in that soft spot babies have right after they're born.

The turn signal sounded off as loud as a freight train shrieking down the track. A hard swallow and my wide unblinking eyes accompanied the little gasp I released when we decelerated and turned.

I dipped my head in his direction checking the gas gauge since we pulled into a service station and up to a gas pump.

"Now, I know your ass is crazy. The tank is half full and you're about to go out there and pump gas? They have guns, crazy ass! Gas is combustible," I stated the obvious, but it didn't stop the suicidal lunatic from smiling, leaning across the seat and placing a kiss on my cheek before he climbed out of the car whistling like deadly criminals weren't following us.

My eyes and neck worked overtime attempting to locate the vehicles shadowing us. Although I didn't spot them, I sensed eyes on us. Brizio was out there leaning against the car with his back to the highway, pumping gas with one hand while he worked his phone with the other.

If he wasn't the most bold and arrogant man I've ever met. It was like he was taunting the men stalking us, inviting them to come and get him. And if they engaged, I'm sure he would get some type of sick pleasure from placing our lives in more danger.

Time ticked by like it was traveling through clouds of molasses. The longer I didn't see the people the more I sensed them closing in on us.

"Finally," I said. My eyes were locked on Brizio walking around the car. Relief swept through me when he climbed in and closed the door.

"Did they stop following us?" I questioned.

"No," he answered while starting and driving us back onto the main highway.

"Both vehicles are on the right side of the hotel across the street," he continued, driving while texting something into his phone.

"Can you see in the dark? How could you possibly know they are at the hotel much less what side of it they are on?"

"While you assumed I was being suicidal, I needed them to stop so I could get a better look at them," he said lifting his phone. "I tapped into CCTV, got an up close view of them turning into the hotel where they had to drive past several bright lights."

My brows lifted, impressed yet again by how smart and resourceful he was turning out to be. He kept this up and that big ego of his would at least measure up to his level of intellect.

"They are armed with their weapons out but they're holding back. I believe they are receiving orders from someone on the other end of the phone the passenger never put down. If they *are* receiving orders it means we need to capture them alive."

I had never done so much neck jerking in my life, his words hitting me like blows.

"What do you mean, we need to capture them? Do I look like a damn certified hitman? A bounty hunter?"

He placed a hand atop of my leg, the simple stroke calming in a strange, twisted way.

"Now, if you're going to be my woman, you can't be afraid to confront enemy forces. Besides, you grew up in the Grind, therefore I know this is not your first hostile encounter. And let's not forget, I had to call my cleaner in to clean up one of your crime scenes."

He had a point. However, there was a vast difference in knowing someone was coming for you versus being forced to fight for your life when surprised or cornered.

My eyes narrowed into slits.

"What do you know about where I grew up?"

I lifted a hand. "Never mind. I don't even want to know how much of my business you've snooped into."

"I was impressed with your background. You overcame a lot of shit. While most teens were partying and not caring about life, you were working, raising your brother, and going to college. If not for my family, mainly my cousin Primo, I would have probably been dead or in jail, so I can appreciate all you've been through."

He lifted his hand, the one with the missing finger. I'd noticed it on several occasions, but it never felt appropriate to comment on it.

"I know you've noticed this. One of the biggest lessons I've had to learn was the toughest of my life. This missing digit is one of the best things to ever happen to me. Primo gave me this."

"What?" my word came out a whisper.

Nevah's Primo?

"He cut off your finger and you're thankful for it? You really are into this torture shit aren't you?"

He chuckled.

"It wasn't like that. I was a hot head. You couldn't tell me that I didn't know it all. My damn ego was the size of Texas because my last name was DeLuca. Always in trouble. Drugs and alcohol were like my food supply. Going to jail was like a badge of honor. However, it took many tough lessons for me to see, to truly understand that I wasn't bringing any type of value to our name, or that I didn't have any type of standards set for myself."

Although we were engaged in a meaningful conversation, our eyes remained peeled. The Expedition and the Altima had reemerged, peeking from behind random cars every once in a while. We were only a few blocks from his club now.

"I believe you have accomplished a lot of the goals you've set for yourself, but the Texas sized ego of yours hasn't deflated one bit," I finally replied.

He chuckled.

"Can't let everything go, right?"

"Right," I agreed, nodding.

He reduced speed, turning into the alley next to his club. Darkness swallowed us when Brizio killed the headlights and drove with the park lights scarcely brushing back the shadows to illuminate our path.

"What now? We wait and see if they make a move?"

"No, we party and hope they are in the mood to party as well," he said, springing his door open and marching around to my side of the car to help me out. I didn't even bother questioning him about wanting to party with the killers that likely sat outside his club waiting for him to enter it.

CHAPTER ELEVEN

Maya

"You want me to do what?" I questioned, not sure anymore if it was a good idea to let this crazy ass man help me. I do believe he was getting off on this shit.

Currently in his office, we spied on the men who'd followed us on his monitors. Two had entered the club and the other two remained waiting in the parking lot of the building across the street. They had no clue the building was under the watchful eyes of Brizio.

He had eyes and ears everywhere. Several calls from his family members were proving that he was a major source of eyes, ears, and information for them as well.

"All you have to do is come up with a way to get them to follow you down to my basement. They have no idea who I am, otherwise, they wouldn't have stayed here let alone walk into my club. Based on their actions so far, they are here for you. For once in my life, I'm not the target and it feels kind of…off," he stated.

Was he upset because he wasn't the one being hunted in this situation? All I could think was, *What have I gotten myself into with this one?*

"Now," he paused and stepped closer, getting in my face. As much as I hated to admit the shit, I liked his rough edges.

He palmed my face, his gaze an intense trap that took away my ability to move.

I jerked my head back when he lifted his other hand. He tapped at his ear, indicating that it was a small listening device. He pinched it between his fingers and held it up for me to see. It was black and no bigger than a tic tac.

He was preparing me to do a CIA type mission. Once he tucked the little device into my ear, he finally proceeded to finish the sentence he'd begun.

"What if you didn't have a man like me that's willing to do whatever needs to be done to protect his woman?"

I stepped close enough for our body heat to mingle. There was chemistry, I didn't doubt it. Too much. But, I wasn't anyone's woman, especially not an egomaniac like him.

"I'm sure, I'd be alright if I hadn't met you. And, will you get it through your thick skull already? You are not my man."

"Stop denying what you already know, Maya," he stated, matter of fact, like we were already set in stone. "Now, get your sexy ass out there and bring those two fools to your man," he said before slapping me on the ass after spinning and shoving me towards the door.

After shaking away a smile I couldn't help, a deep breath prepared me for this mission my fake man had assigned me. I stepped through the door with a plan. Whether it worked or not, only time would tell.

***

I strutted up to the bar right next to one of the men Brizio had pointed out. He'd zoomed in on their faces so there would be no mistakes in identifying the targets.

The bartender on duty tonight was the one I flirted with the last time I was here. He marched over, skipping customers who'd been there before me, including the man standing next to me. I sensed the man's eyes on me.

Good.

"Can I get a crown and coke please?" I stated when the bartender stood in front of me, his smile wide and in-viting. I still didn't know his name, but it felt like I knew him to a certain degree.

"Make that two," the man stated, adding his order before the bartender walked away.

"Coming right up," the bartender answered, grin-ning at me and nodding in the man's direction.

"If you weren't so sexy, I'd be upset that the bar-tender ignored me to help you first," he stated.

Was he really sitting there flirting with me? A smile surfaced and spread across my face.

"What are your plans for tonight?" I questioned, arching an exaggerated eyebrow while staring him up and down suggestively.

He slid closer, damn near knocking me off the barstool he moved so swiftly. His body was against the side of mine now, his hot breath blowing in my face. Thankfully, his breath didn't stink.

This man had been following me and Brizio, so he must have spotted us or me at club Bella Vita. Brizio was right. They had no idea who he was, which meant that I was who they wanted.

"My plans can be whatever you need them to be," he stated. He was flirting hard, not acting like someone targeting me to do harm. Was I picking up the right guy?

"What's your name?" he asked and it wasn't fake interest I saw flash in his eyes.

"I'm Lola," I stated, lying easily.

"Shawn," he offered, rubbing a suggestive finger up my arm. I hated when men touched me without permission, petting me like I was a new puppy. I did as I often did when I wanted something from them. I played along. In most cases, I wanted to get them to a quieter place to question their asses. Tonight, I needed to lure this one into the Devil's Sandbox.

When the man's friend stepped up and stole his attention, I eyed him while he eyed me and whispered something in his partner's ear.

A smile crept across my lips, my gaze scanning the man up and down while my tongue brushed my lips. It baffled me how easily some men could be tempted.

Fooled. Lured by the promise of sex. It was so fucking overrated that I truly didn't get the appeal. It was always a hit or miss when I did decide to have sex, sometimes good, sometimes okay, but most times it was a waste of my time.

My friends assumed I slept around, always spotting me picking up different guys. However, and in nearly every case I would leave with a man and he would leave my ass once I mentioned murder.

Shawn's friend took a step back but remained alert on the other side of him. Shawn smiled at the bartender who stepped up with our drinks.

"On the house," the bartender told me with a wink.

"Fifteen dollars," he told Shawn, giving him a cold glare I didn't miss.

Was the bartender jealous?

Oh my. I was loving this attention.

Shawn slapped a twenty down on the counter.

"Keep the change," he said. His smug grin indicated he'd picked up on the bartender's attitude.

Ten minutes of meaningless conversation was about all I could take. This man had no idea who's club he'd entered and did a decent job of pretending like he hadn't followed me and entered these walls specifically for me.

"Let's get out of here," I suggested while he was complimenting me on my outfit for the tenth, eleventh, maybe even twelfth time.

"Okay. What did you have in mind?" he questioned, standing. His greedy eyes were glued to my tits before he decided to acknowledge that I also had a face.

I leaned into him, allowing the same tits he couldn't stop ogling to bump lightly into his chest.

"I want it," I glanced down suggestively for effect. "Right now. You've managed to get me all worked up." This time I pushed my chest into his harder and inched up on my toes until my lips brushed his ear.

"My pussy is wetter than a rainforest. Let's go down to the little secret basement that only the VIP customers at this place know about."

I tugged him along, my grip tightening around his hand. He followed eagerly without glancing back at his friend who stared after us with parted lips.

I made sure the friend heard the part about me being wet and the secret basement, which may have explained his slack jawed expression. A glance back and wink combo I threw at the friend made him swallow so hard, his Adam's apple appeared to dance in his throat.

The power of the pussy was an amazing tool that turned sane into insanity in seconds. Had these men abandoned their quest to do whatever it was that they were sent to do to me? Only time, minutes perhaps, would tell.

"How did you find out about this place?" Shawn asked, practically drooling.

"I'm a VIP member. This is one of the perks I get for paying a membership fee," I lied with an easy smile while we strolled down the steps, my pace fast and choppy with fake tipsiness.

"Almost there Shawn." I let my hand slide down the front of his stomach to his hard dick.

"Oh my," I cooed. "You got a big one. We are going to have some fun," I added, turning the handle and pushing the door open. The sight of the door caused Shawn to jerk his head back, but my fingers teasing his dick kept him walking.

We stepped through the door together with him breathing down my neck.

"It's so dark. Hit the lights. I want to see that beautiful ass of yours naked."

I dropped his hand and kept going.

"Have you ever been to heaven Shawn?" I asked, my voice smooth in such a disturbing space.

"No, but you look like you can take me there," he returned, fumbling around.

"I can take you somewhere Shawn, but I can assure you it won't be heaven."

"What the…"

It was all he could get out before the *thump* of flesh connecting with flesh sounded. The distinct sound of a gun hitting the floor came next. When the lights did pop on my eyes widened at the sight of Brizio holding the man in a rear naked choke.

His body jerked frantically as he attempted to claw at the forearm pressing against his carotid artery and cutting off the blood flow to his brain. His wide fluttering eyes remained aimed at me while his body went limp. Sleep was not his friend, but it snuffed out his awareness within seconds.

Brizio released the man, letting his body hit the floor like a sack of rotten potatoes.

"You are good," he said, sounding impressed by my ability to lead a man. "I may have to reward you because the other one is on the way down. Come here," he called.

Instead of arguing like I normally did, I stepped across Shawn's crumpled body and stood before him. The man's heavy breathing indicated how far out Brizio had taken him.

When Brizio gripped me by the waist and pulled me in, I didn't know what to expect, but it damn sure wasn't the kiss he planted on my lips. The hot press of his lips melted my damn protest and lured me into the grips of its untamed potency. His hot tongue slipped across the seam of my bottom lip and all I did was part my lips to allow him entry into my mouth.

A low moan escaped, one that came from deep within the pit of my quacking stomach. Instead of pushing him away, I drew him in, my hand filled with the expensive material of his suit at his sides.

What the hell?

Why couldn't I break away from this storm he'd lured me into? When he reached down and caught my top, attempting to take it off. I snapped out of the lust induced trance in which I was stuck.

"What are you doing?"

"Rewarding you like I said I would do. You need to look like you've at least been engaged in something elicit. I need you to open that door with this dress off, so *he* could come in here willingly."

"Oh," I said, not fully recovered from the kiss he'd laid on me.

"It looks like a dress, but it's a top and skirt," I said absently. My lips tingled where my tongue had traveled across them to catch the last remnants of the heat his kiss left behind. Him studying my reaction only served to feed his already well-inflated ego.

I eyed him suspiciously while lifting my arms to let him take my top over my head, leaving me in only my leather skirt. He stopped and fixed his stare so intently on me, insecurity crept into my head for the first time in years.

"Now, I understand," was all he said before he leaned in and placed another kiss, more delicate this time on my lips. Before I could respond and let him know he couldn't just take kisses whenever he wanted them, the lights went out and the door released a low pop and opened a few inches.

"Hello," the man called out.

"Shawn," he shouted his friend's name. Based on the rusting in the background, Brizio was dragging Shawn's sleeping ass, to some dark corner of this room.

"Come in," I called, strutting to the door and easing it open further. His eyes widened at the sight of me in just my bra and my skirt hanging unzipped and haphazardly.

I was just now noticing that Brizio, with his thieving fingers had gotten the button of my skirt open and my zipper down. Therefore, this man was getting a glimpse of a lot of skin which may have explained Brizio's reaction at seeing me shirtless.

The big smile he carried into the room with him died when the door closed suddenly behind him, the lights popped on, and his gaze crept up and over my shoulder.

My shoulders tensed from the chill that raced up my spine. The muffled whimpers behind me caught my attention, but there was no way I was turning my back on the man in front of me whose face was filling with anger the minute he noticed that it was his buddy back there. He had to have been tied up based on the way his straining cries registered as low specs of sound on the auditory system.

Although I'd witnessed these two be searched at the door, I had no idea what other weapons they may have sneaked into the club. At my first step back, he took a step, reached out and snatched me so hard, I spun like a top on ice and collided into his chest.

"You fucking bitch," he spat harshly in my ear. The sight of his friend laid out on what I think was a sex table in the middle of a small stage had me gawking as hard as the man behind me had been. Mere seconds had passed since I'd walked away from Brizio and like a magician, he'd made a small stage appear from thin air and a solid wood table the man lay motionlessly atop.

"Let her go or your last thoughts will end up on that floor," the ominous voice stated, the tone low, dominant, and unmistakably deadly.

Where the hell had Brizio come from? I assumed he was behind me but his voice indicated he had materialized behind the man. The man let go immediately, and I stepped away from his hold. I spun to see Brizio standing behind him.

His eyes were locked on me, while the man stood in front of him frozen.

"Are you okay?" He was more concerned about me than he was the man standing in front of him.

"I'm fine," I muttered. How had he ended up behind us when I'd heard him walking towards us in the dark?

He shoved the man in the back, forcing him forward. When the man refused to move, dragging his feet and resisting, Brizio swept the man's feet from under him and had a knee planted in his neck before his head hit the sand covered floor.

The speed at which he delivered the martial arts type move to control the man widened my eyes, and my parted lips remained open. Just as his friend had shook and jerked, this man did the same, succumbing to sleep from the knee in his neck within seconds.

Brizio gripped the man by one leg and proceeded to drag him across the floor. A quick once over revealed he didn't even have a gun in his hand.

How had he subdued the man so quickly? Surely, he hadn't just walked up behind the man and used his words as a weapon?

CHAPTER TWELVE

Maya

Brizio dragged the man until we arrived at the two wide steps that took him up on the small stage. He didn't bother stopping but continued dragging the man along like he was a prop that needed to be added to his collection of toys. One of the man's limp legs had spread open and thumped loosely behind his body with each jostling move.

Once Brizio had the man on the stage, he stopped, leaving him in place and approached the one laying atop the thick slab of wood. A closer look revealed it was a solid slab with restraints anchored to the top and bottom to keep the man in place.

Resisting the urge to keep watching, I scanned the room. This wasn't the same as the space in which I'd seen him torturing the woman. This space was smaller, the size of a large bedroom, but it was empty of all the sex toys and sex furniture I'd seen decorating the other larger space. How big was this basement?

This must have been door number two to the Devil's Sandbox, giving a different vibe from the sex room. The sex room gave off a more lively feel. This space gave off a vibe that said this was where Brizio brought people to unalive them. Was he about to torture these men in front of me? And why was my sick minded ass standing here like a spectator not saying shit?

If they had information about my brother, I would stand there and let Brizio do whatever he needed to do to make them talk. I accepted the sick idea as quickly as it had popped into my brain. Besides, I needed to know who I'd pissed off enough to come after me, and if it was the same asshole who'd killed my brother.

With one man strapped to the slab of raised varnished wood, Brizio had the friend cuffed on the floor at the head of the table to a medal notch protruding from the wood. The one on the floor woke up with a hard jerk and had a birds eye view of his sleeping friend above him.

I climbed the steps, my movements languid, my eyes darting over the scene while I processed what was about to happen. The lighting remained dim. Only illuminating enough to see the fear tinged with anger in the man's wide searching eyes. He had awakened to a nightmare that left him strapped to some type of a sex table.

I spotted protruding veins, heard guttural strains, and didn't envy their useless struggle to free themselves from the thick restraints viced around their wrists. The hate that filled the gaze of the man on the floor when he spotted me could have been used as a tool to free himself.

"How strong is your stomach?" Brizio questioned. He reached into a small toolbox I spotted aligned along the opposite side of the table the man on the floor took notice when Brizio withdrew a pair of scissors.

"It's strong. I've been up close and way more intimate with death than I needed to be, but growing up where I did, it couldn't be avoided," I replied, never dropping my gaze from the squirming man.

"Good," he replied. When Brizio lifted and aimed the scissors at the man atop the display booth, he flinched away. Instead of going for his skin or a body part, he cut away the man's clothing like a surgeon preparing a patient for a delicate procedure. The material was peeled away until it was splayed out on the table.

Seeing the man fully naked didn't bother me, but I worked overtime, attempting to come up with the type of torture Brizio would deliver to make the man talk. His splayed open legs were chained to the bottom of the table while his hands were chained above his head.

He groaned and continued to make useless attempts to shake himself free. His hand jerked weakly, but there wasn't enough play in the chain attached to the black restraints for his efforts to matter. He was stretched out over the table and would be at the mercy of whatever Brizio intended to do to him. His friend on the floor moved frantically against his restraints, his wide eyes searching.

My gaze darted to the item Brizio picked up from his box of horrors. What was he going to do with that thing?

What was that?

A careful step drew me closer, concentrating on the object in Brizio's hand so hard, I didn't notice I was moving until he glanced over at me. His lips twisted up into a sexy, devious smirk while he snapped on a pair of blue latex gloves.

I squinted at the object for a moment. Unable to guess its identity, my gaze darted back to Brizio gloving up. The chain link connecting to the ends of the object made it resemble some type of sex toy. One end of it could have been a penis pump, and I was positive the other end was a set of white anal beads.

"Are you planning to use sex torture as a way to make these men talk?" I had to know. Curiosity was killing me at this point.

"Trust me, they are not going to get any type of pleasure from this. I'll have him tell us all we need to know and begging me to send him to hell in five minutes or less."

O...kay then.

My head fell into a slow nod, not fully understanding, but accepting that I would have to wait and see.

"Oh," flew out before I clamped my hand over my mouth at the sight of Brizio shoving the anal beads part of the device up the man's ass with no lube.

The man jerked hard, the chain making a muffled clunking sound. His straining moan at the intrusive act bounced off the walls. His wild eyes searched and his head jerked around several times while he attempted to piece together where he was and what was being done to him.

"What are you? Why? Let me go," the man said, attempting to jerk free of the restraints again. The thick black leather straps and metal chains answered his movement, not giving him an inch of play in the straining resistance it offered.

"Let's make a deal. You don't have to do whatever it is you're about to do," the man pleaded.

"Who sent you after Ms. Daniels and why?" Brizio questioned. His tone was low and ominous enough to raise goosebumps on my arms. He didn't sound like the arrogant, shit talker who enjoyed getting on my nerves.

"I don't know. I just received a payment and orders."

"Wrong fucking answer," Brizio replied. He reached down and tweaked the friend's nose. That act looked comical, playful, but I knew better. The man drew away from the touch with a harsh jerk, his wide gaze darting around the space. His chest heaved hard and fast to keep pace with his harsh breaths.

Instead of spewing a bunch of pleas like his friend was currently doing, this man maintained a more calm demeanor, glancing around until he put his eyes on me. They narrowed, and grew intense, deadly.

"What is this?" he finally questioned, glancing up at Brizio who was about to do something with the other end of the item, aiming it at Shawn's dick. He picked up the limp appendage, pinching it between his gloved thumb and forefinger, before shoving it into what I was assuming was a penis pump.

"Now, I'm going to ask you those few simple questions one more time and if we don't hear what we need to hear, I'm turning this on and I'm not turning it off until you're dead or dying."

The men started yelling at the same time, making it hard to understand what was being said. However, I understood enough to know that they mouthed the same old shit about not knowing who hired them and that a third party was involved. When Eric's name fell from one's mouth, I stumbled closer to the table.

"What the hell do you know about my brother? Eric Daniels?"

The man on the table, Shawn, quieted when Brizio put a finger to his lips and aimed deadly eyes at him. My eyes were glued to the man and penetrating enough that I believed I could shake him with the strength of the stare alone.

"Some big shot killed him," the one on the floor spit out. "We don't know who it is."

"All we know is he's covering his tracks, getting rid of everyone who knows about the murder," the one on the table added. He cast a glance in my direction. "We were hired to kill the girl," he muttered, his eyes filled with seething regret, not for what he had to do, but for not finishing what he had to do. He was sorry he hadn't killed me, and I hated to think what these two would have done to me if not for Brizio.

"Who is this big shot? Where is he? Have you killed others on his behalf?" Brizio questioned while I reeled from the knowledge that these men knew about my brothers murder and were hired to get rid of me.

The man shrugged, "I don't know who he is. We are only paid to pull the trigger and not ask questions," he answered, without an ounce of remorse in his tone.

"Wrong answer," Brizio said through gritted teeth, and drew back a fist, preparing to send it into the man's smug face. He froze, dropped his fist and reached into his back pocket. Me and the men starred, our eyes riveted to Brizio frantically scanning the surface of his phone.

When a wicked smile crept slowly onto his face, I stretched my neck to see if I could make out what had captured his attention.

He lifted his head, glancing at both men, the smile on his face demented, a death sentence.

"I like to know who I'm dealing with, so I sent my very resourceful cousin a snapshot of your ugly mugs and he sent back some interesting statistics on you two. Says you've put in wet work for the Soldanos and Vittorio families and are linked to the rape and murder of a sixteen year old runaway. The Vittorio's provided you the alibi that helped you skate away from the girl's murder."

My sense for detecting scum had been right about these two. There was no telling how many murders they'd committed and I had the feeling they didn't care if the person they hunted was innocent or not.

Brizio started pacing, casting death filled glances at the men who'd gone deadly still.

"If there is one thing I can't tolerate, it's hurting and killing innocents. Mainly women, and children. You raped, tortured, and killed that girl, the murder labeled one of the most brutal in the St. Louis area."

Not a sound from me. These men were rapists and therefore deserved whatever Brizio had in store for them and more.

"The way the girl's body was found tied to a motel room bed, pointed authorities to three other unsolved rapes and murders of young runaways girls who were tied up in the same fashion and with the same type of rope," Brizio continued, his eyes grew darker the more he talked.

"I'm willing to bet if I look in your vehicles I'll find that you two evil mother fuckers are still using that same bundle of rope."

The man on the floor blinked. The one on the table had sweat seeping from his pores, his body so tense it appeared a constant current of electricity was passing through him.

"How many girls did you two kill? Did you kill Eric Daniels?"

Their heads shook, but neither said a word. Their eyes revealing some of what they wouldn't say.

"Enough of this shit," Brizio spat. He approached the foot of the table, the area where his box of devil toys were located. He lifted and sat a small sledge hammer on the table between the man's slayed legs, near his left foot.

A chisel was extracted next, thick and all metal. Brizio kept it gripped tight in his hand. His gaze lifted to meet the man laid out in front of him.

"Please man. Look. We work for families that pay us to get rid of people. Mafia families. Some rich families who pay top dollar to keep their dirty secrets hidden. But, we don't know no Eric Daniels," he said, his wide eyes on Brizio who sat his hand atop the sledge hammer while aiming the chisel at the inter part of his shin bone.

"I've always been interested in human anatomy. For some time now, I've wanted to see if I can do a full extraction of the fibula without breaking the tibia. Think I can do it?"

The tip of the metal pressed into his pale flesh, causing the man to shimmy his leg in an effort to ward off Brizio's morbid curiosity.

"Please. Please. We work for criminals. We don't ask questions..."

"Aww!"

"Oh. No!"

The man's wailing cries pierced the air like cracking wind from a tornado when Brizio snatched up the sledge hammer and brought it down on the head of the chisel. The metal sank deep into his flesh, and...

"Shit," I muttered. The metal must have slid between the two bones and pushed at the soft tissue at the outer side of the leg. It was a lucky shot or Brizio's knowledge of human anatomy was better than he was letting on.

"Oh! God. Pl..."

"Shut up before I use this chisel to see if I can separate your mouth from the rest of your head."

The man muffled his howling, his teeth gritted together so hard, there was no doubt he was swallowing chips of enamel. The friend on the floor had closed his eyes and appeared to be praying.

Brizio jerked the chisel hard. Cracking bone mixed with the slick sound of the blood pouring from the gaping wound, set the man off again. His screams lit up the room with a tone that dogs and small animals could hear for miles.

I was rooted in place and unable to turn away. Most people who'd never been an eyewitness to torture would have been remorseful, or at the very least, in some state of shock. I was standing there praying that pain would be the deliverer of truth.

Brizio let go of the chisel and tossed the sledge hammer aside. He and I stood watching and waiting while blood pooled under the leg wound.

When the man's cries dulled to harsh sniffs and whimpers, a low click sounded. My attention was lifted. How could I have forgotten about the funny looking sex-toy torture device? One part was shoved up his ass, and his pale limp dick had been shoved into the connecting part.

The man's body hummed with renewed life, his concentration snatched away from his leg wound. At first the man grew deathly still. The unknown was more frightening than what was attached to his body.

A transformation took place, his face going from expressing fear, to uncertainty, to panic. A glint of horror flashed before his eyes grew wide and his breathing picked up.

"Please. Please." He begged Brizio. He'll kill me if I say anything."

"You're about to die right now if you don't. Who sent you after Ms. Daniels?"

He glanced around frantically, scrambling for something to say, his body starting to shiver from whatever affect the instrument produced.

Brizio glanced down at his watch. "In another minute and a half this pump is going to squeeze your dick until it's pieces of bloody skin and those balloons in your asshole are going to expand until they either start to pop or your asshole explodes, whichever happens first. I'm not sure yet which comes first, the balloon or the asshole. This is a prototype I made last week," he stated, sounding proud of the psychopathic death trap he'd rigged up.

"Aww! Turn it off. Turn it off. Please!" The man's yells grew intense and loud enough for the sound to vibrate inside the room.

"Oh, I almost forgot to tell you the best part. I filled the balloons with broken glass, so you might want to start spilling some beans before your insides get turned into roadkill."

"Don't do this man. Don't do this," the buddy was down there on the floor pleading for his friend.

"Give us the name. Who hired you to kill Ms. Daniels? Who's trying to cover up Eric's murder?" Brizio continued to question him despite the frantic screams he was releasing. I couldn't imagine the type of pressure he felt, his back end blowing up from the inside and his front being squeezed to a pulp.

Holes and deep gashes were being ripped into his wrist and ankles, from his harsh jerks to break free.

"Ettore Gagliardi! Ettore! His people hired us."
The man yelled. "Turn it off. Please man. Please.
Turn...it...off!"

"I'm so sorry for your discomfort," Brizio said, not
sounding the least bit apologetic. "Where can we find
Gagliardi?"

Ettore Gagliardi. I turned the name over in my
head. Where had I heard that name before?

"You know what I'm envisioning right now?"
Brizio questioned. "Those young girls you raped and
murdered. They will finally rest in peace now that you're
paying for your sins."

A sinister smile crossed my lips. I grew up in a
place that never put stock in the judicial system. Street
justice was how disputes were handled. The sight of
these men sickened me and I didn't harbor an ounce of
remorse for either of them.

Gagliardi's name climbed back to the top of my
mental reel. Wasn't he the guy on all those wine com-
mercials? His family was famous for world renown
Italian wines. They were multi-millionaires who'd built a
reputation based on class and elegance and had shown up
in multiple money magazines over the years.

Why would a millionaire want my brother dead?
Better yet, how did my brother get involved with a man
seated at the head of a wine empire? The more we uncovered, the more questions the mystery created.

"Turn it off!" The man's screams drew me from a
well of questions with no answers.

"He told you what you needed to know," the friend yelled.

"No he didn't. I wanted to know who killed Eric Daniels. Were you hired to kill him also?"

"No. We didn't do the kill and didn't ask questions about who we were paid to take out." The friend on the floor yelled in a rush, concern etched his face for his screaming friend when he should have been worried about me. They would have raped me and disposed of me like I was nothing more than trash in a rich man's path.

"How much did he pay you to kill Ms. Daniels?"

The one talking remained locked in Brizio's deathly gaze. The one yelling had allowed fear and pain to dominate his ability to think clearly so he shouted incoherent words that made no sense.

"One-hundred thousand. Fifty a piece," the man blurted. His neck stretched and his wide eyes locked on his buddy who resembled a convict getting the electric ride of his life while strapped to Old Smokey.

Brizio had designed a death trap worthy of hell itself, one that attacked the man from the inside and outside and was centered on specific, precious locations.

"Aww!" the man howled, the sound making my eardrums vibrate.

He twisted and jerked as much as the restraints allowed. His discomfort level drove his erratic actions, made him crazed like a rabid animal who bared teeth and howled with the force of something unnatural. I expected to see blood seeping from his protruding forehead and neck veins the way they pushed against his sheet-white skin like they were desperate for air.

His body shuddered harshly, knocking against the wood he was splayed atop like a wicked drumbeat. Were my eyes deceiving me or was something pushing to get out of his lower stomach?

"Turn! Off! Off! Off!" was all the man managed to spit out, his words a hollow echo to the pain riding him hard and relentlessly. He'd agreed to a monetary payment to take my life, had raped and killed innocent girls. Was it evil of me not to have any sympathy for him? Did I not have the decency to tell Brizio to stop this?

"Like I said before," Brizio said in a calm voice that broke into the shrill yells. "Once I turn it on it can't be turned off. You should have spoken up sooner."

I didn't recall Brizio saying that, but whatever. The asshole was getting what he deserved. The roaring noise he made had me fighting to keep from covering my ears. When blood began to seep from the connection between his legs and leak down his inner thighs, my eyes widened and my hand flew up to cover my gaping mouth.

The horror laced screams became background to the view of his dick being flattened between the thick suctioning rubber surrounding it. His stomach protruded and I swallowed the bile building at the back of my throat, waiting to see if something would push through.

Pop!

The muffled sound, made all movement and sound cease and stretch on for a lifetime. The man's body began to convulse as fluids, either a part of his internal organs or urine, leaked from him and spilled onto the table.

"You fucking devil!" The friend spit out between gritted teeth, anger riding each word. The bloody liquid spilled out in rapid spurts now, flowing at a pace that would reach the angry friend restrained at his head.

When the man stopped jerking and his body froze. Time stopped, allowing the dead to descend to the burning pit awaiting him.

Brizio glanced down at the buddy.

"Your turn," he sang. The enthusiasm in his tone should have been against the laws of nature considering what he'd just done.

"Promise me you'll put a fucking bullet in my head," the man said, his stretched opened eyes glued to his friend. "I'll tell you whatever else you want to know if you promise me a quick one. Not that shit," the man said, shaking his head.

"I promise," Brizio told the man, drawing a pistol from the back of his pants and aiming it at the man's head. His breathing kicked up the moment he saw the gun, his chest rising and falling fast. A hard swallow made his throat jump before his eyes fell closed.

"Gagliardi paid you to kill Maya Daniels, but did he also kill Eric Daniels?" Brizio asked.

"Yes," the man answered, keeping his eyes closed.

"Were you there when he killed him?"

"No, but I was ordered to help take the body away."

Motherfucker!

I took a step closer, not caring about the pungent smell that singed my nose hairs and tickled my gag reflex.

"Where did you pick up the body and where did you take it?"

"We picked it up from Mr. Gagliardi's penthouse inside the Hilltop and transferred it to another suite inside the same hotel. We set it up like it was a party gone wrong type of situation."

They were attempting to trick us into believing Eric had died at the Romano brother's club, switching up the dates to throw us off. They hadn't counted on a back up to their system. The crazy thing about the situation was that Federico Romano wouldn't have known the truth himself if not for the backup recordings. Gagliardi's tech guy was likely already dead for that oversight.

"How many others knew about the murder and helped set up this scene?"

"Part of Mr. Gagliardi's security detail. Me, three others and the man you just murdered," he said. His eyes hadn't opened yet. His restrained hands trembled, a sign that the anticipation of death was riding him hard.

"Why did Gagliardi kill Mr. Daniels?"

"Because he could. He likes to have sex with young men and do torture scenes with them. Sometimes, he takes the scenes too far."

"The fuck," I mumbled, gasping. There was a damned millionaire out there killing young men for sexual gratification. And here I was thinking the mob were the bad guys.

"How many others has Gagliardi killed?" Brizio questioned.

"Two others that I know about," the man said, his voice shaky. Tears shrieked down his cheeks like they ran from the storm of fear filling up his head.

"Open your eyes," Brizio ordered. The man peeled one eye open, squinting up at Brizio. "You are going to live to see another day. I've decided that you can be of use to us," he told the man before stepping to him, lifting the gun, and bringing the butt of it down in the center of his forehead.

The man slumped forward, out cold. How the hell could that rapist asshole be of any more use? I stared at Brizio like he'd lost what was left of his mind.

Brizio glanced up, pinning me with an assessing gaze. "Do you know who Ettore Gagliardi is?"

Deep lines stretched across his face. I nodded.

"Millionaire over a wine empire."

Brizio didn't show on his face what he felt, but I sensed an edge of seriousness at the mention of Gagliardi. There was more to this man than his money.

"He's going to be hard to take out. He has more people in his pockets than we do. But," A devilish smile peeked at the corners of his lips. "No one is untoucha-ble."

I hated hearing this devastating update. Money was better than armor. Being around this DeLuca man was proof enough already that some people lived above the law. Ettore Gagliardi sounded like he was above being touched. Even by the mob, although they were known for handling most, if not all of their *business* outside normal laws.

Now that I knew who killed my brother, making him pay for it wasn't a task that would be easily accomplished, if at all.

CHAPTER THIRTEEN

Brizio

Death. It surrounded me, coated my skin. Faint traces of its scent snuck up my nostrils and invaded my lungs. My scanning eye took another slow stroll around the space until it stopped on Maya. She handled this situation better than I expected.

I assumed she would stop me from taking a life in front of her, but she hadn't spoken a word in protest on behalf of the men hired to take her life. Ones who murdered innocents, and not only knew about her brother's murder but had helped set up the cover up.

Based on the way her gaze had fallen upon the man's dead body with indifference and an uncaring glint, she was fresh out of fucks to give about anyone that came for her and those who had anything to do with her brother's death.

"So you're just going to leave a dead body and a man tied up in the bottom of your club?" Maya asked. Her eyes sparkled with curiosity.

Was she questioning my cavalier nature about dropping and leaving bodies, or how I would keep from getting caught? I couldn't tell.

If she hung around me long enough, she would learn that a cleaning crew was an integral part of the strong DeLuca foundation.

"Let's go shower and I'll tell you all about the importance of a good cleaner."

There was an edge of frustration in the sigh she released. She was ready to go chasing after the man who killed her brother tonight, unaware that serious planning had to be conducted to reach a man on his level.

The ringing phone dispelled the heavy thoughts consuming us.

"Hello," I answered on the first ring.

"I carved out some time specifically for you and Maya. Are you available to see me about what you asked me to do?"

"Yes," I answered, the eagerness in my tone getting Maya's attention. "We'll be there shortly."

"Are you sure you want to do this? That *she* wants to do this?" he questioned with a touch of concern traveling across the line.

"Yes," I lied, clicking off before he started a sermon on what I should and shouldn't be doing. I would talk to Maya on the way over to see him, twenty minutes was plenty enough time to convince her to go along with my plan to keep her safe.

Maya's keen eyes were glued to me, as I hung up with one cousin and dialed another.

"Aurelio."

"I know," he said before I could push out another word. "The text you sent me earlier told me enough to start *looking*. You're going to need a crew for this one. We'll meet up tomorrow."

"Thanks," I said before hanging up.

The silence that followed the call hung heavy in the foul smelling air, and I could feel Maya's sharp eyes on me.

"The shower will have to wait. My cousin has been difficult to track down lately, and he's set some time aside specifically to see us."

"Your cousin? Which one? From what I've gathered so far about you and your family, you have many cousins." She did have a point.

"Tonight we are going to see my cousin, the priest, Father Romigi."

Silence, thick and heavy followed my reply.

***

Maya

My nerves. I wasn't a woman who got rattled easily, but meeting Brizio's cousin, a priest, had me ready to chew the tips of my fingers off with my nails. The speech and reasons he'd given while he drove about protection and safety didn't help my nerves either.

Eyes roaming, head jerking around to catch every detail, I peered out the window at the very large and very intimidating church we approached. There weren't any cars in the parking lot, and I stewed in my unease as Brizio pulled around to the back of the church and parked.

"Are you sure we need to do this?" I asked Brizio, wringing my hands. I read the bible, believed in God, but there were some sacred rituals I'd found difficulty believing in much less seeking out. Having to see a priest to increase the strength of protection this family could offer me was not something I would have ever seen coming much less expected.

Eric. His name echoed through my mind. I needed to see this thing through for him.

Brizio turned off the car and reached over, placing what was supposed to be a calming hand on my forearm. I glanced down at the delicate touch before lifting my gaze to him. I didn't take him for the religious type, and certainly not the type who would go to this length for me.

"Trust me on this. I wouldn't have asked my cousin to do this if it wasn't necessary. We need this blessing. It will go a long way in keeping you protected."

I nodded, believing him. He hadn't steered me wrong yet, and I believed he genuinely wanted to help me.

"Okay, I'm ready," I told him. Uncertainty ate at the volume of my words. I wasn't going to be a chicken. Brizio was positive this would help keep me safe. It meant that I should be grateful, instead of questioning his judgment on what he believed needed to be done.

Brizio opened my door and helped me out of the car before marching me into the back door of the church. We stepped into the hallway of offices that reminded me of a law firm versus a church. We walked, trekking through a maze of halls before he knocked twice on one of the office doors.

"Come in," a male voice called.

Brizio sprang the door open and gestured for me to enter before him. Two steps in and I was stopped in my tracks by the priest sitting behind the desk. The collar was the first thing that caught my eyes.

He stood and the big white crosses stark against the black material of his robe, stood out on his chest. My breath caught. He was surreal, a voice for something we couldn't hear, a sign of something we couldn't see. The sense that he was the real deal who was touched by some ancient deity overwhelmed me.

A real live priest. Words remained lodged in my throat. I'd seen priests on television and in passing, but never this up close.

We eyeballed each other, him taking me in as much as I was him. Was this the same priest Tracy claimed to have seen at Brizio's club?

"Maya," Brizio brushed a delicate hand along my back. "This is Father Romigi DeLuca, my cousin I told you about. Father, this is Maya."

I forced my feet to move me closer and reached out a hand. My eyes fell to the two big crosses on his chest again and lifted to his collar.

"Forgive me for staring at you like I don't have any sense. I've never met a priest in person. It's nice to meet you," I told him while watching his hand, which I expected to be cold for some reason, fold around mine.

"No need to apologize. This collar has shocked many into silence."

It wasn't only his collar, it was him. He didn't look like a typical priest, older with that look about them like they'd never lived outside the walls of the church. Father Romigi looked young, early thirties, good-looking and worldly like he traveled.

There was something within the depths of his eyes that made me believe I could trust him. But, there was something else about him, something that sat at the edges of my knowledge and teased my senses.

"Were you able to make all of the arrangements I asked you about?" Brizio asked him, breaking me out of another mind-freezing stare.

The longer I looked at Father Romigi, the more I got the vibe that he wasn't always a priest, and if so, was he anything like the rest of his family? Brutal Savages?

I fought not to shake my head at how absurd my assumption sounded. He was a legit priest, in a church, there was no way he was involved in the same type of deadly situations as the rest of his family. They probably turned to him for prayer and blessings just as Brizio and I were tonight.

"Are you two ready?" He lifted a hand towards his door. I've prepared one of our prayer rooms."

I nodded and clamped my hand around Brizio's when he took it. All sorts of questions swarmed my brain on the walk to that room. My weak legs shook, my body was a jittery mess, and my mind a chaos filled freeway. Why did it all of a sudden feel like I was drowning in a sea of my own undoing?

CHAPTER FOURTEEN

Brizio

Later, after we had driven home, I walked Maya to her bedroom, trailing lightly behind her. She glanced back with that deadly side eye she enjoyed flashing me. When she opened the door and stepped inside, I followed. A quick spin had us face to face with her palm in my chest.

"Where do you think you're going?" She questioned, the glint in her eyes indistinguishable. "I think you've let this fake boyfriend mess go to your head."

I pushed my chest against her palm, drawing closer, my face inches away from hers.

"You know as well as I do that I'm a lot more than your *boyfriend*. Can you stop pretending like you don't want me and submit to all of this temptation standing in front of you?"

She placed a finger against her lips before glancing up, thinking.

"Well, I've thought about it and you know what?" she waved her hand around to add more depth to her words. "I don't feel the same wants and needs you obviously can't shake. I'm sorry to inform your ego, I mean, you, that I'm not feeling you like you believe I should.

My juices are not flowing for you. You don't do anything for me, B3co."

She was lying her ass off. We had more chemistry than a damn science lab, and she damn well knew it. I gripped her by the waist and slammed her into me. My lips caressed hers so fast she didn't even have time to spit out a protest.

For someone who didn't want me, she was kissing the fuck out of me. Lips smacking, tongue sliding against mine. Hell, she was driving this crazy train and didn't even know it. I was the one who pulled away. She swallowed hard, like she was finally gathering her actions.

"I got you some clothes," I announced, breaking the strange and demanding threads of potent non-sexual desire that slammed into me all of a sudden. I pointed at the closet.

"You got me clothes?" she questioned, eyeing me up and down like she knew I was lying. She strutted over to the closest and sprang the door open.

I nodded at what she saw, allowing every bit of my smug smile to show.

"You got all of this for me?"

Her lips parted before she lifted a hand to her chest at the sight of the closet stuffed with clothes and shoes.

"Whose clothes are these? Don't have me in this house wearing your ex's clothes or even worse, wearing a dead woman's clothes."

I walked up and shoved her ass into the closet.

"Get in there, you apple head ass trick."

"Shut up, you lizard tongue devil," she replied, making me grin.

"This was all delivered today," I told her, pointing to the delivery and packing list sitting on the vanity inside the closet.

"I wasn't there to pick this out in person, but I took the time and ordered every piece."

She lifted a hanger holding a silk top and stared at it for a long moment before her eyes met mine. It was the first time I believe she'd been quiet for more than thirty seconds.

"You got all of this for me?" she questioned, turning and allowing her gaze to sweep around the bedroom sized closet.

I nodded, proud of myself for doing something I believe she liked.

"Why?" she asked without glancing back at me.

"Because you're here. It's not safe for you to return to your house. You needed some clothing, so I got them. It's as simple as that," I said nonchalantly. Truth was I don't even know why I did it. To impress her. To make her smile. So that she'd see me differently. So that she'd be aware that I wanted more than this bantering love-hate pretend situation-ship we had going.

She started browsing through the tops hanging on the opposite side of the closet then the pants and suit sets. A glance back and she eyed me for a long time, her expression unreadable.

"Thank you. I appreciate this. This is...nice. Honestly, one of the nicest things anyone's ever done for me."

"You're welcome," I replied. I wasn't expecting her to be so nice about it. Assumed she'd give me lip about being able to buy her own clothes. I knew she could afford it, but that wasn't the point.

Wait, what was I attempting to convey? The rough edges I could deal with, but I didn't know if I liked the way the softer sides of us made me feel.

"Let's take that shower," I blurted, getting her attention.

She aimed a stiff finger at her door, "You can mosey on down to your room and shower there."

And there she was, the tough veneer was back but her playing hard to get wasn't going to last much longer. The more she denied me, the more she resisted the urges threatening to rip me apart, the more I fucking wanted her. But, two could play her little game. I had something for her stubborn ass.

"Okay," I said relenting. "But, I'll be back. There is some work I need to get done, so I need you to get cleaned up and wait for me."

She nodded, the sarcasm spilling from her eyes and tight expression wasn't missed. Why was it so hard to walk away? I stood in place staring for way too long before I finally turned and walked away, my steps hesitant.

"Be naked when I get back, and I better not have to tell you twice," I called across my shoulder, praying that

if she chose one of my commands to obey it would be
that one.

***

Maya

Damn I wanted to hate Brizio, but the hate
wouldn't stick, it never had. Even now, I twisted my lips
to keep from smiling at his boldness. *Be naked when he
got back.*

"Ha!" I laughed sarcastically out loud. I was starting to believe he was serious about me being his woman.
In his delusional brain, he figured he'd done enough on
my behalf to qualify for the position.

He has, the little voice in my head forced out. Now
that the idea had surfaced, he had done more for me than
any man before him, including my own father. Why?
Why was Brizio DeLuca risking his life and prison time
to help me?

"Stranger things have happened I suppose," I muttered to myself. While exchanging a few texts with
Tracy and Nevah, I kicked off those damn toe grabbing
heels and headed for the shower.

Thirty minutes later, I stepped out of the bathroom
refreshed and for the first time in a long time ready to
fall asleep without a sleep aid. Instead of sleep grabbing
my attention, the half-naked man sitting on my bed did.

His teasing smile didn't have the usual effect. And
his gaze displayed a sparkle I'd never seen in his eyes.

"You actually listened. It's about damn time," he said, nodding approvingly.

I glanced down at myself in nothing but a towel that barely covered my damp thighs. My forehead wrinkled. At times, it was difficult to tell if this man was playing around or serious. If he were serious, what would he do if I finally obeyed one of his commands?

The towel dropped. The damp soft fabric brushed the back of my legs on the way down. I sensed his smile but didn't acknowledge him while stepping closer to the dresser. Not only had the closet been filled with new clothes, but I'd discovered the dresser was stuffed as well. If his aim was to impress me, he'd accomplished his mission.

A sharp gasp escaped, when strong arms encircled me.

"You know what you just did right?"

His warm breath teased my ear, while his hard body pressed against the back of mine and did wicked things to every part it stroked.

"Based on what's pressing against my ass, I'd say I got you all riled up," I replied, my tone breathy, my heart rate spiking along with my temperature.

He felt big, heavy. I prayed the physical representation lived up to the image I conjured in my head.

"Understatement," he replied before pressing his lips against the back of my shoulder and sliding his hand down the front of my stomach.

"This is the first and only time I'm going to ask you this question tonight." His tongue slid up the side of my neck and his exploring fingers stopped right at the top of the airstrip of hair on my freshly washed pussy.

Wet heat seeped and my nipples puckered so tight they ached. We had been dancing around this flame since we met and one or both of us was about to get the shit burned out of us for playing with fire.

"Are you going to ask me the damn question or not?" I asked, eager for him to keep going. The shit-talking mess I was saying about him not touching me earlier flew out the window. He knew I was running my mouth. Wouldn't be the first or the last time I'd have to eat my words.

"How do you want it? All of it. And be very descriptive because after I give you what you want, I'll be in control and don't want to hear anything but my name coming from that smart ass mouth of yours."

Oh hell.

I, Maya-the-big mouth, was tongue tied. Didn't know what to say. This was the first time I'd been asked what I wanted and the simple question threw me off. I usually had to plead my needs out after the sex was started.

Not being one to hold my tongue for long, I mind-mapped my way through all of the I-wish-he-would-fuck-me-like-this scenarios that rarely came true or happened by accident. Therefore, I wasn't going to hold back on telling Brizio what I wanted.

"First, I want you to eat my pussy and not go down there munching on me like you got a mouth full of water either. I want you to eat my pussy like I'm holding a fucking gun to your head. Eat it like your tongue has a damn generator attached to it. And you better make me come too. Hard. And lick me clean like my cream is cotton candy."

"Mmh," he moaned, "I love a woman who knows what the hell she wants. What else?" he asked, licking his lips and shaking his head like my words were echoing inside his brain.

"I want you to fuck me, first in good old-fashioned missionary to get me wet and ready. Then, I want you to switch and fuck me from the back, deep and hard, but not too fast. I want you to go in there and have a come-to-Jesus-meeting with my pussy. I want to be gasping. I want to be running from the dick. I want to be coming so good that I forget how to breathe."

If he could make half the shit happen, I would give him a few points for effort. Most of the men I'd encountered talked a lot of shit and didn't come close to backing it up.

Lord, let him be different, I prayed. Let that ego of his have power behind it.

"Aww!" I yelled out at the hard stinging slap he delivered to my ass before he spun me, manhandling me like he often did. My loose hair swung around and slapped me in the face.

He didn't even give me a second, because he lifted me and maneuvered my legs around his waist so fast, my damn breath hitched and remained stuck in my throat. He hefted my weight up a few times with ease. Was he testing to see how far he could throw my ass?

I landed on the bed with a thud, my breathing mingling with my gasp of excitement and a pinch of fear. My guess about being tossed by him wasn't too far off. His muscles twitched and drew tight, his body a damn turn on all on its own.

Those shorts he wore hung seductively low on his waist flashing me a happy trail along firm abs that beckoned for my attention. His arms, pecks and body were on point, showing off the amount of time and effort he poured into it.

As tempting as his top half was, it was the huge bulge pushing against the stretchy black material of his shorts that had my lips turning up into a deep smile.

"You like what you see?"

Ego in full effect, his ass didn't miss a thing.

"I'd like it even more if you knew how to use it," I told him, not giving a damn about his ego. If his dick was garbage, he just might shoot my ass because I wasn't going to hold my tongue. I'd seen big dicks before, and they were no more than useless vessels if the owners didn't know how to use them properly.

He grinned, shaking his head like I was speaking nonsense.

"You'll find out soon enough," he muttered.

The finality in those words made them sound like a promise.

His hand glided up my legs, the stroke light enough to make my inner thighs quiver. The level of burning desire flowing through me had me a gulp away from swallowing my tongue.

I salivated, begged with my eyes while my hands opened and closed. I desperately needed him to calm the pounding ache in my lady parts that he'd put there.

His teeth sank into his bottom lip after his tongue raced across it. His eyes were glued to my pussy that was leaking like a runny faucet at this point. His eyes lifted while his hands made their journey along the curves of my thighs.

The grin he flashed when his eyes met mine was filled with a fire burning so hot, my lips parted and remained that way. My dry throat couldn't be quenched even if I drank a lake of water.

Brizio leaned in and the first touch, his soft lips against my lower ones, sent a strong jolt of electricity through me. I jumped and gasped at the same time. His tongue circled my wet lips, the movement deliberate before he spread his tongue wide and covered my pussy, lips and hole. The tip of his tongue teased the rim of my opening before it reached my puckered star.

When he licked me all over again with a firmer stroke, I shuttered, fighting not to come from the perfect pressure, the demanding need he elicited, and the erotic sensations flooding me.

"Oh."

I dragged the word out to match the way he was dragging his tongue over me.

"Damn," fell off my lips. The word a breathless whisper, tripping over a throaty moan. I didn't have to ask, or demand or beg, he knew how I wanted it and Brizio delivered, making me grip and grab and pull and tangle my fingers in his hair while I did my best to ride his face.

"Shit," the word was spit out between moans. The tongue had me down to one word chants. One of my hands glided into his silky curls, and I gripped a handful to have something to keep me grounded while my other was balled into the comforter so tight, I was pulling it from the bed.

It got to a point where the stroke was so good, I was afraid to move and I was careful not to move his head because he damn well knew what he was doing without me interfering.

"Right there," I gasped , craning my neck to see the act in progress. The sound of the licks, the sight of him eating me like he was starved. His face light and creamy between my quivering and spread apart brown thighs. It was almost too damn much.

His tongue twisted in a series of loops like he was tying it to my pussy. He tilted his head, showing me what his tongue was doing before stiffening it and sliding it into me, working it in and out until I was tensed so tight, I was ready to pop at any moment. The sweet fucking pleasure of it all spread through my core like warm honey before it ignited like a raging wildfire of sexual domination.

Brizio usually talked a lot of shit, but I noticed while he was putting in this particular brand of wet work, he was all in, doing his job so well I wanted to hire him for a permanent position.

Fuck figure eights, there was no description for the masterful maneuvers he created with his tongue. He made my clit come to life and my walls quacked like it was applauding his effort.

The firm rhythm of his movements, the intricate levels of pressure he applied. It was like he'd taken a class based on the sensitivity of my pussy. The man's tongue stroke mesmerized me, and I couldn't bring myself to take my eyes off him, nor could I stop moaning and cheering him on.

"Fuck," I stretched out the word, like I was singing it. "Good. So fucking...good," my choppy words spilled out, my voice rough, rugged, and flying further and further away.

Those disturbingly demanding eyes of his met my wide lust-hazed ones and I swore he was talking to me through his stare, telling me I needed to come on his tongue.

"Shit!" I yelled out, thrusting my pussy in his face only to have him command the movement by delivering devastating tongue strokes that calmed my ass down before they did me in.

"Oh. Oh," was all I could squeeze out because I was broken, had lost all control of who, what, when, where, and how he'd done what he'd done to me. Time and space were irrelevant. Right now, it was all about the Brizio-sphere.

The raw pleasure, the devastating tongue strokes that plunged in and out of me. Who knew tongue, when wielded the right way could evoke that kind of power over the senses. Forget the pen being mightier than the sword because Brizio's tongue was the mightiest.

"Brizio. Brizio. Brizio."

It wasn't until I was coming back to my senses that I acknowledged it was me chanting his name while continuing to endure the delicious aftershocks of one of the most intense orgasms of my life.

"Shit," I muttered and wasn't even annoyed by the arrogant smirk he flashed when he finally stopped licking me clean.

I was so out of it I didn't even know I was staring blankly ahead until he reached out his hand for mine, my eyes so heavy I fought to keep them open.

"Give me your hand Maya," he commanded. He lifted and placed my fingers over my humming lady parts.

"Touch yourself. Test it for cleanliness. If it hasn't been cleaned to your satisfaction, I'll be happy to do a more thorough job."

"Holy hell," I muttered, running my finger along my sensitive folds, the stroke pleasing while speeding up the ache of need that was returning with a vengeance.

A lazy smile crept across my lips. As much as I wanted his tongue back between my legs, I was getting hot for a more in depth introduction.

"I'm satisfied," I said, pausing to swallow. "With the cleanliness," I added, eyeing him with a heated intensity I knew he felt. He backed off the bed and stood.

"Aww!" I yelled out when I was gripped by the ankles and dragged across the bed like a rag doll. I hadn't noticed how far up the bed his tongue had made me climb until the top of my head had hit the headboard.

Now, he was caveman-dragging my ass across the bed. My eyes dropped at the perfect time.

"What the..."

I swallowed hard enough for the dry gulp I took to make a sound when those shorts zipped down his legs and that beautiful, big, dark-pink monster spilled from those pants.

Damn, was all that kept echoing inside my brain as I stared, too stunned by the sight of him to even move anything other than my tongue across my lips. If be-careful-what-you-asked-for was a person, it damn sure was him.

I don't know where the hell he'd made a condom appear from, but I was thankful one of us was of sound enough mind to use protection.

There was no hesitation when he slid my ass to the edge of the bed until it hung off a bit, gripped me by the thighs and thrusted into me. I swore my soul vacated my body. The sweet ache of pain, the hard drive of pleasure, and the pulsing impact of our bodies joining. This was too damn much.

"Is this what you wanted?" He questioned, his breathing harsh, his hips hitting my inner thighs. He wasn't pounding into me as hard as I knew he could go, but I'd be damned if he wasn't making me so wet and slick it ran down the crack of my ass.

The stroke I asked for had the fat head scraping my slick walls while his shaft massaged them. The biting tension, the sweet friction, the way he sank into me like he owned my body. I was so into this shit, I moaned one second, meowed like a kitten the next, and yelled obscenities a moment later.

"You better fucking, fuck me," I muttered. If he stopped, I don't know how, but I was going to find a way to beat this man's ass. It didn't take but a hot minute for him to work me into a bed of flowing wet heat, so slick, it sounded like my pussy was slurping on his dick.

He stopped. Just stopped. My eyes widened and my head jetted up and down from his glistening dick before zipping back up to the devilish smirk I wanted to knock off his face.

When I was about to say something in protest of him stopping, the air flew out my lungs and my curse word was lost in mid-air. My legs were jerked out, I was spun, and lifted off the bed. I can't recall when my feet touched the floor, but they were down there.

A delicate palm brushed over my ass a few times, him taking inventory I suppose. I turned to see if I could decipher what he was doing but...

Smack!

The smack knocked the fire out of me, the sting sending an electrified charge up my spine. I'd never felt anything like that in my life. His strong hand raced up the front of my body until he reached my throat and lifted me up until my back was pressed against his chest and my neck remained in a vice between his strong hand. Breathing erratic, lips parted, I didn't know if I was coming or going.

He positioned his body behind mine so his dick pressed hard into my back and stirred the ache of my demanding desire.

"Place your hands on the bed and lift up on your toes. I need to see where my dick is going," he said, his breathing as harsh as mine. I had no problem flowing that order.

Like the first time he entered me, he did it this time with no warning. The hard impact of his thrust sent me all the way up on my toes like I'd had training in toe-shoes.

This angle brought on a whole new level of sensations that drove me to the edge of a new high. I cursed and pulsed around him and he took his time, sinking in deep and teased his way out of me, deliberate enough to make me want to chase his dick to hang on to the fullness, the pressure of the pleasing stretch.

When he reached around and used his middle finger to tease my clit, it became my undoing. The full intensity of the downward thrust, the teasing emptiness when he backed out, the sensual slide back in, all while his finger turned a wet loop around my clit.

"I'm..."

It was all I could get out. The orgasm did a sneak attack and took me out before I even noticed how close to the edge I had stepped.

My arms shook, but I remained up on them, jerking with pleasure before it spilled out and consumed me whole.

"Whew," I blew out, wanting to curl up on a pillow and sleep for a week. I never believed I'd viewed Brizio as nothing more than an egomaniac used to getting what he wanted because most people were afraid of his family's name and the reputation it carried. I was being taught not to jump to conclusions when it came to him.

I climbed further into the bed, fully intending to lay my tired ass down, but was stopped by a set of strong hands wrapping around my ankles.

"Where the hell do you think you're going? We're just getting started."

"What?" I questioned, breathlessly. Did he just say that we were just getting started? Did I hear him right?

"My turn," he grinned, the glint in his eyes sending a shiver through me.

My pulse drummed in my ears and my heart continued to hammer in my chest, knocking so hard I was half afraid, I was having a mild heart attack.

The grip around my ankles tightened before he dragged my ass back closer. My knees slipped across the comforter like I was sliding across ice.

My feet barely touched the floor before I was spun and my back was pressed hard into his chest.

"Are you running away from me?" his question was a wisp against my ear, hot and low.

"No," I choked out, lying my ass off. I ran because he'd already given me what I'd asked for and then some. Now, he was talking about it being his turn.

The ache between my legs was evidence that he'd already beaten my shit up good enough. I wasn't sure I could take much more.

A hard shove to the center of my back had me face-planted in the mattress within seconds, the move stealing my breath.

I had literally become the human version of the phrase *fuck-around-and-find-out*, because I was finding out that this man's ego wasn't for show. He damn sure wasn't over compensating for something else.

I believed with all my hammering heart and shivering soul that I was about to find out if he would fuck me until I passed out. And I wasn't sure if my ass would ever wake up again.

"Aww!" The loud smack he delivered to my right ass cheek echoed off the wall, the sting like fire sitting on my skin before edging deeper. The effect of the ass smack remained in full effect when the hot, hard head of his dick rubbed up and down my slick pussy lips.

How the hell was I wet again?

"Holy shit!" I cried, when he thrusted into me. One stroke at this angle didn't take him in fully, but the series of hard thrusts that followed left me panting.

"Don't you dare run now," he said, delivering a harder stroke that snatched my breath. "You got what you wanted, now it's time for you to give me what I want."

He spanked me again, the sting making me yell out. " Fuck! That stings you sick son–of-a bitch!"

He struck again, this time harder. "It. Shit, it feels. Fuck." I couldn't let the word *good* fall from my lips. At this point, I didn't know what the fuck I was saying. Between him dicking me down and spanking my ass, I was screaming 'it hurts' in one breath and muttering that it was 'fucking good' in the next.

"Oh! Brizio. Damn you!" I yelled the first thing to enter my brain because I was…I was. I didn't know what I was.

"That's it. Say…" he punctuated the word with a body slapping thrust that made my eyes cross in my head.

"My…" he gritted out, delivering another devastating thrust.

"Mother…fucking…" he continued, this time issuing out thrust and ass smacking combos, that caused my eyes to shut so tight, water squeeze from the corners.

"Name…" he finally yelled out before reaching up and gripping my hair.

"What…"

I was about to ask what he was doing, but the words got sucked right up out of me. I was at such an odd angle now, I couldn't straighten myself out or angle my head in such a way that I could talk. I was at his mercy and he wasn't giving me anything but a hard-pounding I would never forget.

He drove in hard, and so far up my pussy, I expected to taste his dick.

I was truly fucking-around-and-finding-out. I was finding out that he was without a doubt angling to ram his dick into every bit of space my body would allow...and then some.

I was finding out the hard way that sex on this level wasn't something to be played with. You needed the ability to take the pain and pleasure and have the kind of sexual appetite that devoured both and turned them into a deep, dark, thick pleasure that had its own patent.

"Say my name, now!" He repeated his command because I'd forgotten that he'd even given one.

"Bri. Ze. Yo," I said, chopping up his name into syllables.

"Say my full name, so you can get a clear understanding of who's fucking you," he barked.

"Bri..Bri...," I was so winded at this point, I wasn't sure I could get out anything, much less his full name. I wasn't a quitter. I kept trying until I finally screamed his name, "Brizio DeLuca!"

I was just finding out at thirty years old that I had never truly been fucked, because this shit here was next level. This deliciously savage beating I was taking had blown my damn mind wide open.

I hated the way he was pulling my damn hair and controlling every move. The shit was pissing me off and turning me on at the same damn time. It didn't matter what I liked mentally because my body defied me and responded, cowering to his every demand.

Wet heat seeped, coating him. My nipples puckered so tight, I was afraid one touch would make them shatter like glass. My legs quivered. My inner walls quaked, pulsing against the hard push, the give and take, the in and out, the ass slapping and hair gripping sexual commotion taking place.

The grip on my hair tightened and he tugged even harder until my head was close enough for him to whisper sweet nothings in my ear.

"Tell me you like it," he demanded in a low sexy tone that added to this indescribable scene.

"I...Oh shit!" I yelled out. Did I like this shit? This man had me questioning myself about what I liked during sex. Was I irritated or turned on or was I experiencing a heady mixture of both.

"You know what, you need to fucking stop!" I gritted out. But, just as quickly my mind reeled, and my pussy clenched around his dick. "But, fuck it, keep going, you dirty son-of-a-bitch! You..."

I hated him for making me like this. So fucking raw and dirty. And loving this rough and hard-pounding sex.

"You what?" he questioned between gritted teeth without breaking his impacting strokes. "You didn't finish telling you how much you like this shit."

"I like it. Oh my fucking...I like it!" I yelled out at the top of lungs, my head pulled back so the ceiling was the only view I saw.

His pounding helped push the words out while I had no choice but to accept the most magnificent beat down I'd ever experienced. When he shoved two fingers into my mouth, I didn't know if it was another show of dominance or to shut me up, but I had no choice but to suck on them.

He was making me understand why there was a line of women outside his club, about to attack his guard to get into the Devil's Sandbox. He was making me understand that the line between pleasure and pain became a blur when the mixture was aligned just right.

A wave of pleasure hit me so hard, I swore I was floating. My core thundered with the erotic mix of hard heat. *Pain?* I could pinpoint the ache and never considered that it could bring about pleasure. The thrumming aches set the pleasure riding me ablaze, intensifying the possessive intensity of the sex.

The orgasm took me by force, doing with me whatever it wanted. This wasn't normal. I'd never experienced an orgasm all over my body and rushing through my blood like tiny sparks of electricity. The evidence of the power it wielded over me had goosebumps popping up all over my sweat-dampened skin.

Legs shaking, body quaking, and mind shattered, I was vaguely aware of Brizio yelling out behind me. His body jerked as he pounded into me with reckless abandon.

I attempted, but failed to shake off the heavy haze of my sweetest torture, acknowledging that I wasn't fully conscious until Brizio's hard breaths on my skin registered. His weight bowed my back while his body moved against mine with each of his deep breaths.

When he finally eased up and pulled his semi erect dick out of me, I got the hell away from him. I climbed further into the bed and dived towards the headboard so fast, Brizio couldn't catch me this time. He stood there laughing at my evasive reaction.

He could laugh all he wanted to. I, for the first time in my life, had been thoroughly fucked. Had been screwed. Nailed. Hammered. Ass tapped. I was done. I didn't care about my wet pussy, that I was butt ass naked, or that my hair was all over my head. I didn't even give a damn that he was standing there laughing at me.

I barely had the energy to fluff my pillow before I dropped onto it and pulled the covers up to my chin. The bed jostled and the covers lifted before Brizio slid his hot body along the back of mine. A strong tug drew me into his embrace before he dragged the covers back over us.

Energy depleted, I couldn't move a spent muscle to chase him away even though the odd after sex emotion was creeping into my system. Fatigue dominated me, but my damn mouth must have been powered by a natural resource not yet discovered.

"The thing we just did. It changes nothing. I still don't like you," I stated. My tone was low enough to sound serious. His light chuckle breezed against my neck and his solar powered dick that never went down nudged my ass.

He placed his lips against my ear like he was preparing to whisper something sweet.

"I don't give a fuck if you like me or not. You like my dick and that's all that matters to me."

"Fucking jerk," I called out, fighting not to laugh.

"Fucking bitch," he mumbled before he placed a way too tender kiss on my neck and squeezed me tighter against him. I relaxed into his hold and allowed sleep to lure me under within seconds.

CHAPTER FIFTEEN

Brizio

This shit was getting creepy even for me. Watching a woman sleep.

What the fuck?

The stillness in which Maya slept allowed a child-like innocence to overshadow her tough persona, and her beauty blossomed into a surreal image that drew me in and held me hostage. I couldn't look away. Even her mouth, that I'd never seen unmoving, had finally settled into a relaxed position.

My top teeth sank into my bottom lip and I twisted it to wipe away the smile that surfaced at the idea of our non-physical battles. I loved the shit talking and insults we traded. She was a loud-mouthed vixen, *my* loud-mouth.

Since my customary two to three hours of sleep had come and gone, I remained in an edgy state. My body was drawn to the bed, but my mind roared like a freight train. I leaned in slowly, unable to resist kissing little Miss Sassy.

Did she have any idea I was becoming obsessed with her ass? It had to be an obsession. I didn't know what else to call it. She had grown on me, so much so, I wanted her and not just sexually either. I reached out and stroked the outline of her beautiful face.

It was best to be truthful with myself in this situation. The same bug that bit Primo had flown its busy-body ass in my direction and gotten me too.

My gaze outlined Maya's body under the covers before landing back on her face. I squinted, letting ideas I'd not say out loud flow freely. I was fascinated from the beginning, but she didn't need to know it. Her ego rivaled mine and didn't need any extra encouragement from me.

The first time I saw her, she'd snatched my attention so swiftly, I couldn't resist going out to the dance floor to put my eyes on her versus spying through the cameras.

Okay, enough of this shit.

I had to make myself useful and figuring out how to get to the man who killed her brother was priority number one.

Reluctantly, I walked away, easing the door closed behind me, but not before taking one last lingering glance at who was sleeping in my bed.

***

Maya

I stirred awake, sensing I was alone before I opened my eyes. I blinked against the brilliant glow of the rays flooding in through the tan drapes. I laid there, breathing in the stillness surrounding me. It was too quiet. Where was my...

Thankfully, I caught myself before I spoke the devious shit swimming around in my head. Brizio and I were a means to each other's ends, a temporary fix for each other. He wasn't *my* anything. He coveted the trouble I'd dragged into his life, and I wanted him to help me combat the deadly force meant to stop me from finding justice for my brother.

I rolled onto my back and stretched. A long yawn did nothing to ease the tension that rode me hard whenever the door to my reality opened.

Damn, I was sore, but in that way I wanted the hurt to remind me of the good time I'd had becoming this way. If he had nothing else going for him, at least Brizio was good in bed.

Too good.

Inching closer to the edge, I allowed my legs to spill over the side of the bed. Now, it was time to get down to business since me and Brizio had handled our personal business.

I padded to the bathroom, took a quick shower, and threw on some of the clothes I secretly liked him purchasing for me.

As soon as I cracked our...

The idea was cut off quickly. There was no, *our*. Where was all this talk of *my* and *ours* coming from? We fucked. That's it.

As soon as I cracked the bedroom door open the scent of food, specifically bacon wafted up my nose and my stomach did an alligator roll reminding me that I had skipped dinner last night.

Where was Brizio?

My face bunched when I turned off the hall and found the living room empty. The kitchen was empty of him also, but the strong aroma of food and the warm pans indicated that his cook hadn't been gone very long. I peeked under the pans on the stove and found grits, fluffy eggs, bacon, and toast.

My mouth watered while I fixed myself a hearty helping of everything. Although I hadn't enjoyed this lifestyle long, I would miss it when this mission was done. I had already ran my budget through my head and determined I could afford to hire someone to cook a few days a week, especially if they could burn like Brizio's cook.

"Mmh," I groaned at another crispy bite and flavor of the strip of bacon. Did he like grits too? Otherwise, how would he know that I liked grits?

My lips pursed. He must have been all up in my business when he'd gone to my house to pick me up some clothes the first night I'd stayed with him. Probably was in my bathroom sniffing my dirty drawers.

"You keep groaning like that and I'm going to take it as a sign that you're inviting me to fuck you again."

Hand against my chest, I had to roll my tongue to keep the bacon I was munching on from falling from my open month.

"Where the hell did you come from?" I questioned eyeing him up and down and fighting hard to draw my gaze away from his dick print in those damn gray sweatpants. His arrogant ass had done that shit on purpose, I'm sure of it.

"Is that how you greet your…"

"Don't you dare," I warned with a dangerous side eye. "We promised not to go there or say that, unless it was necessary."

He stepped closer, lifting his hands in surrender but didn't stop his movement until his lips brushed my cheek and swept lower to my neck. I didn't stop him, didn't even jerk away. It meant acceptance.

"I was going to ask if that's the way you greet your protector?"

"My protector," I said, turning the word over in my head and very much aware that he hadn't backed off, his closeness a warm, prickly blanket. His breaths flirted with the tender flesh of my neck. Why were my eyes closing against the sensation?

He finally backed away, his arrogant smile on display. His gaze raked me up and down and something I couldn't decipher flashed in his eyes.

His gaze lowered, taking in my plate.

"I had to look up what a *grit* was," he said before placing his hand atop mine that held the spoon. He used my hand to scoop up a spoonful before bringing it up to his mouth. He didn't chew the grits, but more like swished them around in his mouth in an attempt to get around the texture. He smacked his lips then swallowed, his face awash with uncertainty.

"I can't say if I like them or not."

"I feel the same way about you," I said, licking what was left on the spoon off and eyeing him up and down. He laughed. "Touché," he said before stepping away and fixing a plate with grits on the side.

He sat across the table from me with an easy going vibe about him like we'd done this a thousand times. When seriousness started to darken his facial expression it let me know that play time was over. He knew something. Had another lead?

"What?" I asked, preparing myself for the worse.

"We think they may have found a way into Ettore Gagliardi's circle without causing too much bloodshed. Me…"

He pointed a finger at his chest, "I was all for the bloodshed. However, our family has enough of a spotlight on us due to the crowning of our new Don Enzo and the recent assassination of Don Ermano. All types of goons and goblins are coming for us and we don't handle threats and attacks well. Therefore, we can't blow up shit too badly."

My forehead wrinkled. "You may want to blow shit up, but I don't. I prefer to do this the quiet and drama free way."

"Ha!" he laughed, while munching on a strip of bacon.

"You," his eyes zipped up and down before returning to mine. "Quiet and drama free. Yeah right. That's funny. You were so quiet and drama free, your actions caught *my* attention, damn near got you killed, and put a second body on your resume."

I squinted before my eyes shot up to meet his knowing gaze. How much of my business had he uncovered? Most of my past was undocumented which meant they'd had to scrape some deep wells to find out some of the information he apparently knew about me.

"What do you know about the first body I caught?" I questioned.

"That you did it protecting a woman from being raped. I know that the woman was so out of it that she doesn't know till this day who helped her. I know that the asshole you killed deserved it. I know that his body stayed on the streets for weeks, left to be a stinking example until someone called the city to pick it up because of the stench. Police didn't even label it a homicide, saying it was another crackhead who'd overdosed, although the asshole had been stabbed in the back five times."

"How did you find that out?" I asked. "My friends saw his body, but they don't even know that I was the one who kept him from raping that woman. The police didn't bother investigating because it was hood shit. Street justice delivered to an asshole who'd raped before and gotten away with it. The hood knows, but outsiders don't know off the record incidents like that happen every day to people they believe deserve it. How'd you get that piece of ancient history?"

He shrugged.

"I'm a member of a crime family. We have ways of finding shit out, no matter how old and no matter how secret people think it may be. Secrets aren't secrets unless the person and persons keeping them are dead. And you taking a body for a woman you didn't even know is admirable."

Silence filled the space. I wasn't used to receiving compliments, especially not for something other than my appearance.

"So, how do we infiltrate Ettore Gagliardi and his army of hired hands?" I questioned, getting back to the main topic of discussion and putting an end to the odd sensations coursing through me at his praise.

"We got a copy of his schedule for the week. Gagliardi's assistant was careful, but I know someone who can make being careful look like a mistake and can burn down a firewall within minutes. We'll discuss the specifics tonight at our family meeting. For now, there is more family business I need to take care of. Are you going to be okay here alone?"

A twinge of concern flashed and disappeared as quickly as it had appeared. "I mean, without my valuable company, you probably won't know what to do with yourself. If you need me to stay, just say the word."

My teeth bit into my twisted smile. I didn't want to like him, but I was forced to admit that he was starting to grow on me.

"Handle your business. I'll be fine. I've learned to appreciate my own company just fine. But, I appreciate your hospitality and gracious offer."

The amount of sarcasm dripping off my words was usually enough to flood the floors, but it wasn't there this time, and I believed he noticed.

Brizio leaned in, placing a kiss on my cheek and one on my lips. I believe he'd convinced himself that we were a real couple. What made the action unusual was I didn't pull away. Didn't even have an insult waiting for him.

He stepped back with a teasing smirk on his face and a glint of curiosity resting in his gaze. After an odd moment of us staring holes in each other, he reached out, tapped my arm and walked away.

What was that weirdness all about?

***

Later that evening.

When Brizio mentioned having a family meeting, I assumed he meant us standing around his office at his club casually discussing a plan to catch Ettore Gagliardi. Instead, we were in the basement level of his house in a state of the art office that rivaled something off a movie set.

This shit reminded me of the movie New Jack City. All that was missing was Nino Brown's haircut.

I scoped out each cousin when they entered the room. None were under two-hundred pounds and none less than six-two in height. What were their mother's feeding them as babies, some type of growth hormones?

Big mafia men sat around a thick wooden table surrounded by black leather chairs. My gaze tracked every
move and my mind reeled, remembering bits and pieces
and attempting to process the names and faces.

There was Aurelio, the assassin who I hadn't officially met before tonight but found out was at Brizio's
house the first night I spent there. I'd also heard his
voice over the phone on multiple occasions.

There was Romigi, the family priest who gave us a
blessing I won't soon forget. He was almost too good-
looking for his occupation but pulled it off because his
vibe did feel spiritually authentic. He bowed his head
and his lips moved slightly, I'm sure in prayer.

Lenny and Umberto approached me offering their
hands that I shook graciously. Though their appearance
marked them as different as night and day, they were
brothers. Their bodies were lean and built, but they
looked young in the face. Like they were barely past
their teens.

We were waiting for the man of the hour, Primo.
Nevah would kill me if her man revealed to her what I
had gotten myself into, but it was too late to turn back
now.

The silence in the room was killing me. I folded
my hands in front of me, sat them on the table, placed
them on my lap, before deciding *fuck it* and sat them
back on the table. Although no one glanced directly at
me, I sensed their assessing eyes.

The sound of a distant door creaking open drew
everyone's attention. No one moved and the tension in
the room grew thick enough to clog up my throat. I'd
heard rumors about Primo DeLuca being a ranking

member in his family, but it wasn't until I spent time with Brizio that I fully understood the ranking structure and the amount of power a boss could wield.

These men's reactions, though their movements and expressions were subtle, said more about Primo than words and titles. A few appeared to stop breathing as his footsteps grew closer, like the devil himself was rising up from hell to make an appearance. Brizio and Romigi remained at ease, no doubt his fierce disciples.

The office door sprang open and his shadow invaded the space before he did, drenching the room in a dim overcast. When he stepped inside, smiles formed on faces along with unabashed admiration. Primo's returned smile made every bit of tension inside the room disappear like it had never been there.

I stared, hard. Primo was...overwhelming. He was good-looking like I was finding all of the DeLuca men, but like Brizio, Primo possessed a high level of arrogance that floated off of him like sweet poison.

How in the world was Nevah, with her quiet self, dating *him*? They were polar opposites, but that must have been the appeal.

The men exchanged hellos and even hugged each other, actions I watched in rapt interest. Where I was from men didn't hug or show each other affection at all. This group was of a different breed. The level of loyalty and respect they held for each other was evident in their eyes and gracious gestures.

"Ms. Daniels, nice to meet you," Primo greeted, his smile genuine because it softened his features and made me believe I could trust him.

"Nice to meet you as well," I replied quickly.

The men exchanged a short round of small talk about the days of their DeLuca lives. Silence came alive and lured me into the shadows of my mind until a dark shadow appeared and snatched my attention. Where the hell had Primo come from all of a sudden?

How could such an imposing man sneak up on me like that, undetected? He'd planted his big body right next to me. All eyes including Brizio's were on us.

Primo bent, lowering to my level until his eyes were level with mine. The repositioning was a strategic one meant to make me feel less intimidated. I appreciated it. His big hand gripped the table while his gray or blue eyes, I couldn't tell, were leveled on mine.

"Maya Daniels," he said. The tease in his tone was recognizable although I didn't know him well. My tension eased at the sight of the smile flashing in his eyes.

"You have managed to do what no man or woman on earth has ever been able to do."

My brows shot up fast, and I drew back with a playful hand against my chest, feigning shock.

"And what would that be?" I asked, eager to learn what I'd done now and harboring no doubt that my actions were the essence of more trouble. If there was one thing I was learning about these DeLucas, they didn't run from trouble. They enjoyed it, didn't mind it, flirted with it, and even searched for it.

"You have managed to inspire Brizio DeLuca to take on a cause that has nothing to do with this family.

It's a miracle I never expected to see in this lifetime or the next."

A round of chuckles sounded and Brizio bit into a smile at Primo's teasing. Romigi reached out and patted Brizio on the back playfully like he was finally initiated into a special DeLuca club I wasn't privileged enough to know about.

Primo's stare, intense and fixed, trapped me and filled me with a burning need to know. The raging need had me gulping down the questions at the tip of my tongue.

"I must ask. How did you accomplish such a…" he paused, his eyes lifting like he was searching for the right words. "…Such a difficult and I'm sure daunting task?"

I smiled, flashing my crest white, Invisalign-straightened teeth.

"Look at this smile and these big seductive eyes. Who can resist such a brilliantly, beautiful image when it's bestowed on them?"

The men chuckled while Brizio shook his head and rolled his eyes towards the ceiling. I could almost hear the insult he wanted to hurl but held his tongue.

Primo nodded approvingly, chuckling. He glanced across his shoulder at Brizio before he returned his attention to me. His smile dropped so suddenly, the dramatic change sent my heart into overdrive.

"Has any DeLuca, including that one," he said, aiming a thumb across his shoulder at Brizio. "Has any

DeLuca forced, hurt, taunted, hit, or disrespected you in any way?"

The knowledge that he asked garnered him a lot more respect from me. My head shook slowly.

"No, they haven't done any of the above to me. Honestly, it's been the opposite. Brizio is under the impression that he can boss me around, but I can handle him. Everyone else that I've met has been accommodating, considering I'm an outsider who brought my drama to your doorstep."

He sat his big hand atop mine on the table and leaned in, his voice dropping for only my ears.

"We rarely take on any trouble that doesn't directly impact this family. The level of respect I have for my cousin is the only reason this situation has gotten this far and why I can't rest until it's rectified."

I nodded, not knowing what to say to his comments. His hand remained atop mine and for a reason I couldn't name, the warm touch kept me calm.

"I do apologize for what happened to your brother. Brizio filled me in on your situation. He's willing to die for you. You know that, right?"

Those words hit hard, making all sorts of ideas pop into my head. Primo tilted his head and squinted at me when I didn't reply right away.

"You do understand that, right? If shit went down right now, he would die to save you."

I swallowed hard at the idea. I knew it, but I'd never allowed the notion to sink in that deep. He had put his life on the line from the beginning, and I'd cast it off as him getting off on the danger of my situation. I'd never accepted what his actions meant because I automatically assumed he had ulterior motives for helping me.

"He's saved my ass more times than I can count. He's put his life in grave danger and his freedom on the line for all of us. Every man in this room would die for him and if he is willing to put his life on the line for you, then by default we would die for you also."

"What?" the question dragged past my lips, on a breathy whisper. Primo's words kept hitting me, the impact of them relentless. My mouth dropped open and my lips remained parted, but I couldn't spit out another word.

I dragged my gaze away from Primo's. My eyes darted around the table seeing these men in a different light. They would die for me because of their dedication to Brizio?

The notion floored me as I had never witnessed such blind loyalty and such unrestricted love for family. All that came close to what was now tattooed on my brain and a part of my heart about these men was my willingness to die seeking justice for my brother.

"Say you understand Maya," Primo commanded, reclaiming my attention. After I dislodged the lump in my throat, I nodded.

"I understand. Thank you."

A hint of a smile flashed before he stood and returned to his seat. My damn mind was blown wide open. I didn't want anyone to get hurt or die, but my one-track mind hadn't allowed me to process that I was endangering the lives of these men because I couldn't let go. Now, they were willing to sacrifice themselves for me because of their love for Brizio.

Damn!

The impact of such a revelation had me doing mental stretches so my brain would have the endurance to process it all.

Tears.

The liquid secret-tellers stung the backs of my eyes, forcing me to fight like hell to keep them at bay. My gaze met Brizio's and the space between us along with the other men in the room disappeared. I accepted the heart-warming, heart-aching gesture being presented *to me*. Now that I think about it, the sentiment was always there, but I was too damned blind and stubborn to see it.

CHAPTER SIXTEEN

Brizio

I wasn't sure what Primo whispered to Maya, but it was something profound enough to rattle her. She kept staring at us now with that unreadable expression and what appeared to be tears creeping into her eyes.

Her gaze settled on me for a long time before she dropped her eyes. Was I reading her wrong or was it shame I just saw? I knew Primo well enough to know he wouldn't say something foul to her which left me dying to know what he'd said.

"Okay," I said before standing and walking around the table. "We know through research, double checking, payoffs and more research that Ettore Gagliardi killed Eric Daniels and has gone through a lot of trouble covering it up. He devised a plan to make the Romano family the fall guys. The details on that part are still a little sketchy, but time will reveal the full truth. Gagliardi also used Pasello to clean the original crime scene."

Eyes widened and necks twisted for a better view of me after I dropped that nugget of information. It always amazed my family what I could find out if I really put my mind to it.

Who the hell is Pasello? I saw the question on Maya's face.

"Pasello is one of the best cleaners in the business. Independent contractor. Female," I answered the nonverbal question.

Umberto leaned over and whispered more information to her, the update making her nod. The set of her shoulders eased as well.

"Thank you," she mouthed in his direction.

My cousins knew how to be on their best behavior when a pretty woman was around. Shouting over one another, burping, farting, insults being slung like fists, nothing was off limits. Aside from Romigi who was always poised, when you added a pretty woman to the mix, my cousins would front like they had attended the DeLuca Prep Academy for Advanced Learners.

Maya's eyes followed me now, walking around the table and delivering the briefing like I was teaching a speculative fiction class.

"Now, we all know Gagliardi has a sweet tooth for young men. But, up until Eric Daniel's death, his penchant for murder had never been discovered."

If my mentioning her brother bothered her, Maya didn't let it show.

"Gagliardi will be visiting the exclusive and very elusive club Hiatus. This place is so upscale it makes my club look like a shack and so private, it will take NSA level skills to peek into their security system. Gagliardi's visit will provide a weak point in his security and also provide a vulnerable time slot since he often engages in extracurricular activities at the club. "

Maya's initial introduction to BDSM had gone as I'd expected, revealing her lack of knowledge of the life. She was about to get a crash course because she was about to become an active participant in this mission.

***

Maya

My forehead wrinkled, but I didn't voice the many questions resting on my tongue knowing Mr. Arrogant would provide answers. On his own time.

After the meeting was officially underway, the men continued their silent observations of me. They had perfected the art of looking without putting their eyes on a person. I knew the tactic because I believe I'd mastered it too.

"All we have to do now is work out the details of what happens once we get inside the club," Brizio said, winking and bouncing a finger between me and him.

"We?" I couldn't keep the question from spilling free.

"Yeah, I didn't tell you about that part?" he asked casually, like he had already insinuated that I would be participating in a mission that could unalive us even though it was on my behalf. He knew damn well he hadn't told me a thing.

"Wealthy dominants visit this particular club, mostly to show off their subs. I figured, there is no time like the present for me to finally give you the discipline you desperately need."

My heart sped up at the statement and I fought to keep embarrassment and even a hint of excitement from my subdued expression. Was Brizio really over there choosing this time, in front of his family, at a serious meeting, to show his ass?

Did they even know about all the freaky shit he was into under his club? Did they know me and him were officially fucking? Why did I care if they did know?

Folding my arms across my chest, I fought hard to keep a smile from disrupting my fake frown. Brizio saw my insult coming before I voiced it, expected it and more than likely wanted it.

"You know me B3co," I paused for effect. "Me and discipline are not going to work. Since it's Doms and subs they want, I'll be the Mistress and you can be *my* pet."

His nose twitched, it was supposed to be a frown, but I spotted the smile in his gaze.

"Come here boy. Sit. Sit." I called, clicking my tongue and patting my leg for him to obey my command.

Laughter erupted around the table, catching me off guard. Me and Brizio's banter had quickly become our way of dealing with each other. There was always a touch of hidden amusement woven within our most brutal insults.

Seeing these imposing men laughing, set me at ease and encouraged my smile.

"Damn, I like her," I heard, but didn't see which of the men had made the comment.

Brizio, busy laughing, didn't even snap back right away, and I kind of hoped that he would.

"I think I see a few things more clearly now," Primo commented in Brizio direction, but I didn't understand what he meant by the statement.

After the laughter subsided, I put my gaze back on Brizio who continued to chuckle lightly.

"I don't usually pick up strays, but I guess you'll do ," he finally clapped back, sending the room into another outburst of laughter. Brizio was laughing as hard as his cousins, but his eyes on me at this moment sent something gnawing at my emotions.

The stare, the connecting energy between us, even among this group, it probed deep enough to be acknowledged.

"I'm glad I amuse you," I told Brizio, his smirk teasing, but he was still eyeing me with the strange glint in his eyes. "Dick faced fucker," I muttered under my breath. Romigi's brows lifted at my comment, making me drop my head in shame for cursing in front of a priest.

Scenarios of me losing it and breaking character if I were to play the role of his pet kept popping into my head. I didn't want to be the reason our plan went to hell because I couldn't keep my shit together.

"Have you truly thought this out?" I asked him.
"You know how I am. I don't play nice well and the idea of being your pet has hives breaking out all over my back."

I shivered before rolling and squeezing my shoulder blades together to ward off the idea of the fake attack.

In a few steps Brizio stood right behind me. He reached out and pretended to be inspecting my neck.

"The most stubborn subjects make for the best pets. You'll do just fine. I'll even go down to the local dog pound and shop for you a nice new flea collar," he told me, causing another eruption of laughter to sound.

"Ass mouthed cunt," he muttered next to my ear letting me know he hadn't missed my earlier insult.

"I wish I could be a fly on the wall when you two enter that club," Aurelio stated, mirth flashing in his gaze.

I believed Brizio as well as the men knew that I would do what it took, including being his pet in order to find justice for my brother. That they could laugh at my antics with Brizio brought me to a new level of comfort with them.

"Okay, back to the matter at hand," Brizio stated. "Getting into the club is the least of our worries. I have a membership. It's what we do once we're inside that will lead us to getting our hands on Gagliardi. It will take critical thinking and a well-thought out plan. I'll take suggestions," he stated. His words had me doing a double take at him. Maybe his ego wasn't as out of control as I had initially assumed. Maybe he was only this way with his family since they held him in such high regard.

The sentiment of their willingness to put their lives on the line for a cause that had nothing to do with them as individuals, had nothing to do with their family, but a problem Brizio had taken on a whim, circled back to the forefront of my mind.

Brizio's decision to help me wasn't an easy one, and he'd never voiced a single complaint about why he'd done it. I was the one who'd brought up the question on multiple occasions. *Why?* I still didn't know the answer to the question, but I needed to be more cognizant of what Brizio was willing to sacrifice for me.

The plan of getting to Gagliardi turned circles around my brain and something wasn't adding up. I raised my hand like I was in class. Brizio's head inclined in my direction.

"I know we are going in the club, but to do what, if not to go in there and kill him?"

"Our goal is to get close enough to either plant a tracker on him or drug him. With option two, we don't yet have a way of getting him out of the club without raising suspicion of security and his own protection detail. We want him alive because he didn't pull this cover up off on his own."

"Oh," I mouthed silently. Now, I understood. I would have gone in there and killed the man, and the team of people who helped him cover up my brother's murder would have remained free and clear to keep covering up more murders of innocent victims.

"I just found my way in," Aurelio announced. His eyes were pinned to his phone like it was a big piece of gold in his palm. He kept us in suspense for what felt like an hour, his fingers swiping and his eyes sweeping left to right.

"If I intercept him, I'll be in the kitchen, cooking and taking on the identity of the chef the club is flying in from LA."

"Yes!" Brizio expressed pumping his fist in the air, while smiles and appreciative murmurs came from the others.

"I have the blueprints for the building. Even got a tip on the secret dungeon Gagliardi likes to use every time he visits. Predictability may be his downfall, but the specific dungeon he uses is about as secure as a bank vault. I'm intrigued," Brizio stated.

He was acting like it was no big deal that he and his family were receiving and finding hits on secret information that I was sure the detectives on the case would never uncover.

My forehead wrinkled and my head tilted while taking in every DeLuca face. The level of expertise and mission readiness these men possessed spiked my intrigue and impressed me. They made me experience emotions that men didn't often inspire. Another idea sliced through my moment of quiet appraisal.

"Okay, I'm the novice here," I stated, turning my gaze on Aurelio. "Your ability to get inside and become the club's chef, what does that mean exactly?"

Aurelio smiled and like Primo, his smile was all it took to transform his intimidating features more pleasant and inviting.

"It means that I'll be able to get others into the club as well as bring in the equipment Brizio may need to trap Gagliardi in place, track him, or make him disappear altogether."

Damn!

"Okay." I nodded.

I couldn't have been the only one impressed right now. Who the hell were these people? And shouldn't I be afraid of them? Was I like them on some level since I'd grown up around violence? Or was I a sicko, who secretly enjoyed a splice of darkness in my life? Being around these DeLuca men had me questioning myself and thinking deeper about some of the decisions I'd made.

If I would have been heavy handed with my brother with more rules, would that have saved him? If we had stayed in the hood, would that type of exposure have made him street savvy enough to survive?

A deep breath drew me from my short moment of self-reflection. I concentrated on the plans taking shape that, if executed correctly, would land me face to face with my brother's killer.

CHAPTER SEVENTEEN

Maya

Brizio had finally lost his damn mind. Based on the way I was eyeballing him, he should have been able to feel the sharp side eye I leveled on him.

We had two days for me to be his pretend submissive and there was so much information coming at me, I knew that less than half of it was sticking. He turned a sharp corner, causing me to grip my seat belt for support. He wasn't the most safe driver. Watching him drive was like staring down the barrel of a gun without knowing if it was loaded or not.

"Where the hell did you get your driver's license? The Dollar Tree?"

"Ha. Ha," he replied, sarcastically.

Currently, *he* had decided that *we* would go on a shopping excursion and he insisted on picking my outfit for the mission.

Not that I didn't like it or appreciate it, but what was his fascination with wanting to buy stuff for me? He'd already bought me a closet stuffed so full of clothing, I was still finding boxes that hadn't even been opened. I could have easily pulled something out of that closet to wear tomorrow.

There was also a spark of excitement in Brizio when he mentioned the word shopping that I didn't miss. Who was I to steal the man's joy if he wanted to spend his money on me?

He knew better than I did what would be appropriate attire for this infamous club. I wasn't afraid to admit that I was out of my depth in this strange new world.

Although it was challenging for me to let someone else take the lead in my life, I understood that on this matter, I needed Brizio. I wasn't used to depending on someone in this way. It didn't feel right. It made me feel weak. Helpless. Words I'd rarely allowed myself to accept before now.

You're doing it for your brother.

The constant reminder kept me going, insisting that I needed to embrace the unknown and swallow my pride no matter if I liked it or not.

Brizio was discussing the safety protocols the club had in place and about a thousand other titles and rules about BDSM I was failing to wrap my head around.

"Okay, I got the gist of it about safe words. However, if the dominating party is supposed to be so concerned about his submissive and acquiring permission, why don't they just seek out relationships with people who like their sex rough. One's who enjoy role playing and playing with toys. Isn't that the same thing?"

"Not even close," he said, shaking his head because I was failing to see the point. "It goes so much deeper than you can imagine. You'll understand it better once we start practicing the physical aspects. You're used to being in control, therefore the idea of giving it up terrifies you."

He wasn't wrong.

"I can assure you, if you truly let go, you'll appreciate why there are so many rules. This lifestyle is not for everyone, but I believe someone like you would benefit greatly from it."

My eyes narrowed on him, my stare fixed. Why was he so fixated on pulling me into his little freaky world when I obviously didn't fit in?

"Don't give me that look Maya," he said without taking his eyes off the road. "Releasing the tight grip you have on your control is the best therapy you can give yourself. Thirty minutes with me in the sand box tonight, and if you don't like it, you'll never have to worry about it again."

"I kind of understand, but at the same time I don't. All I can promise you is that I'll keep an open mind and do what I have to do to make sure we give what needs to be given in front of those people."

His other question was still being kicked around in my head.

"And what about the thirty minutes?"

Of course he didn't forget. A long, heavy sigh was released before I voiced my reluctant, "Okay."

His genuine smile surfaced, something I didn't often see from him. His smile was usually teasing, condescending, and often fake.

We rolled up to a little posh boutique called Harlequin's and based on the quick peek I cast into the place, it was a typical high class, over-priced shop.

Open mind, I reminded myself.

***

An hour and fifteen minutes later.

Brizio cracked the door to the Devil's Sandbox open and ushered a hand inside for me to enter first. He marched me past a simple spanking bench and other pieces of sex furniture.

Our march didn't stop until we were deep inside the room. We were feet from the back wall that displayed an impressive array of sex toys, some I couldn't even guess at the purpose.

"We'll start off light and you tell me if you want more or if you want harder or more pain then pleasure. Whatever you're comfortable with."

I nodded. My nerves were being raked over broken glass. I was uncomfortable, but at the same time I didn't want to admit that little bubbles of excitement sparked and brushed against the edges of my curiosity.

Was I betraying some type of oath to myself by being turned on by this place, this scene? Or was it him that had me buzzing with this unfamiliar energy?

Despite not knowing what to expect, I noticed the reassuring sincerity in his tone. I believed the unknown is what was keeping me on edge and inadvertently heightening my state of arousal.

More elaborate displays of sex toys sat on lighted displays and distant shelves. Whips, chain length restraints, cuffs, nipple clamps, and butt plugs were a few that I could name. There were pieces of furniture that mimicked half beds and workout equipment but with straps, restraints, and holes cut into the parts that would allow a person to be stimulated. The edgy vibe of this place was peeling back layers I didn't even know I possessed.

I'd been so busy attempting to stop him from hitting that woman the first time I was in here I hadn't noticed the vast amount of toys and equipment fully displayed in this Devil's Sandbox. Fitting name.

The idea of being tied up and helpless while he did whatever he wanted to me kept me feeling like I was dancing on the edge of a freshly sharpened blade. I sought his eyes, doing my best to read his intentions, but he wouldn't give away a thing.

"Stand right here and face me," he directed, stopping me within five feet of the back wall.

"First we need to establish a few simple rules. If you follow these rules, they will guarantee you a good time. I promise."

Doubt filled my psyche, but I managed a nod.

"First, answer and ask all questions starting with Sir. If you're unsure about something, the word Sir is your best bet, understand?"

"Yes…Sir," I said, trying on the title. It was one I regarded for professional environments like work. This was never how I expected to use the word.

"Good girl," he replied and a flash of something dark and sneaky flashed in his gaze.

"Now, the second rule is you must ask for permission. If you want to speak, it's Sir can I speak, if you want more of something, Sir can I have, Sir can you do this or that or…you get the point?"

I nodded. "Yes. Sir," I answered, playing along and trying hard to be serious about this. If I stop thinking and get out of my own head I may be able to pull this off.

"Once I pick the *toy,* I'll give you the third and final rule."

My brow lifted before I cast a lingering glance around the space.

"We need to get you out of all these clothes," he said, recapturing my attention. "Can I undo these buttons and take off your top?"

His tone was so uncharacteristically charming, he left me no choice but to say, "Yes Sir." His expression was a reassuring smile, one I didn't know if I should trust but found myself returning a reflexive smile regardless.

There was a caring ease about the way he undid my top, like he was being careful not to touch me inappropriately. The lack of sensation made me want it, desire it that much more.

He parted the two halves of my top before he peeled it off with the same careful ease in which he'd unbuttoned it. The shirt fluttered to the floor like a discarded napkin, brushing my leg on the way down.

"May I take those heels and unbutton those jeans and take them?"

I nodded, before remembering to say, "Yes Sir."

His smile and the proud glint he flashed told me he enjoyed me playing along with this little game.

I lifted my leg and allowed him to take my left heel first. He didn't let my foot drop back to the floor. With his hand cupping the back of my heel, he lifted it and brought his lips down, kissing the top of my foot.

The act was simple enough, but it sent a strange jolt of desire rippling through me. I'd never been kissed there before, didn't even know it was a place I'd like to be kissed.

He did the same to the right foot before he stood to undo the button and zipper of my jeans, his thumbs looping into the waistband. When he pulled the two halves apart and peeled me out of them, the act was more sensual than I believe it should have been. Especially with the way he admired my body and kept glancing up to see if I was watching him.

"Sin," was what I believed he'd whispered.

My desire had spiked, my breathing harsh, my nipples had tightened. When had I gotten so turned on by this? He wasn't even touching me in a sexual way.

The yanks, my body jerking, the material sliding along my skin, over the globes of my ass and down my legs was damn near intoxicating. Was it the environment having an effect on me or what?

Once he had me down to my bra and underwear, he stood and stared with his hands behind his back. He took deliberately slow steps around my body, his eyes touching me like his hands hadn't yet.

I swore I felt his eyes on my ass when he stopped and stood directly behind me. When he finally took steps to bring himself back in front of me, he took my hand.

"Over here, I had this piece made special just for you."

I was so caught in the moments of him taking my clothes and attempting to gauge his intentions I didn't notice the device that was standing about five feet over my left shoulder. It was like an hourglass, thick wood at the top and bottom connected in place to a metal frame, but without the glass in the middle. I believe I was meant to be its center.

The sturdy frame was a single thick line of metal down each side that connected the top and bottom. The thick wood bottom had an area where my foot would be strapped. Dangling from the top of the circular wood frame were two metal rings that reminded me of the Olympic steel gymnastics rings.

"Place your feet on the footpads," he directed me, before bending to a stooping position.

I stepped forward and placed my feet where he instructed. The massaging sensation of the foot pads, spread shoulder width apart, brought on a smile. When my feet were fully strapped to the device, I didn't miss the way Brizio's eyes lit at the sight of me.

His gaze climbed up my body with liquid desire flowing from their depths. Maybe because my thin pale blue underwear and bra set didn't leave much to the imagination. Based on the way his tongue ran across his bottom lip and the way his dick print pushed against his gray slacks, he enjoyed the view.

He stood before shrugging out of his jacket and tossing it over a nearby standing bench with dangling straps. I was impressed with the speed and accuracy of how quickly he pulled apart and tossed aside his tie before undoing the first two buttons on his crisp blue button up. He reached up and flipped on a light at the top of the frame, putting me under a spotlight inside the device.

It wasn't lost on me that his shirt matched the color of my bra and panties. Was it a vibe between us or a coincidence?

He aimed a finger above me while inching closer, his body heat merging with the heat falling off of mine. I glanced up at the rings before letting my gaze drop back to his waiting one.

"Third and final rule. Once you take those rings in your hands, you're giving me permission to give you pleasure in whatever form your body tells me. When you hold on to those, no matter what happens try not to let go. Letting go of those rings is the same as using a safe word. It will mean you want me to stop. Do you understand?"

Halfway through a nod, I stopped myself.

"Yes Sir, I understand."

"Oh, I almost forgot. Each time you forget to address me properly, you see those numbers flashing up there?"

I glanced up and saw that the base that held the rings above me also had a flashing digital timer on it.

"Since this is your first time, I'm only going to give you fifteen minutes before I let you come. There is a catch though. I built in a decibel meter and if you're not pleading hard enough for me to release your orgasm this machine will not show me the green light I need to see to release it to you. You understand what I'm telling you Maya?"

What?

"Yes, I understand," I said, despite major doubts running through my head. I was still reeling over the sophistication of this equipment.

The rules sounded simple enough, say Sir, ask permission, and don't let go of the rings. And, I apparently had to scream my ass off for him to let me come. There had to be more to this than those three simple directives and even the bonus rule. Was I missing something?

"Are you ready? Take the rings and whatever you do, try not to let go. Trust me, you'll thank me later."

"Okay."

"Sir." I added quickly, making another proud smile light up his handsome face.

He stepped around the human hourglass he'd turned me into, not saying a thing, but allowing his eyes to roam all over me again. The simple act was a turn on I never expected.

After making me leak into my panties and causing my nipples to push against the thin material of my bra, he stepped away. What was he doing? Where was he going? I jerked my neck around trying to track his movements.

A series of whipping and hard slapping sounds made me tense but kept my desire buzzing. His steps grew closer, the prospect of what would happen next had me shaking.

Whatever he had in his hand slid up my spine, causing a tingle to spring up from down low. He passed the object, a leather crop, under my left arm and around and over my nipple, making me blow out quick breaths. The leather felt good against my tight flesh.

Whack!

The sound, the lick, the sting it delivered to my thigh shook me, made me gasp, hard. There wasn't an ache, but damn it got my attention.

Brizio reached out, gripped one of the metal sides of the hourglass and spun me, the unexpected sensation and sailing around the air left me gasping. I had no idea the equipment I was inside could spin.

He positioned me so that I was no longer facing him. He was at my side now, thick metal between us, but open air exposed my full back and front to him.

The crop popped across my ass twice. Harder than it had struck my thigh. The sting it delivered made a quick, "Oh shit," rush out on a harsh breath.

Two more hard licks followed, one to each cheek, and lower on my ass, making me jerk against the rings I held. The sting, like before, didn't hurt and although my mind was saying this wasn't turning me on, my damn body was saying something totally different. My nipples drew so tight they ached with prickly tingles.

"Do you want more Maya?" he questioned, his tone commanding, husky and flowing over me as much as that resounding sting.

"Yes sir," I answered, sounding unsure but not wanting to give up too soon.

Tap. Tap. Tap. Tap.

"Aww!" I cried out, the bite doing something so unexpected, I glanced down to make sure I wasn't imaging the way it had traveled to my clit and invaded my core, making my lady parts hum.

What the hell?

I swallowed hard. What kind of damn sexual witchcraft was this man casting over me?

Three more licks and my panties flooded. My clit throbbed so hard, it took everything for me not to rub my legs together to get more friction down there.

"If you want more, I need to hear at least a *sir* and a *please*."

"Yes Sir. Please. More," I said without hesitation.

A few licks came, delivered to different parts of my back, the sting allowing just the tiniest bit of energy to travel south. He spun me to face him, the unexpected turn making me gasp.

He passed the crop over my nipples, making them so hard, my legs started to shake. I wanted them sucked bad.

Pop!

The crop struck my left nipple.

"Aww!" I yelled out, the cry pushing through the burst of pleasure and the peppery ache. I swore I damn near came, right on the spot.

"Tell me which you like more, Maya, the pain or the pleasure?"

My throat bobbed hard from swallowing the rush of at least four levels of desire hitting me at once. It should have been an easy question to answer, but I honestly didn't know.

"Should I try again to help you decide?"

"Yes Sir, try again," I heard myself saying, getting into what I'd once called sick shit, way too much.

The crop struck my left nipple, the pop harder this time. A startled gasp helped me absorb the pleasurable ache, but I remained unsure of which I liked. The sting traveled down my shuddering belly until it reached my starving clit.

"Have you decided what you like best? Is it going to be pleasure?"

He reached behind me and delivered two light taps to my ass.

"Or pain?" he questioned, delivering a harder tap to each of my nipples. The licks infused with pain gave a more powerful punch, making me leak so much, my thin panties started to stick to me.

The word "Pain," rushed out on a moan.

"You forgot to say something and whenever you forget the rules in this game, you remember what I told you would happen?"

"I apologize. Sir."

"Thank you," he said, but it didn't stop him from aiming a remote he'd pulled out of thin air and added a minute of time to the flashing numbers above me. Ten minutes ten seconds increased to eleven minutes ten seconds. Surely if the need got great enough I'd come anyway, wouldn't I?

Time told my ass a whole different story. Not only did I not come, but Brizio made me get so close that tears started to sting the backs of my eyes. I wanted to come but my body would just not release on its own. He used three different weights of crops on me, testing my tolerance and bringing me to the brink only to pull me right back to the agony of time.

"Tell me exactly what you want Maya."

"I did. Sir. I asked you to make me come. To let me come. To just fucking go ahead and release me from this fucking frustrating stress already. Sir. Fucking please."

The motherfucker laughed. I was so sexually frustrated, I was ready to let these rings go and finger my damn self. That he had me cursing and saying sir at the same time should have told him I was on the verge of stopping this shit.

"How about if I use this crop to play with your clit? I know it has to be aching like a motherfucker right now. Isn't it?"

"Yes. Sir. Yes. Do that, play with it," the words rushed out while my thighs trembled and the rest of me remained in a state so charged, I felt like I would explode the moment anything, even if a fucking gust of air touched my clit.

A glance up showed me only a minute and a half remaining. At this point, I planned to put a fucking freight train to shame the way I was going to be screaming for the green light and for him to put me out of this damn misery.

He picked up the crop with the smallest popper and eased it between my quaking thighs before lifting and placing it against my clit.

"More Sir. More. Please," I begged, my fingers opening and closing around the rings, but I refused to let go. He rubbed back and forth but he didn't apply enough pressure which was exactly what I needed. I started moving against the thing, but it did no good because he held all the control.

"Sir. Fucking do it. Make me come," I growled at him. I'm sure I wasn't supposed to be cursing him, but the sweet torture of knowing he could get me off and was purposefully holding back from doing so was pissing me off. I'd never been introduced to this state of heightened arousal, not even while having sex.

I tossed my head up. Only thirty seconds left and I swore my damn heart was on the verge of exploding. My sex had grown heavy and throbbed so hard, it rumbled through me like thunder.

My wide eyes landed on Brizio who was just as cool and collected as he'd been when he started this. His dick still pushed at his pants but his arousal didn't seem to have an effect on him like mine.

"What about if I did this?"

Pop!

"Aww!" I yelled out when the leather slapped against my hungry clit that was beating out its own demands louder than my words. Time was up. Four zeros flashed overhead.

"Please let me come. Fucking please!" I yelled, squirming so hard my hand almost slipped from the rings.

"What do you want me to do Maya?"

"I need you to hit me again. Sir. Please fucking hit me again. Please. Please," I begged mercilessly, my throat tightening around the words like I was about to cry.

What the fuck?

Tears teased at the backs of my eyes before, but this time my need had risen to such a state of hysteria, they seeped out.

"Pop!"

"Oh God!" I yelled, when the sweet sting brought me closer to the edge, shoving me, but not quite tipping me over.

"Please. Harder. Sir harder," I yelled, loud enough that I felt my own neck veins protruding.

"Tap!"

"Pop!"

My clit died, saw the light and came back to life with a brilliant tingle that spread like wildfire through my body and sent my eyes to the back of my head. My body jerked. It twitched hard enough to rattle my teeth.

I'd never come so hard in my fucking life. And it was a lasting pleasure, one that lingered low and rose higher until my dopamine levels shot through the roof. My ass was seeing unicorns and rainbows behind my eyes, and I believed humming whatever song the horned horses were singing.

"Thank you. Sir. Thank you," I was saying not even realizing I was speaking until I was able to open my eyes. The floodgates had opened below my waist, making tears leak fast down my cheeks. The intense release, still coursing through me, I believed from the torture of being denied it for such a long stretch of time.

I inhaled, filling my lungs to capacity and allowed myself to breathe through the flood of emotions that rushed me when the sensation of my orgasm dwindled to a low thumbing beat that continued to echo through me. My body slumped, although I continued to hang on to the rings, fearing I'd fall on my face if I let go.

Brizio's face came into view, his smile one of concern and care?

"Are you okay?"

I nodded, feeling bashful for the first time since I was a young girl.

"I'm okay," I replied, my tone low and hoarse. I didn't know how to feel right now because for a reason I couldn't grasp, I felt everything at once.

CHAPTER EIGHTEEN

Brizio

Strong, confident, and self-assured. Those were a few of the reasons I liked Maya from the beginning. If shit hit the fan, she wasn't going to run or hide. She would stand and fight even if it meant laying her life on the line.

However, when it came to her sexuality, sexual freedom, and letting go of the need to be in control, she was about as stubborn as a bull. And, I could understand it.

She'd had to bury her parents and take on the role of an adult to raise her brother all before she turned eighteen. I doubt she ever truly had time to figure out what she liked, much less dive into the world of sexual exploration.

Tears flowed down her cheeks and she didn't blink them away. The knowing in her watery gaze told me she understood the impact of what she'd allowed to happen. She could have let go of those rings at any time, but she never did. She endured what most newbies would never have, lasting that long with a ton of lust and desire bearing down on her.

She probably didn't understand it all yet, but the release she endured was more than an orgasm. She'd let go of a decade of stress, control, and unresolved issues. In that moment of peace there was nothing but blinding pleasure that wiped out all the bad. She sagged, her arms stretched tight to keep from falling to the floor.

Tears didn't usually affect me, but Maya's dropped for reasons I understood and for some she hadn't disclosed to me yet. My hand slid behind her neck.

"Maya, look at me," I commanded. She eased her head up while tears continued to spill down her cheeks.

"It's okay. You unpacked a lot of shit you didn't need to hold on to and it's okay. You can drop your arms now."

She nodded while her teeth sank into her bottom lip. I couldn't tell if her expression was a smile or a grimace or a little of both. Her arms dropped and flopped loud around my neck. With my hand firm around her waist, I held her weight. Her glazed over eyes blinked rapidly but remained on mine.

With my arms around her back and under her deliciously tempting thighs, I scooped her up in one big sweep. Maya was the kind of pressure that could drive me mad if I didn't watch myself.

In nothing but a bra and panties, I carried her out of the sandbox and up to my office.

"Are you okay to stand?"

She nodded. "Yes. I'm good."

She remained upright, but in a wobbly stance until I retrieved her a robe from my closet. I popped the tag off the robe I'd never worn and helped her into it. The essence of her tears still remained, giving her a serene look that I never expected to see on her.

"You're a beautiful woman. You know that?" I whispered while leaning in until our lips met. This kiss, laced with empathy, understanding, and reassurance, was also filled with a potency of something that made me want to relinquish my control to her.

"Thank you." Her words came on a whisper warm against my mouth. And I wasn't sure if she was thanking me for our time in the Sandbox or for the compliment.

The sensual drag of my lips against hers, of our tongues sliding so deliciously across each other's, of the breathless sensations spreading through me. I lost myself in a feeling that should have been forbidden. This was...this was..."

It was a struggle, but I managed to draw my head back, despite my dick down there carrying out a war against my pants.

Maya's eyes were about as heavy and emotionally compromised as mine. We had chemistry, there was no denying that, but we had something else too. Something serious. Something that would never release us no matter how hard we tried to escape it. Something that two people like us would do our best to convince ourselves wasn't there.

I felt it. She felt it. Our gazes remained locked and the sensation of being poured into her forced me to suck in a sharp breath.

"Holy! Shit!"

The impact of what I saw, of what seeped deep into my bones, of what was being communicated between us without words was direct, demanding, and unmistakably present.

My heart raced, my pulse a revved engine ready to race away. Our breathing, long and ragged, echoed through my office. I swallowed, the one indication that I could command myself to do something other than absorb the potency of our connection.

Maya knew what was happening and didn't say or do a thing to stop it. I didn't believe she could speak through the possessive force at play. Did either of us have control anymore?

Brizio fucking DeLuca had fucked around and fell. Was it in love, lust, or obsession? I didn't fucking know because I had no other experiences like this to make a comparison.

This was the kind of shit that never wanted anything to do with my crazy ass. And I didn't know what to do now that it had arrived like a gift I hadn't asked for, didn't even know I needed. I had to find a way to tamp down this overbearing tension driving me to make conclusions that couldn't have been true.

Even saying it in my head sounded like I was shouting it out on a megaphone. Maya blinked, but her gaze remained connected to what she spotted in mine. She'd fallen into the same trance of realization in which I was trapped.

Racked with emotions I didn't know how to process, I was shaken down to my damn blood cells. I couldn't let her see me like this. I needed a distraction and quickly.

I lifted my hands, sliding them up the front of her body until it slid around the front of her neck and folded around her warm flesh into a tight grip that lifted her chin. Releasing her neck, I stumbled back. I didn't feel like having sex.

The fuck?

She had just allowed me to introduce her to my world in the Sandbox. It would take her some time to process it. It wasn't fair for me to take her through another round of sweet torture. *Yes.* That was it. The answer to the fucked up shit I'd said about not wanting to have sex.

"I'll draw you a hot bath and if you're nice, I'll wash your back," I commented, putting more distance between us.

She chuckled at the comment. I appreciated the sound as it was in contrast to the emotions continuing to race through me. I aimed my hand towards the back of my office where there was a full sized bathroom, and a small bedroom.

Even as I busied myself with drawing the bath, I couldn't shake the heavy coat of emotional pressure that had settled within me. I always knew I had a thing for Maya, but now that the connection had manifested and shown its full form, I didn't know if I could handle it.

How could shit have changed so fast? Had it really changed, or was it that I finally admitted to what was there the whole time?"

My fingers traced absently through the hot water. I'd been in my head so long, the water had risen too high in the tub.

"The water's ready," I finally said, glancing up. She'd been standing there the whole time staring at me.

"What's going on B3co? When you're that quiet, trouble is usually brewing."

"Nothing," I lied. "Just thinking about this mission."

"I'll behave and do what needs to be done, if that's what you're worried about," she reassured, disrobing and reaching behind her back to unhook her bra. I stood in a rush.

"Let me help you with that," I told her, reaching around her and bringing her into me at the same time. The hook snapped between my fingers, and I slid the thin material from around her body letting it drop while my eyes zeroed in her tits. Full, round, suckable.

"Your hunger is showing B3co. You need to save that energy for this performance we need to pull off tomorrow."

I chuckled, dropping to a kneeling position to take those panties down and to get a close up view of her pussy. I needed another whiff of her scent.

She wiggled while I tugged, the thin, very damp material slid down with ease. I glanced up into her teasing gaze. Payback was a motherfucker. I wanted to fuck her so bad, I wasn't sure if I was going to be able to stand straight for an hour my dick ached so bad. I got the sense that she knew it too.

I loved how the sound echoed off the walls when I slapped a heavy hand against her ass. It was a reminder of what was to come if she kept teasing me.

"Ouch," she yelped, without an ounce of pain registering on her face.

"You might want to take that bath while I'm offering it. If I fuck you right now, you are not going to be able to walk into that club let alone pull off a performance."

She didn't move at my threat, the challenge in her gaze was telling me to do my best.

"Get your hard-headed ass in that tub woman," I said in a more demanding tone. She moved this time, but I remained in my kneeling position to admire that ass when she walked off. *Damn!*

The mocking smile said she knew exactly what she was doing and she damn well knew my eyes were glued to her. She lifted a leg to step into the tub and my eyes followed her in, even taking in how the warm water and fragrant bubbles wrapped around her.

She eased back, laying her head against the little bathing cushion, eyes closing immediately. I still couldn't stand up, my shit was too hard. I crawled from my position to the tub.

Crawled!

What the fuck is happening right now?

Maya ran the towel lazily along her chest and stomach with her eyes closed. They snapped open when I took the towel.

"Let me do that," I told her, continuing where she'd left off and loving that she was relaxed enough to let her eyes fall back closed.

"I understand better what you explained to me yesterday and today. About letting go of control. It feels like a huge boulder was just lifted off my chest. And as much as I hate to admit it, you were right."

"What the hell is happening right now? Did I just hear Maya Daniels say that I, Brizio DeLuca, was right about something?"

She chuckled, our banter swept away the last lingering knots of the heavy emotional mood I'd allowed to go on for far too long.

"Shit like that will only stumble out of my mouth once, so you better enjoy it while you can," she warned and I believed her.

I eased the soapy towel up, letting it slide across her shoulder and down her back. She leaned forward, and judging by her long, deep inhale, she enjoyed the attention. So did I, too damn much. I couldn't do this for much longer because everything within me wanted to crawl into that tub with her.

"What's your story B3co? How do you fit into this big DeLuca family?"

"It's a long story," I replied.

She lifted an exaggerated brow. "Does it look like I have somewhere to be right now? You're Captain Hooknose ass went snooping into my history, it's only fair that I get some of yours."

I didn't even try to make a snappy comeback. I believed she deserved a little piece of my DeLuca history.

"Our late Don Ermano was my grandfather. My mother Mirabella DeLuca was his daughter. She and my father, who was a respected associate of our family, were shot right in front of me when I was ten. The killer broke into our house, a member of a rival family. He made me watch him kill my parents, and their deaths weren't quick or painless. He told me he was letting me go because I probably wouldn't live past eighteen anyway, and that he wanted what he'd done to torment me."

"I'm sorry Brizio," she offered, her tone caring, her face creased with tension. She placed a hand over mine that held the towel, stopping it from sliding carelessly over her thigh.

"After that night, I never felt like I fit anywhere anymore. I was shuffled around from family member to family member. None had the patience or the know-how to raise me. I was horrible. Arson, beating up on other kids and adults, stealing cars, taking drugs, you name the trouble I was drawn to it.

"It wasn't until I was shipped here to St. Louis and met my cousin Primo that I started adding value to the DeLuca name. I gave Primo hell too, but he ended up being what I needed when I was on a path of self-destruction. In a way, he raised me, didn't abandon me or try to pawn me off when I did dumb shit. Eventually, I allowed the knowledge he knocked into my head to start seeping into my brain."

A smile greeted me for sharing, sweet, delicate, and caring. I'd never seen anything like that on Maya's face, didn't know she was capable.

"You think you were a trouble maker because you were hurting over what happened to your parents?"

I shrugged. "I don't know."

"What happened to the man who killed your parents? Did your family ever find him?"

I nodded. "Yes they did. They sat me in front of him and asked me to identify him. I lied. I told them that he wasn't the right man."

A small dent showed up between my brows.

"Why would you...?"

She paused when she connected the puzzle pieces.

"You wanted to kill him yourself," she stated, matter of fact, picking up on my nature even from the past. "How old were you?"

"I was twelve."

"Brizio," she whispered. "You sacrificed your innocence to avenge your parents. That's a lot to carry. Shit."

She was more perceptive than I imagined. I would have done anything for my parents, just like I know she was willing to do anything for her brother.

"Does your family know that you were the one who killed him?"

"I never told..."

My words trailed off. The realization of how easy it was to tell her one of my darkest secrets hit me like a ton of bricks. I believe she understood the impact of me revealing that secret. She didn't comment, didn't ask me to elaborate, or ask any more questions.

I pulled away from her abruptly. I needed to think about tomorrow. I needed to shake this connection we were developing before I ran out of wiggle room to pull away from it and her when the time came. I left the towel draped across her shoulder, standing.

"I need to go and start setting up a few things for tomorrow."

She nodded, her smile laced with care and what I believed was understanding.

CHAPTER NINETEEN

Maya

The expensive white silk didn't cling, it smoothed along my curves and kissed the tops of my knees. A tiny sliver of cleavage peeked, enticing eyes to linger for more. I had a tough time ripping my eyes away from the first glimpse of the dress on me in the mirror.

The slit up to my thigh was in competition with the chest area, no more than an enticement. Did Brizio buy this dress for his eyes and decided to allow me to wear it out to tease others? It was elegant and sexy, not at all what I expected for the type of club we were about to visit.

The red heels that matched my lipstick were a dare, at least five inches and not platform. The thin stilts that posed as heels would inspire fear in any woman who lacked confidence.

A woman I hardly recognized stared back at me after I slid on the shoulder length jet black bob wig. Jeans, designer tops, and the occasional dress was all you would get out of me.

This whole ensemble put me in the mind frame to exude the kind of confidence that didn't fit the roll I was expected to play tonight. Was Brizio's devious ass testing me?

On the other hand and as much as I hated to admit it, B3co knew what he was doing and could pick out my clothes and buy me whatever the hell he wanted. I wasn't saying shit else on the subject.

"You look…good," I almost choked on the word. "For someone who gets his clothes from the grave yard," I added.

I wasn't used to dishing out compliments, especially not to Brizio. But, there was no denying the way his body filled out that damn suit.

The defined lines of his muscles pushed at just enough of the expensive black material of his suit jacket and pants, giving my eyes a workout. Had I just not been paying attention before or had this man always been that damned fine?

His blown out hair teased his shoulders and had my fingers tingling to touch, pull, and get all tangled up in those thick dark tresses.

"Thank you," he replied. I expected to hear a smart comment, but it never came. Instead, we stared at each other while silence hung in the air like a static charge waiting to zap me.

"Are you ready for this?" He asked. His sly grin made an appearance, but I didn't miss a hint of concern in his eyes too.

"No. I'm not. The lessons you've imparted on me went in one ear and out of the other. The biggest lesson I learned yesterday, blew up my body and flew out my pussy when I came."

He howled at that one, his laughter making me laugh.

"I'm dead ass serious. You don't come that hard and not lose something. Short term memory, a few pounds, part of my uterus."

"I get it, but it's time to be serious now. We have to pull this off."

I nodded although I still believed it was too much to comprehend so fast. How was I supposed to know that this lifestyle had its own world, with rules and guidelines and a library full of do's and don'ts?"

"You'll do fine," he said, reassuringly.

"All I can remember is the part about saying Sir a lot and acting like I don't have the brain capacity to think on my own."

He chuckled. "That's all you'll need. Oh, and remember to look at my dick a lot, same as you did last night."

Brizio was currently the same arrogant ass I'd first met. The version of him that showed up last night after that hourglass session was the most unnerving version of him I'd ever met. It was like being around a live wire plugged into a dimension I wasn't sure I was equipped to handle. I like this version of him much better than the scary, serious one.

***

The drive to the club relaxed me as we tossed around our usual back talking banter. By the time we got done slinging insults, he was the equivalent of the predator in drag, and I looked like a puffer fish hopped up on crack.

We exited the interstate and traveled along a series of streets and highways that pulled us away from the city and deeper into a wood lined area. I gawked out the window, taking in the lack of scenery.

"They are serious about their exclusivity, aren't they?" I questioned absently, barely making out the shadow of what looked like a mansion in the distance."

"Very serious," Brizio replied, driving onto the property and halfway around the large circular driveway. He stopped at the edge of the driveway that led to the side of the house where a valet opened our doors.

"Mr. DeLuca, so happy you could join us tonight," the man greeted before holding up a wrist watch that he slipped onto Brizio's arm. It must have been how they tracked people.

"Andrew will show you in," I heard him say.

Andrew must have been the one standing outside my door. Why wasn't he moving to come and greet us?

Brizio walked around and opened my door, reminding me that I was his pet and no one had a right to put their hands on me.

"This way Sir," Andrew stated. He gestured for us to follow once I was out of the car and my arm was securely tucked under Brizio's. The thick and extraordinarily tall glass doors were pushed open for us. We entered, stepping into an area where there was a security checkpoint reminiscent of one at the airport.

Brizio and his ability to gather information had already alerted me on how tight security would be and of what we could and couldn't carry into the place. The guards were thorough, patting us down like we were being processed into a federal correctional facility. I was waiting to hear one tell me or Brizio to bend over and cough.

Once they determined we weren't a threat to the facility or others, we moved past the checkpoint and entered another area where we walked through a full body scanner.

Damn. Now, I understood why Brizio and his cousins had done so much planning before attempting to infiltrate this place. It would have been easier to break into Gagliardi's house if anyone had been able to acquire the location of which one he would be located at a specific time.

The man had ten houses across three states. He lived at random locations as a security measure. It was more proof that the life he portrayed was a façade. Hopefully, our mission would lead us to his location or provide retribution in the form of his death.

Another thick set of doors made from two-way glass and we finally entered the Club.

Welcome to Hiatus, Mr. Brizio DeLuca. It will be our pleasure to serve you, an automated voice greeted pleasantly. The device must have been reading the watch Brizio was given earlier.

The first few steps inside stopped me in my tracks.

Wow!

It was Cirque du Soleil meets upscale spa retreat. The music was upbeat, but instrumental and the lighting dim enough to inspire desire and even a touch of romance.

Even Brizio stopped to take in the scene for a few seconds before he placed a hand on my back and nudged me forward. My roaming eyes scanned, allowing me to observe the others in attendance.

This place was a full cocktail of Masters, Mistresses, Dominants, and submissives. The sight of a woman walking men like dogs and men doing the same to women wasn't something I saw every day.

The things some of these people used as clothing were items you'd find in a hardware store, like this lady. A leather strap wrapped around her tits covered her nipples and three others fashioned around her lower body covered her pubic area. Having that much leather running down the crack of her ass had to hurt.

My attention was lured around the room as Brizio kept me moving. Some people wore more sophisticated attire like Tailored suits and dresses. Nothing they wore gave me an accurate reading of what they enjoyed or participated in sexually. The subtlety in some of their actions gave me hints.

What the hell?

My neck snapped around. I fought hard to keep myself from gawking. Was that the devil himself? Lucifer, in an all-black suit. He was at least six-eight with a full set of horns that protruded realistically from his head. He held on to two flaming leashes that connected to the necks of two men in nothing but G-strings.

Another man in an expensive suit with his ass out in the back, passed us, gawking so hard, I forgot I was supposed to be more low key until Brizio's voice rang out.

"I can't believe I've only been to this place twice before tonight," Brizio muttered.

"You never had a good reason to revisit, until now," I whispered. The way I saw it there was no reason to put your energy into things that rarely crossed your path. This lifestyle was a good example. I didn't have a need to know about it, so I was never tempted to explore it.

"If you want to keep your fucking eyes, I suggest you look in another direction. Now," Brizio growled, sending a tall distinguished looking man who resembled Fabio away so fast, I believed he was about to break out running.

"I knew I should have marked you," Brizio muttered. I vaguely remembered what marking me entailed, but it was too late for upgrades now. We were here and had parts to play.

Speaking of parts, how the fuck were we supposed to get the attention of the deviant freak who'd murdered my brother? We hadn't discovered the motive behind my brother's killing other than a possible romantic entanglement. I wanted an answer as to why he was killed as badly as I wanted to send his killer to hell.

Another set of interested eyes came from a group of three. A man and two women, but they were respectable enough to look and keep it moving.

My curious gaze followed the group. Which of the three was the dominant? They all appeared like equals or perhaps I wasn't versed enough in this lifestyle to know the differences or how to spot the telling signs.

"Our seats are over there." Brizio pointed at a seating area close to the largest of several stages strategically placed around the open-floor planned space. We had a bird's eye view of the stage from the large comfortable cushioned booth that semi-circled the table. Two reservation signs sat atop our table. Brizio swiped his wrist in front of a small digital scanner built into the table's center piece.

He made sure I was seated before he took his place beside me. His muscular leg pressing against mine momentarily dragged my attention away from the expanding crowd.

The couples and groups continued to file in and I caught eyes full of every type of situation. The best words I could think to use for how some of these people had chosen to enter this place was, situation.

Nakedness was certainly not a problem for some. Others appeared happy crawling around on the floor with collars and chains around their necks. The richest among the crowd flashed expensive clothes, jeweled accessories, and bossed their subs around like they were misbehaving children.

Brizio's hand was a constant comfort, rubbing up and down my thigh with a calming tenderness that wasn't usually his type of vibe. Our eyes tracked the waitress, me looking under my lashes, at her in her thin see-through negligee approaching our table.

"Good afternoon, Mr. DeLuca," she greeted him without glancing in my direction.

"I have a Martini for you, neat and a crown and coke for your *Regina Perfetta.*"

Too fast. His what?

My forehead crinkled, but I was mindful not to question him in front of the woman. It sounded like she just called me *Regular Pig feet.*

And how the hell did she already have our drink orders? Phones weren't allowed inside, so all of our information must have been uploaded in a database before we arrived and downloaded onto Brizio's watch.

My nosey ass was determined to get a peek at the tiny note the woman sat in front of Brizio after she placed our drinks in front of us.

As soon as the waitress departed, Brizio, knowing me as well as he did, faced me. "I'll tell you what I listed as your pet name if you agree to do another session with me, the next one for two hours."

I clamped my lips shut. Did I really want to go two hours with this man in that dungeon of his? His eyes remained on me, waiting.

"I'm good without knowing. It's probably something crazy anyway," I told him.

He shook his head, "Trust me, you're going to want to know what I named you. It was the first thing that came to mind when I saw you. And despite what you may believe, it's not something crazy."

I didn't get a chance to respond, because a man wearing a black half-face masquerade mask approached. A man and a woman followed, walking behind him like he was casting two shadows. When he walked past the table next to ours and placed his wrist against the little digital box on our table, it identified them as our table mates.

"Hello," he spoke, inclining his head in Brizio's direction without giving a name.

"Hello," Brizio replied in kind, not giving his name either.

I couldn't not look at the man. I had to see his face. To me, everyone I came in contact with was a suspect. Would Brizio let me sit at a table with my brother's killer without telling me?

My eyes squinted in Brizio's direction before turning my curiosity back to the man. Upon closer scrutiny his eyes peeking from the mask made me believe he was of Asian descent. I knew from photos that Gagliardi was Caucasian. The man aimed a dismissive finger to the floor, where his subs took their places at his feet.

The act widened my eyes until I noticed others throughout the dimly lit area sitting at their Dom's feet. Although I understood that there was more to Dom and sub relationships, I still wasn't sure I liked this lifestyle.

"It's the seasonal auction tonight. Are you purchasing anything tonight?" The man leaned slightly across the table. He was careful not to touch me, his question meant for Brizio.

Purchasing what?

Brizio glanced down at me, before he lifted his gaze to the man?

"I came to see what's being offered, but do you think I need to make a purchase?"

The man's face lit in a smile, dispelling his pinched lips and tensed jaw. He took a quick glance down at me, before he put his smiling gaze back on Brizio's.

"No," he answered with a chuckle. "I was thinking of trading you these two for her? I must say, you are...blessed."

"Shut up.

"Be Quiet."

"Don't say shit!"

I yelled the commands loudly in my head and was forced to close my eyes against the strong need to tell this man to fuck all the way off. They talked about buying and trading people like they were inanimate objects. The more I found out about this world, the less I liked it.

Brizio insisted it was too soon for me to fully understand and appreciate it, but I didn't think I was obedient enough to even allow it to soak into my quick reacting brain.

When the lights dimmed and the tone of the music lowered, I had no choice but to wait and see what all of this auction business entailed.

.

CHAPTER TWENTY

Maya

It took Brizio's strong hand to keep me in my seat when these disrespectful ass people started buying and selling people like the fucking auction block had been put back into effect. The one thing that kept me sitting and kept my big mouth closed was that no one who was sold was black. I believe they were conscious of what that specific act could signify.

Our table mates stood as soon as the fifth and final auction had concluded. The leader, the Dom of the threesome leaned in Brizio's direction and reached out his hand. When Brizio took it, he added a slight curve of his lip representing a smile. It bothered me that I didn't know the guy, still wondering and not allowing myself to believe that I may have been this close to my brother's killer.

"Nice to meet you, Mr. DeLuca," he said. They hadn't exchanged names because they already knew each other. His gracious tone and slight head nod implied that he respected Brizio.

Brizio inclined his head, an air of nonchalance in the movement.

"You as well, Master Russo."

Master?

What qualified one to be a master in this lifestyle? I couldn't remember.

The man's brows shot up, like he hadn't expected the greeting from Brizio. Was he trying to keep his identity low key? He wasn't the only one in this place wearing a mask. The unknown variables about this specific man was killing me.

He and his pets walked off, heading in the direction in the back of the building steeped in pure darkness until it swallowed them.

"They are going to one of the dungeons to play," Brizio stated. At first I believed he was speaking to me, but his face was aimed straight ahead not focusing on anything at all.

"Okay," he said, confirming that he was either going crazy or communicating with someone through the same type of listening device he fitted me with before. I'd also seen more of the high-tech equipment the DeLuca men would be using displayed on the table at the family meeting yesterday.

Brizio reached out and took my hand before standing.

"We are about to go play too," was all he said before we walked off in the opposite direction than our table-mates had gone.

At least ten minutes had passed and we were just now approaching what I believe was an entryway into something other than another hallway. We'd traveled through at least five hallways and gone up and down a couple of different flights of stairs.

Every time I attempted to ask Brizio what we were doing he'd place a finger against his lips to shut me up. Were we doing all of this mystery walking to find my brother's killer or what? The not knowing was as torturous as having my orgasm withheld.

Finally, we came to a stop outside a door. I prayed we were about to enter it, if only to put me out of my misery.

"Code," Brizio said and a few seconds later he pressed a six digit pen in the little panel outside the door. When the red flashes of light turned green, it cracked the seal on the door, but Brizio had to give it a push to get it to open.

We stepped inside before the room opened to a dimly lit area that was a replica of a back alley, dumpers and all. The realistic view made me question if we had stepped outside.

The sound of the city, cars, people's voices, it all played into this scene from speakers I couldn't see. All that kept me from fully believing we'd stepped outside was glancing up and not seeing the height of the buildings we stood between and finding only inky blackness above our head.

The discarded mask on the floor and the same two subs. This was the man who'd been sitting at the table with us the whole time. Was it Gagliardi?

I couldn't see his face. A long black stick whipped through the air and came down in the face of the man kneeling before him. The man's scream from the vicious blow was not one of pleasure.

Brizio insisted that this BDSM exchange between Dom and sub wasn't about abuse, but *that* damn sure appeared to be abuse to me. At the sound of our approach, the man froze in the middle of lifting the stick again. Was he about to strike the man in the face again?

"This room is taken already," he said. Brizio stepped closer and the abusive asshole relaxed. The kneeling man's shoulders shook and although he refused to release a sound, I knew he was crying. The woman kneeling beside him with her palms lifted, didn't move, not even to look in our direction.

Every emotion worth showing up picked this moment to hit me, kicking up my heart rate so high, my breaths blew out in erratic pants. We wouldn't be in this dungeon if this wasn't *him*. The one who killed my brother. The one I wanted to murder with my bare hands. The one who'd been sitting at the table with us the entire time. Did he know who I was? That I was the sister to the victim he'd slaughtered?

"I usually don't share, but I'll make an exception for you," the man, Ettore Gagliardi handed Brizio the stick without a second thought, eager for him to become an active participant in the sick shit he had planned for his subs. His face came into view when he turned toward Brizio. Despite the dim lighting, I noticed it was eyeliner that misled me about his identity.

Brizio took the stick with a grin I recognized. Did this man have any idea he'd just handed a weapon to an earthen devil?

I remained rooted in place, but I wasn't seeing red like many claimed to see when vengeance ravaged their hearts. A chill swept through me, the icy tingle relaxing in a way that I'm sure wasn't healthy.

With that cold relief at seeing my brother's killer this up close came flashes of the different types of brutal deaths I pictured the man suffering. Bare hands around his throat, hot pokers burning his naked flesh, hung by the neck until he was within an inch of slipping away only to be released from the noose to be beaten into a bloody pulp.

There was no way this line of thinking was normal. Where was my voice of reason? Where was the nice part of me that knew vengeance, torture, and cold-blooded murder was wrong?

I believed the best parts of me had been left on that cold metal table with my brother's mutilated body. I'd not been the same since I saw him. Since he'd started visiting me in my dreams every night begging to be freed from his prison of restlessness.

Brizio had the people in this life and in the entertainment industry fooled, but I'd seen him in action. He didn't glorify death or praise it, he inhaled it like it was his air or a part of his life blood. I believe it was safe to assume anyone bearing the DeLuca name lived by the same deathly values.

"I appreciate it," Brizio told the man, snapping me out of my frozen state of mental gymnastics.

"But, I'm not here for them," Brizio announced, making the man's brows quirk, especially when he aimed a finger back at me.

"We are here for you."

Ettore Gagliardi must have recognized the dangerous edge dripping off Brizio like warm rain drops. I took a step closer and whatever he saw in my facial expression made him go pale. His lips fell apart before he turned his gaze back to Brizio, lifting a surrendering hand.

Before the man spit out the first syllable of his protest the stick he'd handed over came down at his face. The swish of the swing was so hard and fast, I swore it blew my hair back.

The lick struck with a resounding *whack* that sent the man flying back and landing hard on his ass. His pets scrambled out of the way of their fallen master. He cocked hateful eyes up a Brizio while gripping the blooded right side of his face.

Processing what had just happened, what was about to happen to him, his breaths blew out in pants while his wide eyes remained pinned on Brizio.

"What is the meaning of this? Why..."

"Shut the fuck up!"

An ominous silence fell over the space, making me tense my shoulders to ward off the chill that raced up my back. He knew or had an idea why we were here. It's why he couldn't stop looking in my direction. If he was looking to me to be the voice of reason, he was about to find out the hard way that vengeance had no heart in this matter.

Brizio walked up to the man's sub, who cowered at his approach, peeking up at him behind raised hands.

"You can look at me. I don't do abuse. Doesn't do shit for me," Brizio announced before reaching out and cupping the bruised face of the one who'd been hit.

"I'm going to make him pay for that," he promised the man, fingering his swollen and bruised cheek with a caring touch that did not belong in this scene. My eyes fell on Ettore, who's neck swiveled from me to Brizio to his sub and back around the final circle of his life.

"You two can get up and climb into the dumpster," Brizio's commanding Dom's voice rang out over the space. The subs stood at Brizio's demanding tone and moved with purpose, not even casting a glance in the direction of their fallen master.

I was a novice at this life, but I didn't think this was how it worked. You couldn't just walk up to a Master, strike him down, and start commanding his subs?

Could you?

Once the subs climbed inside, Brizio approached the dumpster and peeked inside.

"Whatever you hear, feel free to use the sounds to get yourselves off."

He snapped his fingers, recalling something and making the sub snap to attention. His action had also pulled my death stare away from Ettore.

"I know what a world class asshole this dick has been to you. I've heard about the abuse and have taken it upon myself to find you two a new home with Quinin."

The level of glee they attempted but failed to keep off their faces spilled out into the dim space. I believed their obedience in the face of who they considered one of their superiors was all that kept them from jumping up and down and hugging Brizio.

I don't know who this Quinin was, but she *or he* must have been a sub's dream the way they peered up at Brizio like he was a god they worshiped. Neither gave a word in protest about being traded to someone else, and they still hadn't cast a glance in the direction of their old master.

"Yes Sir."

"Thank you Sir."

Their voices rang low, but I didn't miss the humble timber in the tone.

"We appreciate you Sir."

"I'm forever grateful Sir."

I heard so many *Sir's* I was getting sick of the word. Trained to swallow or hide their emotions, they tempered their joy at what Brizio promised them, but it continued to radiate off them regardless.

This was some crazy shit. Brizio slammed the top down and used the chain and thick padlock to secure it closed.

Mr. Ettore Gagliardi remained laid out on the floor holding his bloody face. Brizio tossed the stick and with one strong hand, swooped in and gripped the man by the arm.

"Get your ass up. I have questions for you," Brizio spat. The edge to his tone matched the icy currents that had numbed my ability to feel empathy.

The man was nearly Brizio's size and height, but he was being manhandled. With choppy steps and my mind caught in a frozen vortex of vengeance, I followed while Brizio led the man to a big cross with chains attached to it.

"I don't know what this is about, but I can assure you..."

"Shut up and talk when I ask you a question," Brizio commanded, cutting him off before flinging him so hard his back struck the thick cross.

"Maya, would you give me a hand, please," Brizio called back to me, drawing my attention away from the wide eyed man. Apparently, he needed my help with strapping him to the cross. The idea made a rush of sick pleasure race through me.

Once the man's hands, feet, and torso were secured to the cross, Brizio didn't go to the display of sex toys hanging on the wall behind us for a torture device. He extracted something from inside his suit jacket and screwed it together. The ringing scrapes told me the object was metal. Was it a gun? How had he gotten the device through the Fort Knox level security of this place?

"How?" My one word question found its way past my tangled up tongue.

"Cousin Aurelio," Brizio answered before the thick medal baton he'd put together revealed its full potential. The instruments on that wall weren't made to deliver the same kind of damage as this piece of thick metal.

Bam!

I jumped, gripping my chest to keep my heart from leaping into that dumpster with the subs. The first lick Brizio delivered was without warning and so hard the man let out a whooping cry that tore through the air and raised goosebumps on my skin.

Ettore yanked his arms against the restraints so hard I expected his hands to be broken and possibly detached from his wrist. His stomach, the area that sustained the impact appeared to be caved inward. Drool dripped from his quivering lips, his body a mass of trembles to combat the aches rolling through him.

"Have you heard the bible verse about thy rod and thy staff?"

The man shook his head robotically at Brizio's out of the blue question that brought up an image of Father Romigi in my head.

"I own both, a rod and a staff, and they are excellent torture devices. I'm going to ask you a few questions, and I'm only going to ask each one once. I want an answer and for each wrong answer or non-answer you give, you will endure the wrath of Kane, my very own rod."

The man was too stunned for words, his body still a trembling mass of flesh, his face pulled tight with a riot of emotions.

"If you piss me off Ettore, I'll be forced to break out my staff and you don't want that."

Brizio glanced down at the metal stick he called Kane and an evil smile danced across his lips. "Kane is my favorite though. Where my staff, Able, delivers swift death, Kane is more deliberate and will give you time to think about what you need to say."

The metal tapped against the inside of Brizio's palm, the sound as intimidating as his words. "I must warn you, the most hits from Kane that anyone has lived through and not suffered permanent damage or death, is unlucky number seven."

What the hell was in that baton to make it *that* deadly? And why was I edging closer to see what type of damage it had delivered to Ettore?

"Oh," Brizio lifted the baton, aiming it at the man's head. "Make sure you start or end each of your comments or replies with *Sir.* Do you understand?"

"Ye-Yes, Sir," the man's voice trembled while drool, tinged with blood drizzled down his chin. Blood also wet his upper abdominals and lower chest region of the cream colored silk top he wore.

The man wheezed from one hit, meaning a rib or two was cracked. It had just occurred to me that Brizio had chosen this method of death for Ettore because he'd seen pictures of my brother, knew that he'd taken a brutal beating before he was killed.

"Did you kill Eric Daniels?"

My brother's name kicked up my heart rate and my eagerness to hear him admit to what had led to my broken heart, to what had slowly started to turn it black. The need to know intoxicated me, drove me to almost repeat Brizio's question.

"No. I p-p-promise you. I don't…I don't know him. I didn't kill him," the man pushed out the words, stuttering between coughs and wheezes.

"Wrong fucking answer. And where's the fucking discipline. You didn't say Sir."

Woop!

"Shit," I muttered when a chunk of flesh and blood particles from the man's arm flew through the air. Brizio was wielding a stick that was built in hell and forged by the devil himself. Kane was no joke.

The intensity of the man's cries made the sound vibrate off me and bounced off the surface of the wall behind the cross he was strapped to.

"Where did you kill Eric Daniels?"

"Please. Sir. I beg you. I didn't…"

Thump!

This lick struck his leg this time, ripping the material of his pants and tearing away flesh. Blood ran down his arm, rolling past his armpit and down his side like it was in a hurry to meet the blood wetting the side of his leg.

His body shook so badly at this point, I doubted Brizio would understand a thing he said when he did speak. I'd seen some wicked shit growing up in my hood, but I'd never seen anyone bludgeoned to death.

This was the kind of shit I'd seen on the old movie classics like *Scarface* and *Casino*. The DeLucas lived up to the hype of their mafia reputations.

The stench of blood and the unmistakable scent of urine found my nose. Several long breaths calmed my constricting throat and rolling stomach.

The atmosphere around us was chocked full of fear, the air stale, the only sound the cries of a dying man.

"Why did you kill Mr. Daniels?"

His voice hoarse, his breaths, quick spurts blown out from overworked lungs and a pain ravaged body.

"Sir. He...st...s-stole from me. I accidentally strangled him."

"Wrong answer," Brizio told the man, lifting Kane high above his head.

"Stop!" I yelled out, stopping another vicious strike, one I believed would add to the internal damage the man may have already been suffering.

"Brizio," I called in a low tone. I didn't have to step any closer to share with him what was on my mind. I was just now realizing I was no less than three feet away from the bloody flesh the man was becoming. Brizio lowered the blood soaked piece of death metal in his hand.

He leaned in and the evil devil faced monster that was beating a man to death seconds ago disappeared and was replaced by the handsome devil Brizio played so well.

"I don't think he killed my brother," I said, my words a harsh whisper.

"What?" Brizio questioned, jerking back a bit at my words. He glanced at the rod in his hand and at the man on the cross before glancing back in my direction. His stare was so potent, I could read his questions before a word was spoken.

"I identified my brother's body. A lot of evil shit was done to him. I sat with Eric for hours looking at his mutilated body, talking to him, promising him that I would find out who did that to him. That I would make them pay for every cut, bruise, and contusion. Security eventually came in and pulled me away from my brother."

I shook my head at Brizio. "Eric was not strangled. You've either beaten this man senseless or he's taking the blame for someone else."

Brizio didn't reply but he instead cast a speculative eye at Ettore. I reclaimed his attention by continuing my explanation.

"You saw pictures of the staged crime scene," I reminded Brizio. "But I was with my brother long enough to know that he was beaten to death. That he put up a good fight. I know what a strangulation looks like. Eric didn't have any of the tell-tale marks around his neck, no petechiae in his eyes, nothing." I aimed a stiff finger in Ettore's direction. "He's lying. I believe he may be covering for someone he's willing to die for. Ask him who he's covering for?"

Brizio nodded, before turning back to the man, whose clothing was dark red at this point. He was bleeding out, proof that Kane was no regular stick. I glanced down at it in Brizio's hand. What was it made from?

"Ettore Gagliardi," Brizio called out, getting his attention. It took effort, but he pulled his chin off his bloody chest and peered up at Brizio, tears tracing through the blood on his face.

"New information has come to light. We don't believe you killed Eric Daniels."

The man's eyes, popping from their socket, zeroed in on Brizio and then me.

"Who killed Eric?" Brizio barked.

"Me. I killed him," he swore, his tone low, shaky, breathy.

Crack!

"Oh shit," I muttered, covering my eyes and peeking through my fingers. This blow was to his opposite shoulder as the injured arm. Instant dislocation. The bone had slipped from the joint and left his arm hanging on by skin and tissue based on the unnatural curve of his sleeve and how the arm swung listlessly from the restraints.

The epic cries were a noise that brimmed with an otherworldly sound. He begged for help and pleaded for mercy. Muscles pulled taunt, eyes wide as silver dollars, and body jerking to expel the hurt stabbing through his bones.

The screams were like nothing I'd ever heard, the tone piercing time and space and reaching a disciple that made my ears ring. Why hadn't he passed out already?

"You can give up one person or give me permission to kill your whole family. I don't like any of you entitled ass Gagliardi's anyway."

The offer cut through the pain and got Ettore's attention. "Your wife is a Karen to the tenth power, your daughter Jennifer is following in her footsteps. Your son, well he can win the entitled and snobbish asshole of the year contest. I understand why people like you turn to BDSM as a means of escape from lives that will bore you to the point of knocking on the devil's door. So, what's it going to be, give up the one who killed Eric or risk me marching your whole family to the gates of hell?"

"Sir. Please," he begged.

"Who killed Eric Daniels?" I asked the question this time, unable to help myself.

"My...my...," What was he saying? I couldn't make out the second word he spoke.

"Speak up!" Brizio shouted.

"Brock, my son," the man sputtered.

"He...they hung out a few times with the potential of Brock becoming an investor in some company or something. The young man didn't want a relationship, told Brock that he wasn't gay. My son...he...he kept pursuing and pushing anyway."

The man swallowed hard, fighting the biting aches and stabbing pain that must have been eating him alive.

"Brock stalked him, he'd done it to others. But, this young man turned the tables when he...he refused to be bullied by my son."

He paused again, his body trembling.

"He started investigating Brock. Had gathered enough to discover some of Brock's secrets. When Brock told me what he'd done to him the last time they met up, I covered it up," he admitted.

Rich, entitled, asshole sons-of-bitches!

How many crimes had he covered up for his sick ass son? The knowledge let me know Ettore Gagliardi was just as, if not sicker than his son to allow him to commit a vicious murder and not seek to punish him or even get him some professional help.

"Please Sir. Don't hurt my wife and daughter. Please."

Brizio narrowed his eyes and cocked his head at the man.

"What the hell do you think I am? Some kind of devil? Of course I won't hurt Karen I and Karen II. But, I have a date with Brock Gagliardi. Your demented son has an appointment with death."

The man managed to flinch in the midst of all the trembling when Brizio aimed Kane at him.

"I did some research on your family while I was digging up all your dirt. I should have caught on, but it didn't occur to me to suspect your son since you've done such a good job of covering up his crimes. Is Eric the first person Brock has killed?"

The shaking man was a breath away from passing out, I sensed it. His somewhat good arm was stretched taut with the heaviness of his drenched body. The other swayed from the restraint holding it in place, the bloody material of his shirt dipping. He no longer had enough strength to keep himself upright."

"Answer the fucking question," Brizio yelled, making the man jump despite his loss of focus and strength.

"How many? How many others has he killed that you've covered up for him."

I leaned in, wanting desperately to know the answer. Brizio lifted Kane when he took too long to answer.

"Three…" he spit out. The confirmation made all that happened and would happen to Ettore justified in my book.

"And you believed it was acceptable for your son to go around hurting and killing people? That you and your family's privilege gave you the right to get away with murder?" I blurted, walking up to the man, so that he could look into my eyes.

"You covered it all up like nothing happened, like the lives he took didn't matter to someone's family member. Probably assumed sweeping it under the rug was perfectly fine, fuck who was hurt in the process of those victim's death. Fuck that the people your son killed meant something to someone else." I spat the angry words at the man. Tears stung the backs of my eyes and fell hard and fast, but they weren't tears of regret. This was uncut, flaming hot rage coursing through me.

I aimed a finger at Brizio. "He has a problem killing women, but I don't. I will find your wife and your daughter and I will kill them slowly," I promised the man, loving the fear overriding the pain in his eyes.

I had no intention of touching his wife or daughter, but I wanted him to believe that he would lose them all. Brizio was at my side, sliding a caring hand around my waist. He glanced up at Ettore with murder in his gaze.

"I wouldn't have a problem if your spawn had been killing rapists, child molesters, or even other killers, but he killed because he didn't like being rejected. His superiority complex couldn't take the devastating blow."

Brizio shook Kane at the man to drive home what I believe was a departing speech.

"You're going to die because you didn't raise your son right. You believed that you and your family had a right to not be punished for the wrong you did. You didn't see a damn thing wrong with covering up the murder scenes of your serial killer son."

Wack!

My eyes went saucer wide at the sight of the sprays of blood splatter and the man's hair raising reaction. Ettore was a human piñata, being broken apart with every devastating blow delivered.

Bam!

I jumped at the loud sound of the fleshy lick that was accompanied by the man's haunting screams. My eyes never strayed away from the bloody sight of the mangled flesh and bone the man was becoming.

"Pop!"

The echo and shadow of a portion of Ettore spilling to the floor was accompanied by a splattering sound that entered my ears and stuck to my mind like glue.

Brizio stopped at the seventh blow. Ettore no longer moved, and if he wasn't already dead, I had no doubt that the injuries he'd sustained would rush him to death's door.

The scent of blood and exposed internal organs thickened the atmosphere and grew so suffocatingly strong, I choked on the aroma, squeezing my nose to block out the stench.

Brizio cleaned some of the blood and matter off of Kane before he thoroughly cleaned himself with cleaning supplies he reached into some dark space and retrieved. He faced me, smiling like there wasn't a whole dead man, mere feet away in our peripheral.

Was I as sick as Brizio? Shouldn't I feel guilty? Shouldn't we have at least considered turning our findings in to the police?

A little voice in my head roared the answer. *Fuck no!*

For all I knew, the police covered for the rich pricks whose monetary reach brought their justice. Therefore, street justice in my opinion, was justified.

"Ready dear? We have places to go and people to visit," Brizio stated, holding out his arm in a gentlemanly fashion. Again, he acted like there wasn't a mutilated body hanging in pieces on a cross behind us and two submissives who'd obeyed so well, I hadn't heard a sound from them while their master was being tortured and beaten to death.

"You're just going to leave him like that? What about all of the security in this place? And the subs? They saw your face and my face," I reminded Brizio.

"Aurelio," was all he said before taking my arm and tucking it under his like we were about to go on a date. All these years I knew I had a spark of crazy in me, but Brizio had turned that spark into a blazing flame.

The way he smiled said he truly didn't believe he'd done anything wrong or disturbing. The way I walked off with him and didn't look back spoke for my new level of crazy.

CHAPTER TWENTY-ONE

Maya

"Wait," Brizio said, stopping us right before we approached the door to exit.

"What? Did you forget something?"

Why the fuck was Brizio looking at me all funny and shit? Was it lust I was seeing? The lighting was dim, but it wasn't dark enough for me to miss desire, clear as day in his eyes.

"Maya. You have to admit. This is a beautiful scene. One that inspires…."

His lust heavy eyes and the devilish smile he flashed said it all. Was Brizio serious right now? The man was good, so good, I hadn't stopped thinking about him fucking me since, but now?

I pointed at Ettore, "There's a fucking mutilated body about twenty-five feet behind us. The man's evil soul feels like it's lingering in here looking at us."

"Forget him," Brizio waved a dismissive hand at the body. "Let him watch. I saw how turned on you got when you were watching some of the performances in the auction. And, we can't let a dungeon like this go to waste," he said, closing the last bit of space between us and running a strong hand up my side.

"I think you even got wet watching me beat that fucker to death," he whispered.

Why the fuck are my nipples tightening and my pussy pulsing to this crazy ass shit?

A strong hand clasped my arm before Brizio directed me towards a sex table I hadn't even noticed before he stopped us.

"Up," he commanded, spinning me to put my back to the table before he lifted me with ease. I was atop a wooden box, a cube that served no other purpose than to be a prop.

In the corner of my eye I caught the sight of a wall of sex props. Some bore the resemblance of knives and guns and I prayed they were silicone and plastic. Otherwise, it meant that this hell-scape we'd entered allowed the participants to act out any depraved fantasy they dreamed. They were probably in here fucking each other with guns and knives. Why did my fucked up brain wouldn't have minded seeing some of the sick shit?

Gears and ropes and other specialty pieces of equipment I couldn't name hung in the dim background. I was the one who warned others to be aware of freaky white boys, and here I was in a fucking live action BDSM snuff film type situation.

Sitting up on the square, Brizio didn't command me to lie down nor did he tie me up. He stepped between my legs like we were at home alone. My pulse kicked into overdrive at the feel of his hands sliding up my legs.

My inner thighs rested against the side of his abs, adding weight to my heavy desires. He didn't stop his approach until his forehead rested against mine.

If his goal was to claim my attention, it worked because I was more interested in what he was about to do to me than the dead man in my peripheral vision.

"Aw!" A quick gasp escaped when he jerked me by the thighs, pulling me flush against him. His hands gripped hard, the rough touch pulsing with a hum of energy that quickened my breath and hardened my nipples to the point of hurting.

What the hell?

I shouldn't be this damn turned on. Should I?

His strong hands traveled up until I felt them sliding over my chest and higher until they were sliding around the front of my neck.

"Oh!" I yelled out when his fingers tightened around my throat at the same time as he pulled my head back with the tight grip he'd taken of my hair. I hadn't realized he'd gotten a hold of my hair until I felt the rough tug. My wide eyes remained fixed on his but my uncontrolled breathing sounded off in this room that was becoming a tomb of sex and deadly violence.

The delicate kiss brushed my lips. It was too sweet to compliment the chokehold and the sharp hair pull that had my skull humming with tension. It was the sort of ache that should hurt, but under the circumstances made me want to tell him to yank harder so that I could feel the pain. So that I could be punished for just standing there watching him kill someone without making even a futile attempt to stop it.

What the....

My mind was playing dirty tricks on me. I could have sworn I saw the body move in my peripheral vision, but I refused to turn away from Brizio's demanding gaze. Part of my brain wanted to decode the storm raging in his gaze, but the other part of my brain liked being left in the dark about his intentions.

His hand slipped away from my neck and my hair was released. The ease of pressure in each area was noticeable, missed, while his hands maneuvered deliberately over me until they wrapped around my shoulders.

Rip!

The loud gasp I released rattled my chest. The cool air met my back from my dress being yanked down. His hand pressed against my bra covered chest, nudging me back.

I went down willingly with him remaining between my restless legs. There was no problem helping him take the ripped material or lifting my ass off the table so he could take my soaked panties.

A fleeting thought crept into my demented mind. Was the hard breathing I believed I heard coming from Ettore who may or may not still be alive or the subs inside the dumpster?

Was there some secret little cut-out that allowed them to see us? I was learning that sex furniture held secrets, just like some of the people using them. Had the subs witnessed Brizio's brutal beating of their master?

None of this shit made sense, but I couldn't help being in the moment of it. I would have to ask my questions later because I had to answer the calls of my demanding body. Brizio repositioned me so that the back juncture of my knees spilled over the side of the table. I wanted to know, needed to know what came next.

The devilish stroke of his strong hand on my body had me choking on a broken dam of desire. His hand slid sensually up my body, across and between my breasts. The tip of one of his fingers raked over my nipple and sent a pulse of hot need straight down to where I prayed any part of him would end up.

He was in my head now. I wouldn't have cared if the whole city stood behind us, I responded to every caress, every nudge.

"Oh...," I jumped, letting the sound slip when he palmed my pussy, making a sweet gush of liquid seep from me. I think I was supposed to say Sir in a situation like this but, I couldn't remember all the rules. I couldn't even think past the overpowering sexual energy flowing through me.

He leaned in real close, while my pussy was literally humming in his palm, my clit throbbing with a desperate need that made me want to cry out.

"You remember when you said you would never allow me to dominate you, especially in this way?"

I nodded like a kid afraid of not getting a scoop of her favorite ice cream.

"Answer me the way you're supposed to," he gritted out, his face serious enough to make fear peek through the cracks of my lust.

"Yes Sir. I remember," I said, fearing he would stop when things were getting good.

"This is the kind of sweet torture you've been missing out on and I know you like it because I can smell your arousal," he continued, moving his palm a fraction of an inch to make me fight the urge to move against his hand or hop up and punch his ass in the face.

A pinch of resistance remained within me. I didn't understand how it broke through the thick haze of lust that had a chokehold on my senses. I was beginning to understand how lines could get blurred between, pain, pleasure, and a number of other irrational emotions.

His middle finger turned slowly, deliberately circling around my clit, but there was not much relief in the slight movement that served to make me squirm harder than I already was, my legs shaking, pussy aching, and my body a river of fire waiting to explode.

"Oh!" I yelled out when he stopped teasing my clit and increased the pressure of the hand he had clamped around my pussy.

"Beg me for more," he commanded. "This type of pleasure has to be paid for and the only currency I accept comes in the form of discipline. I accept gifts like, please and Sir and you're the fucking best to ever touch me and so on and so forth."

This time he wasn't whispering. He wanted to make sure my hard headed ass heard every word while I was at his mercy and prepared to beg my way into an orgasm.

He undid his pants and the sight of him springing free, hard and ready and big enough to cause my pussy damage had me swallowing whatever words that had formed in my head. The sense of being watched brought on a wicked sense of pleasure.

What the hell is wrong with me?

Was I high? Drunk? Drugged?

"Aw!" A loud scream escaped when I was dragged to the edge of the table, my ass cheeks spilling over the edge, my legs pinned in the air by his strong hands. He was so stiff the tip of his swollen head pointed right at my dripping pussy, so close I was tempted to inch closer just to feel the hot head stroke my wet flesh.

"I don't hear any motherfucking begging," Brizio stated, his demanding gaze pinned on my heavy one.

"Please…" my voice sounded hoarse, rough. "Please Sir, I need more," I said louder, not giving a damn about my ego. I'd deal with that bitch later. Right now I needed this man to make me come.

"Louder. I need to feel your desperation. I need to taste it on my tongue."

"Sir please, fuck me!"

"I need your voice to make my dick harder."

Fuck!

The desperation coursing through me was going to kill me. Now, I was getting the full physical definition behind all the begging. It wasn't for show. It wasn't faked. You became desperate enough to sell your damn soul to ease the ache of this type of arousal.

"Sir, please. Please, fuck me hard. Fuck me now. Just fucking fuck me," I cried out sounding like my ass was about to cry, voice cracking and all.

The teasing grin on Brizio's face didn't match his scanning gaze. Was that enough? Was I begging right? Was there a special way to beg to make him listen faster?

"Oh, my fucking…" Roared from my throat when he thrusted into me so hard, it left no doubt that my damn soul fainted, had passed out and was snoring.

"The next time you want some of this, you better fucking make me believe that you need it more than oxygen," he said, fucking me while he was talking.

"Yes. Yes…"

I was trying to say yes sir, but dammit if this man wasn't fucking me so good, the words I needed to say were being banged right out of my head.

"Now, how are you supposed to answer me Maya?"

"Sir. Yes. Sir. Oh God. Sirrr…" The last word dragged on so long it drew all the air from my over-worked lungs.

"Next time you want some of this, how are you supposed to ask for it?" he questioned, using his words as a fucking weapon. I was being held at gunpoint because the dick had me straight up possessed.

And I was there, at the pinnacle of the highest mountain, about to come so hard, my body tense at the notion. Just a few more pounding thrust and…

"No the fuck you're not!" Brizio shouted, slowing his stroke down to a crawl. "If you want to come on this dick show it some respect."

"Please Brizio fuck...I'm. Sir." I tried to wiggle, but his grip on my hips had me pinned. The best I could do was constrict my pelvic muscles, but it wasn't enough.

"I respect the dick Sir. I respect it. Please!"

"That's what I fucking thought," he said, pushing each word out with a thrust that pounded into me and delivered the type of pleasure that made you pray you survived it with your mind intact.

I shattered, body shaking, chest racking breaths, eyes slammed shut, and a chill that covered my body and seeped into my blood. If Brizio came, I was too far gone to feel it.

Finally, I could breathe without praying for a breath. My eyes cracked open, my lids lifting like they were weighted down with bricks. My gaze met his penetrating one. I bet he was measuring how much further he had dragged me into this lifestyle.

I glanced down at the way I was spread across this table, remembering where we were and what had taken place feet from us. My pussy still throbbed around his semi hardness, the pulse keeping pace with my erratic heartbeat.

I hated to admit an obvious truth, one that I feared would change me forever. My pussy was being programmed. My body, conditioned. My mind transformed.

Begging was the least of my worries. What else was I willing to do for this? I didn't even know what to call this type of sex. All I knew was that Brizio had marked me and based on the big ass grin forming on his face, he knew I would be willing to do just about anything for what he and his big magical dick could do to me.

CHAPTER TWENTY-TWO

Brizio

Aurelio and his ability to track anything that moved had us in place and waiting at the restaurant's location for Brock Gagliardi to arrive. Maya and I stood at the valet booth, after I told the attendant, an associate of the DeLuca family, to take the rest of the night off.

The black Ferrara F8 Spider we were looking for rolled into the garaged valet area like clockwork. A twenty-five year old who hadn't worked a day in his life driving a three-hundred thousand dollar car. Fucking shame.

I walked up to the door after he sprang it open. He climbed out, shoving his keys in my chest with an arrogant smirk on his face. The keys fell to the ground with a *clink* while I reached up and snatched his ass by the collar.

"Get your spoiled ass over here," I said, seizing a hold of him with such force he jumped a few times to regain his footing.

"What are you doing? Are you fucking crazy? I'll slap a lawsuit…"

Slap!

A backhanded bitch slap was just what the doctor ordered for this sick prick.

"Shut the fuck up and respect your elders," I yelled at him although I was only four years older. The hard lick echoed through the air just as Maya was driving from within the garage in the outbound lane.

The car, a black Mercedes Maybach belonged to another privileged prick I wanted to lead to the gates of hell from the Moretti family. Unfortunately, I'd have to let that pot of rage simmer for a later date, but it felt good taking one of his most prized possessions.

Murder flashed heavy in Maya's gaze when the window came down. She stared so hard at Brock's approach, I prayed she'd have enough restraint to remain in the car and drive us to his final destination.

For good measure, two more licks and a swift kick in the ass would give Maya a little relief as she glanced in the rearview mirror at us. I couldn't imagine how she felt coming face to face with the man who brutally murdered her brother, especially after she revealed how she was dragged away from his mutilated body by security. The reason behind the senseless killing is what would have this sick fuck begging one of us to kill him.

Once Maya figured out how to open the trunk, I delivered a stiff elbow to the back of Brock's neck. He toppled into the trunk and left me the task of lifting and tossing his legs inside.

"Are you okay?" I asked Maya as soon as I climbed into the passenger seat and pulled the door closed.

She nodded, biting deeply into her lip. I know what that specific lip bite was all about. She was ready to fuck up someone's life. I loved that my woman had a temper. She would need it to live in my world.

"How do you feel about taking his life?" I asked, attempting to get a sense of where her head was before I dragged her deeper into my dark nature. Back at the dungeon, I was sure she would stop me from fucking her, but she'd gotten into the scene as much as I had.

"If I'm supposed to be feeling guilty, it's not here. Right now, it's taking everything within me not to tie that frog faced fucker to the back of this car and drag him to death," she said. The jagged edge to her tone let me know she meant every word.

"Take the next right," I instructed her, to get us to the quickest route from the city.

"If dragging him behind this car is what you'd like to do, we are heading to a place where you can make it happen."

She jerked her head quickly in my direction, making the car tires give a little screech.

"No shit?"

"No shit, but might I suggest another place that is near and dear to my heart." I placed a tender hand over my chest.

Although she peered straight ahead the little quirk of her lips revealed her excellent side-eye vision.

"And what is this den of hell that you speak of...*Sir*? And will we be using your rod and your staff?"

I groaned, grabbing a firm hold of my jumping dick. She'd not only said Sir, but I loved the sexual word play on my instruments of destruction.

"If you want to make it to where we're going without a bruised ass and a sore pussy, you better stop turning me the fuck on."

My dick was harder than the fucking engine block under the hood of this car. A deep breath and a long, gradual release didn't help ease my tension. I couldn't even remember what we were talking about. Maya was clueless about the way she affected me. Controlling myself was hard enough but hearing her talk like that was a whole different story.

"You can't be serious," she said, shooting a quick glance in my direction. "You're turned on while that killing asshole is in the trunk and we are on our way to do the unthinkable?" Her words were breathy.

"Aren't you?" I answered her question with a question. The long pause she let linger answered for her.

"I guess I am, but isn't that some sick shit, to feel…like having sex while in the presence of death? In this case, death is a few miles away, waiting for the one in the trunk."

"It's normal. The line between life and death is so thin it makes the margin between feelings and emotions and wants and desires blurry."

I didn't know if it was normal or not, but all types of sick shit about death and fucking and sex and life was rolling through my cross-wired ass brain. But she didn't need to know yet, that I got off on shit that probably made normal people cringe, sick, and probably run. She didn't need to know that I had just fucked her while watching Gagliardi die on that cross.

"I guess," she finally replied.

I directed and she drove. The low thump of our passenger registered as we neared our destination. I had found this location by accident a few years ago, when Primo and I had christened my club with its first body.

The location was as close to off the grid as one could get. We drove along the outskirts of St. Louis near the small town of Hazelwood. There was nothing but farm houses and ranches spread between large stretches of wide open plains and woods.

I directed Maya to turn off onto a dark, deserted dirt road. No street lights and a thick curtain of trees stretching and bending along the narrow passage marked our path.

"Brizio," Maya called out, breaking into the constant thumping and muffled cries coming from the trunk. She eased her foot up off on the gas.

"It's okay," I told her, spotting the vehicle she was eyeballing. "It's our ride back to civilization. It also has a few supplies inside that I asked for."

I sensed her eyes on me now.

"Don't look at me that way. You should know by now I make every effort to be prepared."

She didn't say anything, but I sensed her smile. She eased up next to the dark gray Volvo SUV and stopped.

"Are you ready to do this? This is not like self-defense. Once you cross this line, it can't be uncrossed."

"He brutally murdered my brother because his ego was bruised. If you think I have doubts about what's about to happen, you can think again," she said, snapping the door open and climbing out.

She was talking about committing first degree murder. A normal man would have been alarmed, made attempts to stop her, but not me. She needed this closure or she would never be at peace.

"Let me make us a fire," I said before marching to the back of the Volvo and taking out the campfire essentials I'd asked Umberto and Lenny to pack. The rumbling and bumping and cries and shouts going on in the trunk of the Maybach had increased. It wasn't a nuisance of sound like I expected but made for excellent campfire music.

I withdrew a few portable chairs from the trunk and sat them in the area where I intended to build the fire. Maya stood in place a few feet from the noisy trunk, staring at it like she was in a daze. I took her hand and escorted her to one of the chairs I'd set in place.

"You sit and think about all you want to do to make him suffer, and I'll build us a fire."

"Thank you," she said. "You're such a gentleman when you want to be."

At least she still had her bubbly personality, a good sign given the situation.

"I'm a gentleman all the time, just not the typical kind," I replied before walking away to gather tender, firewood, and rocks.

Ten minutes later and we had a campfire. I returned to the SUV's trunk and grabbed the bag of marshmallows and graham crackers that my thoughtful cousins had packed.

"I've never been camping before," she admitted. I handed her a stick to use to toast her marshmallow. "This is actually kind of fun."

"Anything for my woman," I replied, unable to keep a wide grin off my face. Thankfully, she didn't think I was taking shit too far with the campfire fun while she was planning out an execution that I'd suggested.

I took the seat across from her before reaching out my thin branch and letting the fire sear the outer layers of my marshmallow.

"Have you reached any definitive conclusions about how you intend to avenge your brother?"

She nodded. "At first I just wanted to do it fast, shoot him in the head and get it over with. But, that would be too kind. My brother suffered," her voice cracked. "I believed it was for hours. I want that rich asshole to fight for his life too. I want him to know what it feels like to be helpless, to beg. I want him to apologize to Eric, to acknowledge he was wrong, not only for my brother but for the others he's hurt and killed. I want him to suffer until I decide he's suffered enough."

A devious smile rested on my lips.

"Might I suggest we take him to church?"

My question broke into the evil little plots I sensed swimming around in her head.

"Church? Why would you want to take him to church?"

Face squinted, her eyes shimmered with intrigue against the firelight.

"My cousin Romigi, remember him?"

She nodded, showing me a small smile.

"Besides being a well-respected priest at St. Andrews, he has a few secrets that give a whole new meaning to the term man of the cloth. For example, he has his own prison."

Her brows shot up high on her forehead and her head tilted slightly while waiting for me to continue.

"His prison is a place that is near and dear to my heart. It's a quiet place where people go to suffer, and trust me, Romigi has the patience of a monk when it comes to allowing those who need long-term pain and suffering to serve out their time."

Her wide eyes were all that moved, searching mine to determine if I was serious.

"He doesn't look like the typical preacher. I got the sense that he didn't always do fatherly things, but he feels spiritual."

I nodded. "He is as dedicated to helping good people as he is to punishing the bad ones. Who do you think made Kane and Able for me?"

Her mouth dropped open.

"Wow! Your family is off the chain. It's like they have every category of killer checked off of a killer checklist. Priest. Assassins. Business owners. Doctors."

I chuckled.

She pointed at the car. Our noisy tribute sounded like he was attempting to rip the truck open with his bare hands. It rocked hard against the man's desperate attempts to free himself.

"Aren't they going to be able to track that car? And what about his car that we left running in the middle of the valet lane?"

"What good is having cousins that are genius level tech geeks and trained mercenaries if they can't make it safe for me and my woman to do what we need to do?

I handed you the keys to that car because it had undergone a few *adjustments*. Brock's car has been conveniently destroyed by now."

Was that pride resting in the wide smile and expressive eyes she presented?

"You DeLucas are no joke. Can I ask you something? And be honest."

I pursed my lips. "Have I been dishonest with you yet?"

A smile, she tried but failed to hide surfaced before she lifted her gaze to consider my question.

"I don't believe so," she finally answered. "But." The one word was followed by a long pause and a squinting stare. "If you didn't want to sleep with me and rein sexual domination over me, would you have found a way to have gotten rid of me already? I could have messed up a lot of things for you and your family by stirring up trouble the way that I did."

My smile dropped. "We DeLucas are capable of a lot of things Maya, but hurting innocents, children, or women is not one of them. It's a line we vowed to never cross unless it can't be avoided. And just to be clear, you are more than some woman I want to have sex with, and I believe you know it."

She had to know there was more to us than lust and sexual desires. I tossed my stick and my uneaten marshmallow into the fire and stood.

Suspicion crept from the sharp gaze she leveled on me. I approached and stood peering down on her before I tugged her to her feet.

"Tell me you know that we are more than lust, and desire, and hot ass good...wet...sex."

She fought a smile, her eyes unblinking, teasing.

"Even though I want to believe that is all we are, I know that there is...more," she admitted. "No man in his right mind is going to do all that you've done for me just to have kinky sex. My mental reach goes much deeper than I might let on. I knew early on that there was a mutual attraction, but I haven't pinpointed a specific reason behind our connection or your desire to help me."

I stepped closer, folding her into my embrace until our bodies kissed. She reached up and slid her hands across my shoulders, letting her nails rake lightly over the nape of my neck.

"You want to know what I think the connection is?"

She didn't answer. And the flick of panic that flirted within the depths of her gaze said she was as afraid to know than I was to admit it. Admitting to things of a sensitive nature, like feelings and emotions wasn't our thing. But, like all fears, we had to face and overcome them or they would eventually consume us.

"What?" she questioned when I took too long to answer.

"Let me out! Someone help!"

Though muffled, the sound broke through our locked gazes and the tension that had flooded our bodies. I believe we were more afraid of our feelings than any other obstacle we could ever face.

I leaned in and she met me halfway, our lips brushing lightly before pressing into a deeper kiss that conjured up those feelings we were avoiding speaking of out loud. I backed off, wanting more, but I needed to adjust my focus to the matter at hand.

"Are you ready to do this? And if so, what's your plan?"

She took a moment, letting her gaze scan the starry sky before answering.

"I seriously contemplated the church prison, but I'll pass. I want him to suffer, but I don't want to drag it out too long and be stuck with knowing he continues to breathe. First," she paused, lifting a finger. The devious little smirk on her face gave me chills, the good kind.

"First, let's pull that shit stain from that trunk. Then, I'm going to need to borrow Kane."

"Oh shit. Okay," I said a little too excitedly.

She didn't have to tell me twice. I retrieved my rod and handed it over. She tested the feel and weight of it, moving it from hand to hand and closing and loosening her grip around it.

Seeing it in her hands, knowing what I'd just done with that rod, had me getting hard. I shook off my sick desires and turned in the direction of the noise.

Aiming the key fob, I popped the trunk while marching closer. My fist was cocked when the trunk sprang open. The center of Brock's face connected with my knuckles when he attempted to hop out like I expected.

The loud *humph* he released was followed up by a spray of blood and spit that I dodged. He rolled over the edge of the trunk. His wobbly feet hit the ground but wasn't strong enough to hold him upright. He stumbled to the ground and scrambled into a sitting position.

"Please," he spit out. "I'll give..."

"Shut up!" Maya snapped, cutting off his words. "Money is not going to get you out of this. Your money was apparently not long enough and your father couldn't cover up your crimes well enough for you to get away with murder this time."

He stared at Maya, but his begging eyes and pleading words did nothing to lift the dark cloud of vengeance pressing down on him.

"Your father gave you up," she revealed to him.

His lips parted while his wide, regretful eyes remained fixed on Maya.

"He's dead and it's all your fault. The great Ettore Gagliardi was beaten to death, the same way you beat my brother to death."

Brock shook his head, tears sliding down his cheeks, one bloody, one pale white. I didn't know if the tears were for his dead father, that he was caught, or for the knowledge that his father was who had given him up.

Maya admired the rod before placing her deathly glare back on the sniveling man. I was riveted to this scene and impressed with her level of calmness intwined with the deadly way in which she was handling Brock.

"Your father was beaten to death with this rod. It's still wet with his blood. I can still see pieces of his skin on it, the hair beaten from his scalp still sticking to it."

Damn!

Brock's head shook so hard a few of his tears flew through the air and sparkled against the moonlight. His eyes were already wide, but doubled in size at the sight of Maya lifting the thick piece of metal, smeared with his father's blood.

"You beat my brother to death, a man who would give someone his last dollar or the shirt off his back to help them, all because your ego was bruised when he turned you down."

"Please. Please." His hands came together, begging. His wet eyes glistened. The fire behind us gave off enough light to see all of his features, his legs tucked beside him, his arms up and pleading, his body teetering left and right.

"You have to believe me. Things got out of hand. It was an accident. It didn't..."

"You better think long and fucking hard about the lie you're about to tell. You killed my brother because he didn't want to date you. Tell me it's a lie," she dared him, her eyes wide and deadly. Her chest rose up and down hard and fast.

Brock shook his head, fast and robotically, his shoulder length hair flopping all over his head and face, wet with sweat and tears.

"I tell you what. I'm going to beat you to death and I'm going to take my time doing it. And guess what?"

His pleading grew more intense. Each of Brock's words were laced with regret as the air around us thickened. One more quiet step drew Maya closer. She was within striking distance now.

A hard swallow made Brock's neck tremble like he was attempting to choke down the boulder of lies he wanted to tell. She had asked him a question, but he must have been too afraid to answer.

"I'm going to beat you to death and I'm going to take my time doing it. And guess what?" she repeated for him.

"What?" he muttered, ducking back and glancing up at her under the thick cloud of fear surrounding him when she lifted the solid metal rod and used it as a pointer.

"It's going to be an accident too. I'm going to use all of my strength to hit you over and over with this piece of hard metal and accidentally beat the skin off your bones. I'm going to hit your head so hard it will crack your skull and the broken bones will protrude through your scalp. But, I'm not going to stop there. Nope," she spit the words at him, eyeing him under long lashes. "I want to see the inside of your head, to see if it is as empty as it must have been when you believed it was okay to torture and kill an innocent man and go on living like nothing ever happened."

She smiled and nodded, shaking the baton at him. "It's all going to be a friendly little accident, and I'm going to go on and live my best life while the insects are dining on your brain and the crows are picking your heart apart to munch on your arteries."

Holy Hell! She was vicious. And why were her words making my untamed dick jump?

If I didn't know any better, I would have figured she'd done this before. Maya was a DeLuca, she just hadn't accepted it yet.

"Tell me this. I need to hear it from you. How many others did you kill?" Maya asked him.

My neck jerked and my eyes widened at the first hard and unexpected blows that landed against Brock's back and shoulders.

The pounding she delivered accented each of her words. Hard *thumps* tore relentlessly into his tender flesh. The thin expensive cotton shirt he wore didn't offer a thread of protection against the attack he nor I saw coming.

The first few licks landed like she was using a bat to tear open his arms. The man wailed, flopping around on the ground like he was already dying.

"Please. Oh, please God, don't do this. Don't kill me!" His voice echoed off the trees and anything solid and dispersed into the wide open blackness of night.

Maya backed off, letting him wallow in his discomfort.

"I'm sorry. Please. I'm sorry," he begged, spit hanging off his lip and glistening against the firelight.

This would be a campfire I wouldn't soon forget. Highly entertaining, riveting, I was already giving it a five-star rating even if she stated she wanted to stop right now.

"Brizio," she called for me over the man's cries.

"Will you be a gentleman and align him so his legs are flat on the ground like so?"

She used the rod, dripping blood to point out the direction she wanted the man aligned. I gripped him by the shoulder and turned him despite his poor attempt to break free of my grip.

I glanced up at Maya. What was rolling through that beautiful head of hers?

"You said you want his legs flat?" I questioned.

"Yes, please. And drag him a little to the left about a foot."

I did as I was told, although getting him to keep those legs stretched out would be a task. The man wouldn't stop wiggling. And his yelling was starting to get on my damn nerves.

"Keep your ass still," I yelled at him, kicking him in the top of his left thigh so he'd keep his damn leg down. "My woman has plans for you, and I don't need you messing them up."

I stomped on the other thigh, driving the heel of my hard bottomed shoe into the muscle. Bet he kept those legs down then.

When Maya stepped closer, the man's screams lit up the sky, so loud his voice vibrated off my skin. The constant chirps and insect calls in the background had gone silent, allowing Brock to have the floor where it concerned sound.

"Will you keep him right there?" She asked, staring down at me struggling to keep the man under control.

"Please. Please. I'm sorry," he cried out, staring up and acknowledging that she was the keeper of his fate.

"He possesses a good set of lungs. Probably could have been a good swimmer or a singer or something if he'd taken an interest in working. Keep him right there."

Her comments, so casual and out of the blue, pulled my attention from Brock so that I could get a good look at her.

"Yes Dear. He's not going anywhere," I assured her, holding the squirming man in place as my curious gaze tracked her movements. She climbed into the car and a devious smile danced across my lips. If I wasn't sure about anything else, I was sure that Maya was a DeLuca, through and through.

"Keep your ass still before you miss out on all this fun you're about to have," I muttered, pushing my feet down harder on Brock's legs.

The smooth engine of the car purred to a quick start and the squirming man froze.

"No. No. No," he kept repeating before his twisting and squirming revved up again. Like with the first licks she delivered to him, Maya gave no warning.

I saw the white flash of the reverse lights and the next thing I knew, the tires were scratching up pebbles. It appeared she was aiming to take us both out, but Maya was on point. Right before I let go of the man and scrambled out of the way of the fast-approaching ass end of the car, Brock lifted his legs in an attempt to keep them from being crushed under the wheels.

Crack!

Wrong move, he lifted his leg right before the tires rolled over them. The car's back end lifted before folding his legs into a heaping mess of crushed bones and flesh.

Shock hit Brock like a mac truck. His abrupt silence sent a chill up my spine. The car's back tire crushed his legs, pinning his bottom half to the ground. The rest of him was in an odd upward position like he was making an attempt to lift the car off his legs. He wasn't ever walking again.

"Aww! Oh Please. Father God! Please. Help me!"

"There he is," I muttered under my breath, shaking my head at the mangled sight of his legs. The campfire gave me a good view of how much worse the position was from him lifting his legs at the last second.

"I know that shit hurts, huh?" I asked him although I didn't expect him to answer. Shaking my head at the horrific sight, I was glad it wasn't me.

"Help. Somebody help me!"

His pleas went unanswered as I'm sure Eric Daniel's pleas had been ignored by him. Maya hopped out of the car, leaving it running. She stepped back to take a peek at her handiwork. "Hmm," she muttered at the sight of him struggling, but still alive.

"I'm sorry. I'm so sorry. Please." Brock continued to uselessly beg, each of his words drawn out, the sound carrying on into the night like he was singing his own departing hymn. Instead of saying Lord, deliver me, he was singing Devil, light me up.

"That's my woman," I felt the need to yell into the night, making Maya shake her head and cast a smirk in my direction.

When she stepped away and returned with Kane, I could hardly take the damn suspense. I hadn't been this entertained since Primo took out four of the Vittorio family in their own warehouse about three weeks ago.

She tapped the baton against Brock's back, reclaiming his attention. It took him a few seconds to acknowledge that death stood at his back. When he did manage to glance back, his cries stopped on a dime and the white shining from his wide eyes gave the fire a run for its money.

"Please. I'm sorry. I was wrong. Mercy. I was wrong. I'm so sorry," he repeated, his voice hoarse and choppy from the waves of agony wreaking havoc on what was left of his mind and body. His soul was already halfway to a pit of everlasting fire. I hope he was seeing the faces of the innocent people he'd hurt and killed. I hope they taunted him for the rest of eternity.

"We are going to play a little game," Maya told him. I'm going to lift this baton and you're going to try to move out of the way before I can hit you.

"Vicious," I said, shaking my head. She was coming to the next torture session Primo or Romigi would eventually have because I believe she would add valuable input into the torturous shit they enjoyed doing to people. She didn't have to know I was one of the founding members of the DeLuca torture squad.

"Ready," she asked the screaming man, lifting Kane high in the air.

Thump.

He dodged it from connecting with the top of his skull but it caught the side of his neck and lower chin, bouncing off the bone hard enough to open his skin. Maya bent, aiming a languid stare and shaking her head.

"I'm so sorry. That was an accident," she stated sarcastically. I bet he was sorry he ever laid eyes on her brother because Eric Daniels was getting avenged to the tenth power.

"Ready, here it comes."

He tried to move but was too broken in mind, body, and spirit to save himself from another devastating blow.

The metal struck the side of his head so hard, I expected his jawbone to fly clean off his face and land in the campfire.

I hadn't noticed how closely I had inched up to the action until Maya lifted Kane and made me jump back to keep from getting splattered with blood.

Whack!

The sounds, the deathly blows, and the man's whaling screams, ricocheted through the thick dark air. The fire crackling in the background added depth to the scene and Brock's roaring screams.

Each side of his jaw was shattered, but he still released cries, some gurgled, but still managing to break through the heavy cloak of nightfall. Maybe she was right about him making a good singer if he'd done something better with his life.

Maya DeLuca was not to be played with. The sight of her beating Brock to death made me wonder if she would avenge me as fiercely if the day ever came. This scene, in my humble opinion, could put the best Opera to shame. It took the discipline I'd built up over the years to keep from coming in my pants at her debut performance.

CHAPTER TWENTY-THREE

Maya

Two weeks later.

When people said getting revenge didn't make you feel any better, they lied. It did. The sense that my brother could finally rest in peace also soothed my restless soul.

I was still with B3co, allowing him to continue to integrate me into his world and the D/s lifestyle. It was hard to believe that a man like him would be happy with one woman, but so far, he was making me eat my doubts.

Who was I kidding? He was fucking, teasing, screwing, taunting, tickling, torturing, sexing, and disciplining away every emotion that threatened to disturb my peace.

"Are you almost ready?" He yelled for the third time. "Forget about it and pick something else if you're trying to get something over that big ass porta potty head of yours."

I couldn't help but chuckle.

"About five more minutes. I'm trying to look like a fucking lady, you fucking spider faced mole-rat."

He chuckled. It was like we had earned degrees on how to sling insults at each other.

Tonight, we were having dinner with Primo and Nevah. We decided it was time to reveal to them that we were a legit couple now.

The drive to the restaurant, Lorenzo's, involved me keeping Brizio's eager hand from wrinkling my dress. Not that I would have minded the action, but I wanted to look nice for this dinner.

I hadn't seen Nevah in nearly a month and a lot of shit had changed. Like her getting married, me torturing and killing someone, not to mention the state of my current sex life.

Despite his rude and sometimes impulsive and ego driven disposition, I had to give Brizio credit for being a gentleman. He walked around to my side of the car and helped me out, stopping the valet when he was heading in my direction.

He tucked my arm into his before we strolled towards the restaurant's entrance. The pride coming off him in regards to me, and the way he made me his priority whenever we went anywhere blew me away. The notion endeared him to me more each time.

I spotted Nevah and Primo, all cuddled up against each other like one had just flown in from a deployment overseas. It was gag-worthy, and I was thankful I didn't have to worry about falling victim to that type of PDA with Brizio.

When they did spot us approaching, Primo eased back and Nevah's hand covered her wide smile at the sight of me. I bit into the big grin filling my face.

Nevah jumped up and slung herself into me, gripping me so hard, I had no choice but to match her language that consisted of a series of giggles and squeals.

"I missed you. Don't you ever scare me like this again. You hear me?" She questioned, shaking me a little within the embrace like a worried mother would her child, loving on me and scolding me at the same time for not returning her calls. I nodded and pecked her on the cheek when she eased up on the hug.

"I'm sorry. I won't worry you like that again," I told her, letting my gaze stroll over Primo and Brizio who stood off to the side watching us.

"I had proper help. Trust me, I'm in good hands," I assured her in a tone only for her ears when she kept that motherly gaze locked on me.

She nodded, understanding that the DeLuca men didn't play about the people they cared about and had no problem adding to their body counts.

We took our seats and like the gentleman I was learning that they were, Primo and Brizio helped us, not sitting until me and Nevah were comfortable.

"Primo. It's good to see you again," I greeted, offering a friendly smile.

"Maya," he returned with a twisted smile and a hint of something in his eyes I couldn't read. Nevah reached over and shook Brizio's hand, since our reunion hug had stopped the initial introduction.

Small talk about the restaurant, the menu, and food carried the conversation until Nevah asked.

"You said on the phone that you had something to tell us." she casted a quick glance at Brizio.

Are you together now?

She didn't have to say it out loud for me to know that was the question on her mind. It appeared she wanted to know the state of me and Brizio's relationship more than she wanted to hear the full story about why I had been dodging her calls and was with Brizio in the first place.

"All that time that I've been staying away, I did it because I didn't want you or Tracy getting involved, *again*, in what I couldn't leave alone."

When I'd first started my quest to find out what happened to my brother, Maya and Tracy helped me without question. When I realized I may have to do some illegal business to get answers, I didn't want them involved. Nevah reached across the table to take my hand at my prolonged pause.

"Brizio knew that I was in over my head and decided to help me. He kept me from doing something stupid that might get me killed. He along with…"

I glanced at Primo, not sure if he wanted me to reveal that he'd been involved in helping us also. His head dropped in a nod.

"…Primo and some other DeLucas helped me find closure to my brother's death."

She smiled. Which was odd. Usually when I did something impulsive and crazy, she and Tracy treated me like a teen who needed discipline.

"I know. Primo told me everything and that Brizio was helping you," she said. I aimed a cocked gaze in Primo's direction.

"He did. Did he?" I questioned through gritted teeth. I'd specifically asked him not to worry Nevah with my antics.

He bit into his bottom lip to fight a smile before he released a low chuckle at how I narrowed my eyes at him. He lifted up a hand, preparing to make a point.

"First, I didn't make you a promise. Second, I may be a member of a formable family, but there's one thing I'm not doing, and that is fucking with, fucking up, or fucking over my wife in any way. She needed to know that you were being helped the way you needed to be helped."

I didn't miss the way he'd put stress on the word help. The DeLuca brand of help was not normal and if they couldn't protect who they cared about, they would break hell loose and use pieces of it to torture people.

My pursed lips turned to an appreciative smile at Primo. He loved my friend hard, and it made me respect him that much more. Nevah was always the one taking care of everyone around her and it warmed my heart to know that she had someone to take care of her now.

"I. We," I said, grabbing Brizio's hand under the table and squeezing. He was too quiet and whenever he was silent, that brain of his was thinking up ways to torture people or sexually torture me.

This time Primo's brows shot up at my unfinished words. Nevah placed her elbows on the table, her eagerness to know my news sparked in her gaze that bounced back and forth between me and Brizio.

I cast Primo a devious side eye. I bet his telling-shit-to-his-wife ass didn't know the tea Brizio and I would spill at this table tonight.

"About a month ago when things began to heat up and my life was in danger, Brizio stepped in to help me. We made a decision early on that would guarantee my safety no matter what. It was a decision I struggled with making because I couldn't picture that type of thing for me. I still give myself the heebie jeebies thinking about it. But, despite all the crazy that has surrounded us we've decided to keep things as they are."

"Yes! Yes! Yes!" Nevah whisper-yelled, calling the attention of a few other diners. She lowered her head and placed a hand over her wide smile.

Primo appeared to be frozen in place, his eyes the only movement as they bounced back and forth between me and Brizio.

"You two are going to be a couple. I knew it," Nevah blurted. She was genuinely happy for us.

Primo remained silent, staring at us like he was putting together a totally different conclusion than the one Nevah jumped to in his head.

"We're not only staying together," I blurted. Brizio lifted my left hand and flashed the emerald cut, halo diamond, he'd given me last week when we made the decision to stay together.

"We've decided to stay married," Brizio finished, kissing the back of my hand he held up.

"What!" Primo hollered. He was calling attention to us this time. Nevah took his place in the silent realm, her mouth hanging open.

Sharp narrowed eyes were aimed with laser precision at Brizio. Primo lifted a hand like he was preparing to direct a choir.

"Married," Nevah mouthed, but the word made no sound. She glanced at Primo and knew from his expressive outburst and what I believed was panic that he had no idea of me and Brizio's marriage.

"How long have you been married?" Primo asked, his words a little breathy.

"Three weeks, six days, twelve hours, and..." Brizio glanced down at his watch. "...two minutes, thirty-six seconds."

Why were they so damn shocked? Was it that unbelievable for me or Brizio to be serious? Isn't that why Primo and Nevah had married so soon after they met, for protective reasons?

I glanced at Brizio who shrugged off their reactions before lifting my hand to his mouth again and pressing his soft lips to the back. The gesture brought on an instant smile. I leaned over the table, not wanting others to hear my words.

"Brizio assured me that it was the best way to keep me safe, especially with the kind of danger I was facing. If my last name was DeLuca, it would make me protected in the eyes of other families."

"You two got married? A month ago?" Primo asked, like he didn't hear Brizio the first time.

"Surely, you don't think you're the only DeLuca who can put a ring on it?" Brizio asked. It sounded like a taunt to his obviously stunned cousin.

"Congratulations," Nevah spit out, a smile easing its way across her face as the notion of me being married soaked into her brain. I was least likely of our group to ever get married, so I understood her reaction better than Primo's.

"Thank you Nevah," I said, before Primo's murderous expression, aimed at Brizio, caught my attention.

"You got married a week after we did," Nevah added, her smile spreading wider.

"You tricked her into marrying you?" Primo asked. The deep crease between his forehead meant business.

Tricked?

My head spun to Brizio so fast, I expected it to spin off my shoulders.

"What is he talking about? Tricked?" I questioned my *husband*.

"I didn't trick her. I explained the situation and she, though reluctant, agreed that it was the best thing to do at a time when tensions were soaring and bodies were dropping."

Primo bared his teeth, talking through them. "Did you also explain that you two didn't need to be married to have the full weight of our protection?"

"Wait. What is he talking about?" I asked, my eyes on Brizio. My nostrils flared and I took deep breaths to calm myself.

Brizio's devious smile surfaced like the pieces I was putting together in my head weren't detrimental to his health. Considering my side-eye, sharp enough to slice through glass, he hadn't dropped the smirk.

I was a nervous mess the night Brizio had taken me to meet his cousin Romigi for *the blessing* as he had called it. The story he had fed me about marriage providing the ultimate layer of protection had been a clever and convincing one. Right now, I wanted to knock that smile off his handsome face.

"Technically, you fell under our protection the moment I agreed to help you. But, in my defense I wanted to make sure that there were no questions where it concerned my intentions towards you."

My hand tightened around his under the table, so hard he yelped. I leaned into him, my lips at his ear.

"Honey, tonight we are going to fucking *switch*," I muttered under my breath, through teeth gritted so hard, I was sure Primo and Nevah saw chips of enamel flying through the air.

Brizio's mouth dropped wide open, his eyes even wider for what I was suggesting. He was about to be my fucking submissive tonight.

"That's right motherfucker, I've been studying," I mumbled for his ears only, my sharp gaze pinned to his, my smile for Primo and Nevah's benefit.

"It doesn't work like that," he had the nerve to say.

I squeezed his hand harder, shutting him the hell up.

"I don't give a fuck how it works. It's going to work like the fuck I say it's going to work tonight," I muttered, aware that Primo and Nevah had taken up a slight lean over the table, no doubt wondering if we would hurt each other.

Brizio nodded.

"Is everything all right?" Nevah questioned. Concern put a deep crease in her forehead and a touch of fear in her roaming gaze. Primo had taken on a different expression than his wife. He smirked at us, I believe having an idea that I was going to make Brizio pay like only a true DeLuca wife would.

"Everything is going to be just fine," I finally replied to Nevah, all while fighting to keep, whips, chains, paddles, ball gags, and all types of sick shit I planned to do to my husband out of my head.

"We are going to go to the club after we finish having dinner with you guys and work it all out," I said, smiling at Brizio lovingly. "Isn't that right honey?"

"Yes, we are going to work it all out," Brizio repeated, looking like he was ready to get up from the table and run.

EPILOGUE

Six months later.

"The alarm has been disabled," I whispered so the person on the other end of the earpiece would hear me. This was a long time coming. I enjoyed spying on the people I knew I would eventually kill. This one lived his best life while scenarios of the different ways I would go about killing him danced in my head for months.

I eased the back door open and entered. The usual sound of the alarm tripping didn't go off due to a severed connection. This wasn't the first time I'd entered this house and could therefore get around inside of it with no problem.

Absolute trust was something I extended to my family. Everyone else, whether they were an associate or someone who worked for me, was disposable, replaceable, a tribute to my Savage desire, especially when they crossed me or my family.

The soft glow of the television peeked around the dark corner I tipped around. A smile teased my lips at the lack of sound trailing. The closer I came to the living room I noticed a lamp's glow. The light hadn't been on when I was strolling across the lawn earlier and awaiting the freeze frame on his cameras to be confirmed.

Had his sixth sense kicked in and warned him that danger lingered, primed and ready to deliver a savage death?

I crept closer until I spotted him sitting on his couch. He grinned at something funny playing out on the screen of his phone.

He focused on the phone so hard, I entered the room fully without him sensing or noticing me. He glanced up when I stepped in front of the television about eight feet in front of him.

His loud gasp sounded before he leaned across the arm of his recliner for one of the two pistols he kept hidden in his living room. He came back up empty handed, unaware that I'd been in his house a few days ago. He was careless and hadn't checked his hiding places. Complacency had him defenseless and at my mercy.

"Brizio. What are you…"

"Don't," was all I said, cutting him off.

"You know as well as I do you gave me doctored up recordings meant to lead me down the wrong path. You know me. I could have easily left that path lined with bodies and you would have slept well at night with the web of deception you helped spin?"

"Brizio. Let me explain."

I picked up his remote from the coffee table and muted the television, aware that he was sizing me up to see if he could take me in a hand to hand battle. I prayed he would make the mistake. I love being tested.

"There is nothing to explain," I finally replied.

"Greed led you to this point. They say everyone has their number. The amount at which they are willing to test the devil himself. Five hundred thousand was the price tag you placed on your life. Fucking shame," I said shaking my head.

His gaze went to the twitch I couldn't control under my left eye.

"You've met Detective Lincoln Marx. Have you ever noticed how he always has a hard on to catch a DeLuca slipping, always has just enough information to make the department *think* he's a step away from catching us slipping?"

He froze, his gaze pinned on mine.

"I don't trust a motherfucker, especially you slimy ass cops. I had you thinking you were my eyes and ears inside the department, but Marx has held that title since before you transferred to the precinct. Who do you think gave me some of the leads on tracking down Gagliardi? We even managed to find the tech fool who doctored up the recordings you tried to use to lay the murder at the Romanos' doorstep."

His face twitched, him attempting to keep his anger in check.

"Marx has made several arrests against your family," he pointed out.

"Arrest that we allowed to happen. You'd be surprised how many DeLucas will volunteer as tribute for this family. As long as we take care of them inside and outside many will volunteer to do a year or two without batting an eyelash. Hell, we've had two in the past three years who volunteer for five or more, knowing that if they wanted out, nothing would stop the rest of us from breaking them out."

It appeared he didn't know how to process the information. Especially now that he knew he was nothing but a pawn on the DeLuca chessboard.

I noticed the moment his gaze dropped to my hands and searched the surrounding area of my waistline. I didn't have a gun or any other type of deadly weapons.

So that he could satisfy his curiosity, I spun and lifted my shirt.

"You aren't going to die by my hands Johne," I revealed to him and enjoyed the flicker of intrigue that flashed in his eyes from my pronouncement. He wasn't easily intimidated and it was a quality in him I'd once appreciated.

"However, seeing your death play out live and in living color is probably going to be the most satisfying thing I've witnessed in a while," I finished. He glanced at his window, thinking I had a sniper on him.

"You knew who killed Eric Daniels the whole time and you let me go off searching down the wrong lanes. But, that's not the part that's going to make your death so satisfying to watch. You also watched Maya Daniels walk into that precinct countless times inquiring about her brother's case and did nothing to help her. You knew she was investigating his death, which you didn't mind because if she went off and got herself killed, it would make your life easier."

My head shook slowly, remembering my wife's dark side, the side I didn't have to teach her, a side she'd unleashed all on her own.

"Maya Daniels was a whole lot more capable than you gave her credit for, and I believe she would have survived your and the Gagliardi family's attacks all on her own and eventually found you."

His lips spread further apart.

"I also managed to find out that you were the one who found the DG6 assassins Gagliardi sent after Maya to get her off their trail. You did a lot for a half million Johne. You sold yourself short, traded your life for the almighty dollar. Now, you're about to be food for the devil."

His eyes kept darting towards his front door, his window, and his kitchen doorway.

"I want to officially introduce you to someone, Johne."

His gaze went haywire, glancing in every direction, except the right direction.

"I'd like to introduce you to my wife, Maya DeLuca."

Two silent steps brought her out of the darkness and into view right behind him. The press of her gun to the back of his head, one I'd been personally training her on, made the man go deadly still. His hard swallow pierced the thick silence filling the room.

Maya stepped around him. The all black form fitting jumpsuit I'd insisted she wear had my heads battling each other for control. My head tilted, the one on my shoulders that allowed my gaze to trace the curve of her ass when she stepped in front of the wide eyed cop. She was face to face with the man who'd helped cover up her brother's murder and hired the assassins, one she'd had to kill.

He lifted his hands, his eyes bouncing back and forth between me and her. She didn't say anything, didn't threaten him, didn't gloat, didn't even make a face. Her lack of a verbal response had him squirming harder, his legs jumping, fingers gripping the arms of the chair, body almost dancing in the seat.

"I think you were right about how I should go about this," Maya said, looking at him but talking to me.

"Will you say that a little louder," I replied. "The part you said about me being right."

She ignored my condescending remark and re-turned to her position behind the man, his neck twisting to track her movement. Once she was positioned behind him, he closed his eyes expecting the gunshot.

He obviously didn't know my wife. The blood pumping through her veins was as savage as mine.

"Will you hold this for me honey?" she called sweetly, lifting her gun. When terms of endearments came from her, death would surely follow.

"Only if you promise to hold mine later and handle it as well as you did that one at the range today."

She grinned.

"Deal," she replied, tossing the gun after I lifted my hands to catch it. Catching a loaded gun with the safety clicked off. Yeah, we were that kind of couple. I shoved the gun down the back of my pants, not even bothering to aim it at Johne.

Was I being arrogant? Sure the fuck was, didn't know any other way. Maya didn't move after tossing me the gun and neither did he.

What is she doing? Meditating?

Her stillness had dear ole Johne about to jump clean out of his skin, a sight I enjoyed immensely. Maya had a temper, but she was a much more patient killer than I was, something I was still learning to control about myself.

Patience added an edge to the way she did things. It was an edge that should have concerned me, but all it did was turn me on.

"Aw..."

The man's cry was muffled by the thick plastic bag Maya had managed to toss over his head without me or him knowing what was coming. He fought, his arms flailing as she twisted the bag in a tight grip around his neck, refusing to allow him air.

"This shit is harder to do than I assumed," her choppy words were flung into the air. He was putting up a good enough fight that the chair groaned under his harsh movements, inching closer in my direction.

"He's nearly double your weight baby, you have to control him with leverage." I instructed, while fighting to stay in place so she could handle this business herself.

Despite the circumstances, if he hurt a hair on my wife's head I would kill his ass slowly.

"Prop your foot against the back of the chair and use your body weight." She followed through, doing as I instructed. She was getting better at taking my commands and had even played dungeons and dragons, a new game I'd invented, with me a few days ago.

Feet kicking, chest pumping hard, and body swinging from left to right, Johne fought hard. However, the lack of oxygen was taking its toll on his strength.

Maya remained relentless, not giving up the hold on the plastic, choking the life from the man even as he landed a few wild shots to her arms. It would leave a bruise and for that I wanted my turn to kill him.

Any bruise she collected would be temporarily tattooed on her by me, and only me. It didn't matter if I was making her come while she agreed to my commands. A yes was a yes, especially in our relationship.

The kicks lessened, his arms too heavy for him to lift. He was fading fast, his skin growing paler by the second. He slumped in the chair, his body jerking in its attempt to find air, but Maya wouldn't allow him a single drop.

He settled into his final position. I waved a hand under my throat, letting her know that she could let go, but she held firm. She stared down at him long and hard before releasing the bag and dropping the leg she had propped against the back of the chair.

She walked around the chair, eyes glued to the man until she stood beside me. I handed over her gun.

Tap!

Tap!

"One to the head and one to the heart. That's my girl," I commended, observing the way blood coated the inside of the bag like it was a sealed bubble around his damaged head.

"No matter what method you use to kill them, always make sure that they are deader than dead."

She flashed a questioning glint.

"Deader than dead?"

I nodded. "You take their asses beyond the dead point to deader. You don't want to send them to hell and leave them to make it on their own. Nope. You want to escort them right up to the devil's door, knock and wait for the beast to open it. Even after that, you shove them into the devil's hands. Just like what you did to Brock. You walked his ass through the door and tossed him in the pit of fire for the devil," I told her grinning.

She shook her head, and I could already sense her conflicting ideas about our behavior on matters where it concerned death. I was a bit of a sicko, she knew it and accepted it.

"Are we what normal people would classify as psychotic or sociopaths? Why doesn't this bother me? Shouldn't I be remorseful? Upset? Disturbed? I mean, I don't like killing people like you and your cousins, but…"

I finished. "It's all a part of being a DeLuca. Now, come here and kiss your husband before you let him spank that ass and cuff you to a set of prison bars in the dungeon of a gravesite while letting tortured prisoners watch."

Maya's brows lifted at the images my words conjured, but the devilish glint in her eyes revealed her Savage bloodline.

End of Brizio DeLuca

Acknowledgement

A special thank you to Author Siren Allen and Author Shani Greene-Dowell. I'm eternally grateful to you for spearheading the mission that earned us the title, USA Today Best Selling Author.

Thank you to the group who agreed to read my short notice ARC copy and Beta Read of Brizio. I appreciate your time, feedback, and your amazing insight.

Author's Note

Readers. My sincere thank you for reading Brizio DeLuca. Please leave a review or star rating letting me and others know what you thought of Brizio and Maya's story. If you enjoyed it or any of my other books, please pass them along to friends or anyone you think would enjoy them.

Other Titles by Keta Kendric

The Twisted Minds Series:

Twisted Minds #1
Twisted Hearts #2
Twisted Secrets #3
Twisted Obsession #4
Twisted Revelation #5

The Chaos Series:

Beautiful Chaos #1
Quiet Chaos #2
Hidden Chaos #3

Stand Alone:

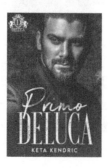

Novellas:

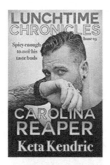

Paranormals:

Audiobooks:

Connect on Social Media

Subscribe to my <u>Newsletter</u> for exclusive updates on new releases, sneak peeks, deleted scenes, and much more. Join my <u>Facebook Readers' Group</u>, where you can live-chat about my books, enjoy contests, raffles, and giveaways.

Newsletter Sign up: https://mailchi.mp/c5ed185fd868/httpsmailchimp
Paranormal Newsletter Sign up: https://mailchi.mp/38b87cb6232d/keta-kendric-paranormal-newsletter
Instagram: https://instagram.com/ketakendric
Facebook Readers' Group: https://www.facebook.com/groups/380642765697205/
BookBub: https://www.bookbub.com/authors/keta-kendric
Twitter: https://twitter.com/AuthorKetaK
Goodreads: https://www.goodreads.com/user/show/73387641-keta-kendric
TikTok: https://www.tiktok.com/@ketakendric?
Pinterest: https://www.pinterest.com/authorslist/

Made in the USA
Middletown, DE
29 December 2023